OVER THE EDGE

Mart Baldwin

 For information address Vivisphere Publishing, a division of NetPub Corporation, 675 Dutchess Turnpike, Poughkeepsie, NY 12603.

ISBN 1-892323-64-8
Library of Congress Catalogue Number 00-190718

OVER THE EDGE

CHAPTER 1

Hattie Mae Gulledge stirred the grits, lined up the sausage links in their pan, wiped a spot of grease from the steam table and patted her short gray hair. Then she gave the bright, warm room a final check. The yellow chrysanthemums on the faded beige formica tables all held their heads up nicely. The floor, mopped last night, shone. The little islands of salt, pepper, ketchup, mustard and hot sauce on each table squared with the table edges, and the ashtrays were empty. She nodded approval then went to the front door and unlocked it.

Two men were waiting on the porch. Behind them fog in the dark parking lot made the lights at Jimmy's Texaco station and bus depot nextdoor fuzzy red blurs, and the rocking chairs on the porch dripped dew. The rush and gurgle of Brightwater Creek across the road seemed amplified by the fog.

"About time, Hattie Mae," one of the men said. "You're two whole minutes late."

His companion blew on his hands. "Ah, she don't care about us. We could freeze our butts off out here, and she wouldn't —"

"Hush up, Jimmy, or I'll put pepper sauce in your coffee. Come on in."

Hattie Mae, whose brown eyes barely came up to the men's shirt pockets, went back to her place behind the serving counter and waited for the day's first customers to shed jackets and slide trays down the line. A pickup eased into the parking lot outside the front window. A car followed, then another pickup.

During the next half-hour the Rocking Chair would fill with working people and a few early-rising tourists. Hattie Mae could almost set her watch by the arrival of the regular customers. The clatter and hum that would fill the café later in the day was always subdued in the very early morning. The carpenters, road crews, truck drivers and salesmen who started their day in the dark preferred to just sit and stare at coffee cups. Fewer people smoked these days, but the room still became hazy from cigarettes.

Even after thirty-five years of dishing up grits and fried chicken at one or another of Blue Ridge's eating establishments, Hattie Mae enjoyed her work. The prospect of another day of watching people and trying to figure them out was enough to push her out of bed when the alarm clock rang at a quarter to five every morning. All people interested her. She had realized long ago that everybody turned out to be different from what you first thought. You just had to peel off a little bark to get down to real wood.

At 6:25 Harold Pell, a local photographer and one of the few customers Hattie Mae could actually look straight at without tilting her head back, came in and picked up a tray. He had pale blue eyes set in a small-featured, red-cheeked face that was almost pretty. His thin, silky, gold-colored hair was neatly combed and, as usual, he smelled like a flower garden. Today it was lilacs.

"Morning, Mr. Pell," Hattie Mae said. "You're early."

"Morning, Hattie Mae. We're going up in the mountains for some shots of the fog in the valley. Have to get an early start. Just toast and coffee for me today." He flashed his quick, bashful angel smile, then carried his tray to the table nearest the door.

Aunt Ola Simpson, a tiny, white-haired, wrinkle-faced, black-eyed mountain granny so picturesque the Rocking Chair could have hired her just to sit on the porch and attract tourists, was next. She took her daily grapefruit half, single biscuit and coffee to the table right in front of Hattie Mae, close enough so the two of them could talk. She studied Harold Pell for a moment and turned back to Hattie Mae. From the down-home expression on the old woman's face, nearby tourists might have imagined a conversation about apple pie recipes, but what she actually said was, "I wouldn't trust that one around my granddaughter. Or my grandson."

For the next twenty minutes or so, as the crowd slacked off and tourists and morning joggers began to dribble in and raise the noise level, Aunt Ola would carry on a running murmured commentary about the people in the room. Hattie Mae's problem was to keep from laughing out loud as this one or that one of the breakfasters got skinned alive and pinned to the wall by the sweet-looking little old lady.

At 6:40 the town's chief of police for the last twenty-three years, James Hackett, arrived, right on time. "Chief" to most, "Hack" to a few friends, "Hawg" to the tobacco-chewing citizens of the town, Blue Ridge's number one cop wore, as usual, the same kind of clothes that most of the early workers wore — khaki pants, plaid shirt and brown high-top snake-stompers. His shirt today was red. The only evidence of his profession was a silver badge pinned to his left shirt pocket. He had curly dark hair with a little gray on the sides, thick black eyebrows and a ridged scar across his left cheek that pulled that side of his mouth down and made his usual expression an ominous scowl. When the other side of his mouth grinned, as it often did, his face became that of a lop-sided, happy wolf man. The happy look was scarier than the scowl to those who didn't know him.

As the chief collected silverware the tourists in the room gaped. Hattie Mae could read their thoughts. Here was a real mountain man, their looks said, somebody straight out of "Deliverance," somebody to tell their neighbors about, back home in East Lansing or Chicago or St. Petersburg.

"Morning, Chief, you proposed to her yet?" Hattie Mae had to bend her head way back to look him in the eye.

"What you talking about, Hattie Mae? If I do any proposing, you know it'll be you that gets proposed to."

"Aw, you can't fool me, you might as well just go on and propose. She ain't going to wait forever, whichever one she is. Which one *is* she, by the way? You can tell me, I can keep a secret. You're taking her to the church supper Sunday night, of course."

"You been talking to Melba again? You know I haven't got time for things like church suppers, I'm much too busy with all our crime."

"Ha! Crime. We ain't got enough crime in Blue Ridge to butter a biscuit with, and you know it. This ain't Dee-troit. All you do is pester tourists and retirees. Lord knows they usually need pestering but, Chief, everybody in *town* knows you need a wife to take care of you, so why don't you just go on and propose?"

"What kind of church supper?"

"The singles' supper, but you know all about it, don't try to kid me. Melba told us."

"It's all news to me."

"It'll be a great place to propose, Chief, do it between the mashed potatoes and the peach pie, maybe. Real romantic."

The chief leaned over the counter, gave Hattie Mae his best grin, reached out and touched the end of her nose with his finger, and whispered, "Marry me."

"You! Get out of here. You want sausage or bacon with your eggs today? How many biscuits?"

The chief carried his tray to Aunt Ola's table. Since the old lady knew everything about everybody who had lived in Blue Ridge since the government chased the Cherokees to Oklahoma, he claimed that having breakfast with her was worth at least two extra detectives on his force. After unloading his tray and adding sugar and cream to coffee, he sat back and pointed to the half-smoked cigarette his companion held between tobacco-stained thumb and forefinger.

"I thought you were going to stop all that smoking, Aunt Ola. It's going to stunt your growth."

Without taking her eyes from his face the old woman took a sip of coffee, raised her cigarette, deliberately filled her lungs with smoke and blew it from the side of her mouth.

"Won't make no difference," she said. "I'm so old I'm starting to grow backwards, getting littler all the time. Used to be big as a rabbit, now I ain't even a squirrel."

"If you don't stop smoking you'll wind up a mouse, or maybe a cricket."

"Huh. You'll be glad to know I did quit cussin', though. Hell, cussin's too much trouble, not worth the damn effort."

Hattie Mae always listened to their conversations, which usually wound up with the chief posing some off-the-wall, unanswerable question, something completely unexpected from a man whose appearance evoked stock car races and coon hunts more than philosophy. Hattie Mae thought he did it mainly to agitate Aunt Ola. Sometimes she reacted, other times she squelched his philosophy before it got its first good breath.

"Aunt Ola," the chief said, "there's something I've been wondering about."

"What's that?"

"Happiness."

"*Happiness?*"

"Yeah, you're always talking about how *happy* you were back in the old days. Back when —"

"Huh. I don't know nothing about that." She waved her hand before her face as though chasing a fly. "I hear there was another fire up at the college last night."

"Oh? How'd you find that out? Who set it?"

"My nephew's brother-in-law's uncle is a night watchman up there. I don't know who set it."

"You don't? I'm disappointed, Aunt Ola. I thought you knew everything."

"Humph." The next smoke billow was aimed straight across the table.

Four customers came into the café then and Hattie Mae had to stop eavesdropping and turn her attention to them. From their accents and suntans she decided they were early autumn-leaf-peeping Yankee retirees up from Florida. Before long the mountains would be crawling with their kind.

The gray-haired couples peered suspiciously around the room before taking trays and silverware. Tourists usually did that. Hattie Mae wondered what they were looking for, or what they were afraid they might see. Dirt and dead flies? Maybe some kind of inbred mountain depravity just waiting to grab them?

After their look-around they bravely passed, ungrabbed, through the serving line. A truck driver on his weekly Cincinnati-to-Atlanta run was next, then a line crew from Duke Power, then the Blue Ridge postmistress.

Next in line, an hour and ten minutes ahead of their usual breakfast schedule, were Paul and Frances Winoski, retirees who had moved down from New York some years earlier. The Winoskis were dedicated rock hounds who spent much of their days wandering the mountains looking for emeralds, rubies, garnets and sapphires. This morning they wore jeans, long-sleeved shirts and thick-soled, rock-climbing shoes.

"Morning, Frances," Hattie Mae said. "Looks like Paul's planning to make you climb cliffs today."

Frances laughed. "He might try, but I'll wait at the bottom, thank you."

"You going to bring me back a diamond?"

"No diamonds in these mountains; you have to go to Africa for that, or at least Arkansas. Rubies, though, that's for sure." She turned to her husband. "Paul, why don't you tell Hattie Mae about —"

He frowned and gave a barely perceptible head shake.

"I'll have scrambled eggs and sausage. No grits," he said. They collected their trays and without further talk went to a table by the window.

Rock hounds from all over the country, all of them a little crazy to Hattie Mae, flocked to the mountains around Blue Ridge. Their utter dedication to rocks amazed her. It was the same with fishermen and their trout flies, hikers and their fancy backpacks, bird watchers and their binoculars, and photographers and their cameras.

At the thought of cameras she looked at Harold Pell. He answered her look with a quick, mouth-only smile then got up and left.

At Aunt Ola's table the chief, as he often did, was trying to convince his breakfast companion to tell him the names of the people who grew the little patches of marijuana that kept turning up in the woods around town. It was a game they played. The chief would probably be disappointed if Aunt Ola were actually to name anybody.

"I'm sure you know who they are," he said, "probably your cousins or nephews or in-laws. I realize that, but even with relatives, you've got a civic duty to —"

"Civic, schmivic. I know who they are, of course, but I don't care if they grow the stuff or not. Hell, it's honest work. Beats makin' moonshine like their daddies did."

The chief grinned and signaled to Hattie Mae for more coffee. His refilled cup was half empty before he spoke again.

"Aunt Ola, really. Tell me. I want to know. You're always talking about how hard life was back in the old days, a hundred years ago, say. Back when you were a sweet young thing — not that you aren't still sweet, of course. I mean back before you started smoking. I understand how hard you worked, but were you *happy?* Were you —"

"You going to start that sort of talk again?" she said. "I don't know nothing about things like that."

"No, come on, tell me. Were you —"

"You asking me if I wished I still had to chop wood? Or spin thread and weave cloth?"

"No, no, no. Just tell me, were you *happy* back then, or was everybody always *miserable* because they had to slop hogs and wash clothes in the creek and build fires in the fireplace? I really want to know. And don't blow any more smoke in my face."

"Of course we were happy. You finish dressing a big old bear in the fall, see all that meat hanging in the smokehouse, it was enough to make you want to break out the moonshine jug and start singing. But if you think I'd want to go *back*, well, you got another think coming."

Hattie Mae, having heard the chief's "real happiness" talk before, stopped listening. Most of his questions plain didn't *have* answers, so why did he keep asking them? What that man needed was a *wife* to take his mind off that kind of stuff.

Outside the café the fog had thickened, but early morning light had begun to take the edge off the darkness. She heard the grind of a heavy engine; then headlights pierced the mist as a dimly seen bus turned in and crept toward its assigned parking place. "There's the 6:43," Aunt Ola said. "Only ten minutes late." She stubbed out her cigarette, winked at Hattie Mae, then turned to the chief, beaming her most grandmotherly smile.

"Say, Chief, I hear you're goin' to the church supper. Well, all I can say is, *good.* You better not mess around too long. Who you takin'? You can tell me, *I* can keep a secret. You better —"

A harsh squeal of air brakes caused everyone in the room to turn to the window. The bus jerked to a stop in the middle of the parking lot. Its front door swung open and the uniformed driver scrambled down the three steps. Several passengers followed. One of them pointed to the ground in front of the bus.

"A deer in the parking lot, probably," Aunt Ola said. "Must have hit it. Too damn many deer these days. Don't know what —"

A stranger slammed open the café door and cried, "There's somebody out here! Bleeding!"

The chief jumped up, told Aunt Ola to call the rescue squad, and ran outside, with Hattie Mae right behind him. The bus driver was kneeling beside a dark-clad body lying face down on the gravel in front of the bus. The hood of a black sweatshirt covered the body's head. A small pool of blood, more black than red in the glare, showed on the gravel next to the body.

A few feet away a bicycle lay on its side, the front wheel slowly turning. The brilliant headlights of the bus made hard shadows in the fog and gave the scene the unreal quality of a bad TV movie. The driver stood up and moved back when he saw the chief, who took his place and lifted a limp wrist. Hattie Mae saw that the wrist was small and thin.

"Alive?" she asked.

The chief looked up but didn't say anything.

"I didn't hit him," the bus driver said in a tight voice. "He was just lying there. I almost ran over him."

One of the passengers who had left the bus said, "Yeah, that's right. I saw it. He was lying just like that when we turned in."

A siren sounded from the direction of Blue Ridge. Aunt Ola, who had joined the group, reached down and gently pulled back the hood. White hair spilled out. Hattie Mae moved to her right and leaned down to see the half-hidden face.

It was a woman's face. Her eyes were closed. She wore no lipstick. Her smooth cheek was the color of uncooked gravy. And her hair wasn't white, it was very light blond.

CHAPTER 2

"Move out of the way, Chief!"

Hack stepped back and watched the four young white-clad EMTs ease the dead woman onto a stretcher. In the ambulance's spotlight, he had his first clear view of the slack, chalky face.

Without warning a hollowness formed around his heart and spread through his chest and into his mind. It had happened before, he knew the signs. He was about to faint. He turned and walked the dozen feet to his pickup and leaned, head down, on the cab. The reason he felt faint was that the dead white face on the stretcher was his wife's.

No, no, no! She didn't even *look* like Mary! Mary's hair was dark brown, not white. They weren't the same at *all.*

But Mary's face, when he reached the accident scene that rainy night three years ago . . . the same gray cheeks . . . the same white lips . . . Mary's eyes had been *open* when he got there. It was just that they couldn't see. And the driver of the other car, mumbling and whimpering, so drunk he could hardly stand, had . . .

Stop *thinking* about it!

"Chief . . . you all right?"

"Oh. Yeah, Hattie Mae, I'm okay."

He turned to the little woman who had come to stand beside him, and read the concern in her eyes. He reached out and put his hand on her shoulder.

"I'm okay. Really."

The leader of the EMT crew called from inside the ambulance. "She's alive, Chief!" Seconds later the square white vehicle, red lights flashing, modern warning system warbling and honking, left the parking lot and accelerated toward town and hospital.

Hack got into his pickup and sat, hands on the wheel, staring straight ahead. Hattie Mae watched him for a moment, shook her head, then went back into the café.

He began to force his thoughts, deliberately, away from forbidden scenes. He had learned to prepare himself in advance for the shock of bad car accidents and didn't think people noticed their effect on him, but the sight of the dead woman — no, she wasn't dead yet — had been so sudden, so unexpected. He hadn't had time to brace himself.

He had to be a cop, always, a hard cop who never showed emotion. That was his role in life, the one he'd chosen. He must never allow himself to be a man who had once looked into his wife's dead eyes.

Stop feeling sorry for yourself. Get over it!

He sat up straight, rubbed the scar on his cheek with his knuckles, looked deliberately at the blood on the gravel in front of the bus, and began to think like a cop again.

To start with, it was clear what had happened to the woman. Her wound was a pulpy mass of blood and tissue surrounded by shredded black fabric from her sweatshirt, high on her right shoulder, away from the neck. That kind of wound was all too familiar to him. Someone had shot her at close range with a shotgun. But the aim had been poor. An inch higher and the charge would have missed completely, half an inch lower and she would have died quickly, instead of slowly.

Hack reached for the radio and called the station, where Melba Johnson had taken her usual place as day dispatcher. He told her what had happened.

"Oh, how awful! Who is it, Chief?"

"It's that woman from out at Hope Springs Shelter, the one that rides a bike all the time. Gerry Smith is her name, according to Aunt Ola. You've seen her, late thirties maybe, light blond hair. Send Billy up here. If he's already checked out, call him at home."

"He and Sam are at the shopping center, at the donut place. Fender bender, nobody hurt. Will she live?"

"Don't know, doubt it. Tell Billy to drop what he's doing and come on here, leave Sam there. I'll wait."

"Okay, Chief. You want me to call Hope Springs and —"

"No, I'll go by there from the hospital. Don't call."

All of the gawkers except Aunt Ola had gone back into the Rocking Chair. She stood by the fallen bicycle, staring at the gravel.

Hack rolled down the window. "Come wait in the truck with me, Aunt Ola."

She managed to climb up to the seat without assistance, then with steady hands lit a cigarette with a match from a little box she carried in a dress pocket. Only after she blew out the match, felt its tip with her fingers and put the dead stick in Hack's clean ashtray, did she look at him.

"Messy, messy, messy," she said.

"What do you know about the woman?" he said. "What would she be doing out here on a bike, in the dark, dressed in black? Where does she live?"

"What do I know about her? Not a whole lot. 'Gerry' stands for 'Geranium,' by the way, somebody over at the courthouse saw it when she had to sign some papers. They joke about her name, but only when she's not around. They don't think she'd laugh."

"Geranium Smith. Flower power? She's the boss out at Hope Springs?"

"Yes. Came down from Boston last year to take over when the last manager quit, or got fired, or whatever. Very dedicated, works all the time, isn't very friendly. I hear she's not all that fond of men. She lives in a trailer or cabin back up there somewhere on Jeter. That's all I know."

"Another damn do-gooder." Hack drummed his fingers on the steering wheel then lifted his watch to the light.

"You ever notice how the do-gooders *never* have a sense of humor?" he said. "And most of them probably hate men, too. They come down to save us poor, ignorant Appalachian grunts, hookworms and all, then after a little —"

"Well, *all* of 'em ain't bad."

"I'm not so sure of that. But, I'll admit, being man-hating do-gooders isn't a reason for somebody to *shoot* 'em. Not a good enough reason, anyway, not quite. Why did somebody shoot *her?*"

"Dunno. Probably thought he was shooting somebody else."

Aunt Ola finished her cigarette and ground out the butt in the ashtray. Hack looked at his watch again and called Melba.

"Billy coming?"

"On his way, Chief," she said. "Five minutes. There was a little problem with one of the drivers at the accident. Sounds like he wants to fight somebody or something. Sam'll cope."

"Okay. I'll go from here to the hospital. Don't know when I'll get to the station. Anything happen last night that I should know about?"

Hack's official working day — breakfast with Aunt Ola was often the most *important* thing he did all day, but it wasn't official — began at the police station with a rundown of the night's events from Melba, who on the town's organization chart was listed as his secretary. Not listed on the chart was the fact that the tall blond mother of three little boys was also day dispatcher, jail keeper, confidante of every member of the force, and runner of the department when Hack was away. And when he wasn't away, for that matter. Hack sometimes thought that if the town council had any sense, they'd make Melba the chief and let *him* take care of the jail.

"Not much last night, according to the log," she said. "The fender bender you know about. It happened at 6:30 in the fog. Both locals. And the library found Willis Cheek passed out drunk on the steps again this morning. Billy brought him in. He's downstairs sleeping it off. There was another complaint from the trailer park, loud party, 3 A.M. Billy checked, but everything was quiet when he got there. And the college called a few minutes ago. There was another fire last night, in the auditorium, in a wastebasket. No damage, the guard spotted it in time, but they're sure it was set."

"I know about the fire. Aunt Ola told me."

"Well, I told the college you'd call them. That's about it. Fairly quiet night. No more butchered cats at least."

Melba switched off. Aunt Ola had just started another cigarette when Billy's cruiser pulled into the lot and parked by the pickup. Hack met his second-in-command by the fallen bike. Lieutenant Holloway's shirt was unwrinkled even after a night of patrol and drunk-wrestling, but he needed a shave. He listened without comment as Hack told what had happened.

"Get somebody to come pick up the bike," Hack said. "Handle it carefully, there could be prints. Have them hose down the blood. Then you drive up the road and look for . . . whatever. Look for where she was shot. I don't know how far you should go, at least to the top of Jeter. She lives up there somewhere. Cabin or trailer. Ask around, find where it is, check it out. I'm going to the hospital. Let me know if you find something."

CHAPTER 3

As the ambulance crew unloaded the unconscious Gerry Smith at the hospital, across town Harold Pell was making final preparations for his fog-in-the-valley photographic expedition. He carefully rechecked his favorite camera, noting the number of shots left on the film roll, then attached his most powerful flash and replaced the camera's two little round batteries.

The battery replacement wasn't really necessary, but the flash was too important to take any chance at all. He zipped the camera in its black leather case, carried it out to the car, put it on the back seat and glanced at his watch. Two minutes to wait.

Fog nearly obscured the woods around him. Leaves and rocks and tree trunks glistened in the dim light. Drops falling to the forest floor from high branches made the only sounds. The air was heavy with the clean, damp smell of decaying leaves.

He followed the second hand of his watch as it crept around to the top. At the tick of seven he turned back toward his studio. His photographer's eye, which seemed to operate independently of his mind, suddenly framed a picture, a great shot almost under his nose — the studio.

The small, squat, shingle-roofed stucco building seemed to crouch, green and softened with moss, half-hidden by fog, ready to . . . to . . . jump. The two windows were eyes, the door a mouth. If he were to wait for the exact moment when the sun broke through the fog, if he shot from here, included . . .

". . . the gray beech trunk and . . . don't talk to yourself." More and more often lately Harold had found himself speaking to trees or to his camera. Or to the air. Scary. Talking to yourself could be a sign of losing your mind. He didn't think he was going crazy, but then probably nobody ever did, even the ones in padded cells.

He went into the studio, stood before the full-length mirror installed for clients, and held out his hands. They were shaking. He willed them to stop. Slowly they did, and the tension lines in his face softened. He picked up the phone and called the house. His wife, Corliss, answered after one ring.

"Hello."

"You ready?"

"Just about, honey, but don't you think it's too gray to take pictures?"

"No. Fog down here, sun up there, that's what we want."

"Mama hasn't finished her coffee, give us a couple more minutes. I'll bring you a cup. And a muffin. I made blueberry."

"That was nice, dear, but I've already been to the Rocking Chair. I'm really not hungry. But thanks anyway."

The thought of food made his stomach lurch. He imagined Doreen at the kitchen table with her special purple Dollywood cup of too-hot black coffee, her breakfast. She always reheated the coffee in the microwave to the point where she had to sip it. Harold hated the sipping sound. He also hated the way she held the cup, her little finger stuck out like a pissing dog's leg. And her two hideous cats sitting on the table watching her. On the table!

He stepped out of the studio. At 7:17 he heard the house door slam, then crunchy footsteps on the gravel path that led down through the woods to the studio, then voices.

"My feet are getting wet," Doreen said.

"Harold says we'll be in the sun in a little bit," Corliss replied. "They'll dry."

He met the women at the car. As they emerged from the path he was struck once again by their resemblance. Doreen had started to shrivel and droop in places where Corliss still bulged, but otherwise daughter was a copy of mother. Both weighed twenty pounds more than they should and always wore too much makeup, and their reddish-dyed hair clashed with their green eyes. When

Harold married her twenty-one years earlier Corliss had been pretty. Despite her added weight she was pretty still, he supposed. It had long since ceased to matter to him.

Mother and daughter were almost identical, but not quite. One difference between them was that Corliss dearly loved Harold, while Doreen thought him a spineless nothing who was wasting her daughter's life. A second difference was that Doreen owned land worth $2 million, while Corliss owned nothing but Harold. Doreen talked about "her land" all the time, about how valuable it was and how it would all be Corliss's some day, but she wouldn't even *consider* selling an acre.

She didn't need to, she said. Harold was the man in the family, he should support them. And he did, though barely.

With Corliss running the business side of their enterprise and Harold taking endless pictures, they kept food on the table. His calendar was always full: weddings, school classes, family gatherings, anniversaries, church groups, even people's pets. He worked constantly, and he hated his work with an intensity that seemed almost to choke him at times.

Freedom to practice his art, to follow his genius, that was all Harold wanted from life. He wanted to photograph people as they *really* were, not the made-up dummies that faced his lens. Real people. Men and women . . . and children. He had once mentioned, barely whispered, the possibility of nude models. Near hysteria had followed from Corliss and, from Doreen, threats.

Actually, he should have had his camera ready then. Doreen's expression when he spoke the word "nude" was marvelous. The whole story of his suffocating life in one frame. Title: "Not in *my* house!"

"You've got the Carleton wedding this afternoon, you remember, honey," Corliss said. "And the Guess's family reunion at the Methodist church tonight, at 7:30. And the kindergarten class in the morning. Arlene Jordan's engagement picture is at eleven. I'll clean up the studio for that this afternoon. And the Smiths called. Mitzi's kittens arrived. They want you to take the whole family. Can you go out there tomorrow after supper? I'll go with you."

"Okay, dear."

Harold felt that his life, the only part of his life that mattered, was being sucked away, chewed, swallowed, used up by stupid-looking people and their idiot animals staring at his camera. He had evolved a game that helped him get through his days. He imagined that his camera was a gun.

"Okay, now look this way. Look at me. Smile. Say cheese." Bang!

He pictured the face collapsing around the bullet as it bored in through the tip of the nose. Then the back of the head would explode. Blood and brains would fly out. A high-speed setup with a photo trigger would catch it all.

"Okay, that was a good one. Now one more. Remember the magic word. Sex." Grins. Click. Bang. Splat.

"I'm ready," Doreen said, "if we really have to do this. But I've got to sit in the front. Or I'll get car sick."

Harold hated it when she sat beside him. It was her perfume, always the same. He had never seen the bottle it came out of but was sure the stuff must be green. Harold was a connoisseur of aromas. They mattered to him. Bad perfume made him ill.

He held the front door for Doreen, then opened the back door for Corliss. "You ladies both look very nice this morning."

Nice. Harold let his mind create images. Yes, ladies, you look nice, like fat Poland-Chinas in skirts, like French toads wearing lipstick, like half-rotten watermelons with mascara eyes, like cracked Humpty-Dumpties with wigs.

Doreen settled herself in the passenger seat and clicked the safety belt.

"I decided to wear slacks," Corliss called from the back. "It might be windy up there. A skirt would blow. What's this rock doing here?"

"Oh, it's one of my props."

Harold was *positive* the rock wouldn't be needed. He realized he would have to climb down the path and check, and that if the fall hadn't . . . he'd have to . . . use the rock. Of course, if it came to that, there would surely be rocks on the ground that he could use, but there *might* not be.

He absolutely *had to* avoid using his hands, at all costs. Because he knew he wouldn't have the nerve to do it with his bare hands. It was crucial that rocks did it, not Harold.

His first plan had involved a gun. He'd gone all the way to Atlanta and bought a pistol, but as the actual execution date approached, his courage had weakened and finally failed. Just this morning, only three hours ago, as he mentally walked through the faked burglary he'd considered, he stopped struggling with himself and accepted the fact that he would almost surely not be able to pull the trigger when the time came.

With a rush of relief, he'd set the horrible gun aside — it was under his car seat now, wrapped in a cleaning rag, waiting to be thrown away — and switched to his alternative plan, the nonviolent plan, the one he should have followed from the beginning. The accident.

"Well, if we're going to go, let's *go*," Doreen said.

Harold realized he'd been standing by the car frowning at the fog — for how long? At least he hadn't talked to himself. He shivered and slid into the driver's seat.

At the end of the long driveway through the woods he turned left on Eamon Road and four minutes later pulled up to the full service pump at Deal's garage. Jimmy Deal came out from the lubrication bay.

"Morning, Mr. Pell. You want me to pump it for you today?"

"Please. Fill it. Regular."

Jimmy filled the tank, cleaned the windshield, checked the oil, then came to the window.

"That'll be thirteen twenty." He gestured to the camera in the back seat. "You not planning to take pictures in this fog, are you, Mr. Pell?"

"We're going up on the Parkway, get on top of the fog."

"Well, I guess."

Harold found he had only eight dollars and change. "Uh . . . Corliss, could you . . ."

"How much you need?"

"Five dollars."

"Here's ten. Keep the rest."

Jimmy Deal would remember — probably yack all over town about how Harold had had to beg from Corliss again. But that was good. Harold wanted everybody in town to know what he was doing. What, when and how. He'd already told Hattie Mae at the Rocking Chair. No secrets, nothing to hide. Accidents happened, all the time.

Some people might suspect, including the police. Well, they could suspect all they wanted, but they couldn't prove anything. Because there would be nothing to prove. It *would* be an accident. Really. He wouldn't have even *touched* them.

Not touching them was very important to Harold.

CHAPTER 4

Because of the opaque, almost viscous fog in the valley, Harold had to drive very slowly — sometimes barely creeping — until they emerged into blinding sunlight just below the crest of the Pisgah ridge. Water droplets on the leaves and shrubs above the fog sparkled, and mist rose in little swirls from the damp surface of the road. Harold turned onto the Parkway, north, toward Asheville. No other cars were in sight. He knew that on this Monday morning, a week after Labor Day, before the leaves had started to show much color, there would be little traffic.

Lack of traffic was crucial. There obviously mustn't be witnesses even if it *was* going to be an accident. There would be a short period, when he was at the bottom checking, when somebody looking over the edge . . .

But even if it happened that way, no real problem. All he would have to do would be to call out, "Help! Accident! Get an ambulance!" The end result would be the same. It was just that he must respond immediately if somebody showed up, but sometimes these days he felt so indecisive, almost incapable of acting.

Well, not today. Today, he was certainly acting.

The Parkway followed the crest of the ridge. To the west an unbroken sea of white stretched to where, fifty miles away, the peaks of the Great Smokies poked up through the cotton. Or it was buttermilk. Or whipped cream. Yes, whipped cream.

"Slow down, Harold. And don't go so close to the edge."

"Mama's right, Harold. Don't go fast. Lord, if we fell off here . . ."

"Okay. Slow it is."

He must *not* let his mind drift like that. Composing shots of cotton and whipped cream at sixty miles an hour on the edge of a cliff! He eased back to thirty-five. It would take ten more minutes at that speed, but there would still be time enough.

"By the way, Mama," Corliss said from the back seat, "they're having a sale on underwear at the outlet. I'm going there after I get my hair done this afternoon. You want to go?"

"Well, I guess. I don't need . . . maybe some panties. But we can look, if we finish this in time. Not so fast, Harold. Is this going to take long?"

"No, it won't take long."

"That curve up there looks slick," Corliss said. "You'd better slow down, honey. And don't forget to turn on your lights in the tunnel. Why don't we just stop and take the pictures here, with the tunnel in the background? Don't you think that would work?"

Harold's heart had begun to hammer his chest. His hands were wet and cold but he willed his voice calm. "No, the sun's not right. I want the light behind me, with the fog in the background. I know the place. Everything's right. This is the morning."

"If you say so, sweetie. I'm about to starve. Mama, you sticking with your diet? I dreamed about cinnamon rolls last night, but I've lost two pounds."

"Oh, it wasn't working for me. But there's this new one I read about at the beauty shop. Mostly just cottage cheese, the no-fat kind. And apples. Slow *down*, Harold! Good lord."

Two point one miles to go.

Five minutes later he turned left onto an unmarked gravel logging road which followed the crest of the ridge for a quarter mile then plunged down the mountain to the valley below. Just before the twisting descent began, the road passed through a jumble of fresh boulders, the remains of a rock slide from the past winter that had been bulldozed to the side. Just beyond the boulders was Bear Wallow overlook, a favorite observation point long before the Parkway was built.

Harold stopped the car well back from the low stone wall and rolled down the window. They listened for a moment to silence — utter, unsettling silence — and watched fog that had climbed the mountain from the west pour in an endless mute river across the Parkway, through a gap in the ridge and down into the white ocean to the east. The air was crisp, almost cold.

"Perfect," Harold said softly.

He got out and opened both doors for the women. While he adjusted the camera Corliss walked to the wall and looked down.

"Ugh. You can't even see the bottom in the fog." She came back to the car. "It's cold up here, even in the sun. I should have worn a sweater."

"Wish I had a cup of coffee," Doreen said.

"Okay, come over here by this rock. We'll get the peak in the background. Doreen, you stand here. Corliss, put your hand on her shoulder."

The rock, an automobile-sized boulder that showed reddish crystalline streaks where it had broken from the cliff above, would contrast wonderfully with the harsh blue of the cloudless sky. Harold arranged the positions and faces of his subjects.

"Good. Now both of you look out toward the Smokies. Look far, peer. You know. Right!"

He clicked, then took a repeat. They would be great pictures. Of course he wouldn't be able to use them, at least not right away. But, if he waited a year or so . . . after all, he wasn't hiding anything.

"Hurry up," Doreen said. "I'm freezing."

"This won't take long. Now change places. Hold your head up, Corliss, stick out your chin, open your face. Don't hug yourself. Don't smile this time. Be pensive. Good!" Click. "Now the wall. Sit over here."

Corliss walked over and felt the stone. "It's wet. I must already be turning blue with cold."

"No, it's just damp. You can sit close together. We'll do one with both of you looking right into the lens, toward the sun. I want you to squint a little. Come on."

Doreen joined her daughter on the wall, patted her hair in place, then turned and looked down.

"Oh lord, Corliss, look — no, don't look. Hurry up, Harold. No, wait a minute. Corliss, your hair's sticking out." She tucked in a strand, then turned and smirked at the camera. Harold rearranged their expressions, took three more pictures, then checked the camera. As planned, there was one more shot on the roll. "Okay, now get up on the wall."

"Stand up? *Here?* No sirree, no." Doreen shook her head and waved her hands. "I'm not going to stand up there. No *way* I'm getting up there."

"It could be dangerous, honey, it's so rough," Corliss said. "Don't you have enough pictures?"

"Come on, up. Hold on to each other. The wall shots are the key, what we've been building up to. Mother and daughter and the void. They'll be the ones that sell the whole series. Up. Here." He held out his hand to his wife.

"I don't know," Corliss said, but took Harold's hand and, carefully not looking beyond the wall, stepped up onto the irregular gray surface.

"Come on up, Mama, it's not so bad. Just don't look down."

"This is insane." Doreen shook her head but stepped up, clutched her daughter's hand and stared at Harold.

"Good," he said. "Hold still." He raised the camera. "I'm going to count to three, then you let go of each other and look toward that rock over there. Be awed by the scenery. Can you look awed?" He took a step forward and focused.

"One, two . . . three." Click. The camera began to buzz as it rewound the finished roll.

"Okay, now help us down," Corliss said.

"Not yet. One more, a close-up. Faces, expressions, the most important shot of all. Hold on, I'll reload."

Harold turned his back to the women, opened the camera and removed the exposed film roll. Now, according to his plan, he would close the empty camera, arm the flash, and . . . and . . . miss the last picture? No. No! He simply *couldn't* waste the opportunity. He *wouldn't!*

He took a new film roll from his coat pocket, reloaded the camera, set the focus to its shortest distance and armed the flash. He stepped toward the women on the wall.

"Okay, last picture," he said.

"Don't get too close, Harold."

"Honey, you're too close!"

Another step. Another.

"Harold! What are you doing?"

"Back up, Harold! I'm getting down!"

He thrust the camera to within inches of their faces and screamed, "Smile!"

The flash exploded.

CHAPTER 5

A nurse, one of Melba's army of cousins, met Hack when he entered the hospital.

"Morning, Chief," she said. "Melba told me what happened. Why in the world would somebody —"

"She still alive?"

"I guess so, at least they're still in the operating room. I'll let Dr. Davidson know you're here. You want to wait back in the office?"

"No, I'll stay out here."

When the nurse left, the waiting room's only occupants, a middle-aged couple and a thin, gray-haired woman, all murmured, "Morning, Chief." Their gray faces bespoke a sleepless night, and the eyes of both women were red and puffy. Hack spoke to the couple.

"How's Bobby?"

Mr. McMurtree, owner of Ace Plumbing Supply and long-time First Baptist deacon, responded. "Broke his arm, and his face is all cut up. They think that's all the damage, but they're doing some more tests."

"He was drinking, Chief," Bobby's mother said. She pressed a balled-up handkerchief to her face. "I just can't understand it. It's not *like* Bobby. He never . . ."

"Uh, Chief," Mr. McMurtree asked, "are you going to have to . . . to . . ."

Charge him with drunk driving? Yes, sir, I sure am. The book. Knock some sense into him. Scare the hell out of your little Bobby-boy. Do it now, before something a whole lot worse happens.

Sometimes Hack's shock treatment of hormone-infested teenagers worked, sometimes not, but he thought that making them look right into the eyes of reality was the most valuable service he did for the community. He didn't mind dealing with the teenagers, but he dreaded facing their parents.

"We'll talk about that later," he said. "Right now, just get him home, and be thankful."

Hack crossed the room and sat down beside the gray-haired woman. "You got troubles, Mrs. Jolly?"

She turned toward him, her face stiff with fatigue and, Hack thought, resignation. "It's Henry," she said. "Chest pains. Bad. I've told him and told him and *told* him if he don't quit smokin' . . . They come out here a while ago and said he'll make it. This time. They told me to wait."

Hack couldn't think of anything to say. In the same situation other people would say, "I'm sorry," or "That's too bad," or "I'm sure he'll be okay," but for Hack the words wouldn't come. He didn't know why. He reached over and put his hand on the old woman's shoulder.

"Thanks, Chief," she said.

Hack thought that an emergency room is the saddest place in the world. His work brought him here often, usually after midnight — the "dead of night" — when the ugly things in life seemed to prefer to happen. This morning, sunshine on a bed of yellow marigolds just outside the window should have made the scene more cheerful, but the brightness somehow made the gloom inside even deeper.

Mr. McMurtree coughed then stood up and went outside. Through the window Hack watched him light a cigarette, methodically smoke it down to a nub, and grind out the remains on a shoe sole. He scattered the shreds among the marigolds then came back inside and resumed his seat. A green-smocked nurse carrying a tray bustled into the room from the hall at left.

She called out in a loud, cheery voice, "Hi, Chief, what you doing here *this* time of day?" then bustled away down the hall to the right. Nurses always bustled. Or hustled, or scurried. And they were usually cheerful.

Hack loved nurses, all of them, even the grouchy ones. His love affair had started with his own Vietnam hospital time and continued through a quarter century of police work. He didn't know how much nurses were paid these days, but was sure that whatever it was wasn't enough.

Ten minutes passed in silence, then a doctor in operating room garb came to the door and motioned. Hack followed him into the hall.

"Your shotgun victim will be okay," the doctor said. "She's lucky. You want to see her?"

"Is she awake?"

"No, but I can show you what we've done. Here, we found these." He held out a glass vial that held two little black spheres. "Bird shot. In a case like this it's usually buck shot."

They went into the dim recovery room and crossed to the only occupied bed. The doctor pulled a coarse white sheet back from the woman lying there, uncovering a thickly bandaged right shoulder. The woman's pallid face, colorless lips, sunken cheeks and closed eyes were those of an unembalmed corpse. The only sign of life in the whole scene was the steady drip of clear fluid from a suspended bag.

"She's doing fine," the doctor said. He pointed to the bandage. "The shot just clipped her here. The only real problem was loss of blood, the wound isn't too bad. Lost some muscle tissue, but no bone damage. She'll have a lot of pain for a while, but it'll work out. A little lower down, little more bleeding, and that would have been it, though. A shotgun can do real bad things. But you know that better than I do."

"Has she been conscious at all?"

"No."

"When will she be able to talk?"

"Couple of hours, can't say for sure. She'll be very weak. Maybe later today."

Hack looked at his watch. "I'm going to have somebody come and wait outside her room," he said.

"Why?"

"Doctor, somebody tried to kill the woman this morning. I don't want . . ."

"Oh."

They left the recovery room. Hack paused. "How are Bobby McMurtree and Henry Jolly doing?" he asked.

"The boy'll have scars, that's all. Mr. Jolly'll live, I think. This time."

Hack called Melba from a phone in the office and said for her to send Sam Bailey. When Sam arrived Hack told him what to do, then left the hospital and drove the three miles out Brevard Road to Hope Springs Women's Shelter.

The building, a red-brick cube that had started life as a schoolhouse for farm children in the 1920s, looked forsaken when Hack drove into the empty, gravel parking lot. Weeds almost hid a low white sign with black stick-on letters that read:

H PE SPR N S SHEL ER

After the county closed the school in 1979 the building sat vacant until four years ago, when a charitable organization in Boston got permission to turn it into a refuge for battered women. After a much publicized opening, the founders gradually ran out of money or enthusiasm or both. Current rumor had it that financial support for the shelter had shrunk from a river to a drying-up trickle.

Hack sat in his pickup for a minute looking at the building. A large orange cat with a sparrow in its mouth came out from the underbrush at the edge of the gravel and, after giving the pickup a long, unblinking stare, slunk up the cracked concrete walkway that led to a low front stoop. It disappeared around a corner of the building.

Hack got out, followed the cat as far as the front door and pressed the bell. After the third unanswered ring he tried the door, which was locked, then walked around the building to a porch in back. As he raised his hand to knock, the door opened. A woman, fortyish, with stringy brown hair and suspicious eyes, peered at him. In the room behind her babies were crying.

"What do you want?" she said.

"To speak to the manager."

"She's not here."

"Then to whoever's in charge."

The woman hesitated. "That's me, I guess, Chief. I'm Violet Turner. Come on in."

She opened the door and stepped back. Three other women, two middle-aged and rail-thin, the third clearly young enough to be in high school, sat, together with two babies in highchairs, around a scarred wooden table in the middle of the room. The young woman, who overflowed the edges of her chair, wore a too-tight blue tee shirt and too-small jeans. The babies, who had stopped crying when they saw Hack, had their fronts covered with big plastic aprons decorated with red and blue polka-dots. Their faces were smeared with what Hack remembered from his own daughter's baby years as a mixture of oatmeal and strained peaches. Behind the table a little boy holding a half-eaten piece of toast sat on a battered wooden rocking horse. Every eye in the room fastened on their visitor.

"Morning, folks, where's Gerry Smith?"

"I don't know," Violet Turner said. "She hasn't come in yet."

"What time does she usually get here?"

"Around eight o'clock. She doesn't go home until after midnight."

"She have a car?"

"The shelter has a van, but she rides her bike. Is there something wrong?"

After years of trying, Hack had never found an easier way to give bad news than directly.

"She was shot on the way down the mountain this morning," he said. "It looks like she'll be okay."

Violet Turner took a step backward. Her right hand moved to her face and her eyes widened. "Somebody shot Gerry?"

"It happened around six o'clock, in the dark. Any reason she would have been coming to work that early?"

The bulgy girl in the tight tee shirt started to cry. One of the babies joined her; then the little boy on the rocking horse let out a wail. Suddenly a long jet of steam spurted from a kettle on the stove. A piercing whistle followed, and the other baby tuned up.

Hack moved the kettle off the burner. The whistle stopped. He stepped over to the boy and ruffled his yellow hair. "Hi ya, cowboy, can you make that horsey go fast?"

The child stopped crying and, after a level look at Hack, dropped his toast on the floor and began to rock as hard as he could.

"How about a cup of coffee?" Hack said as brightly as he knew how. "That possible?"

Violet Turner seemed to wake up. "Coffee. Sure, Chief, but it's instant. You want cream and sugar? Sit down. This is Arlene Scoggins — that's Bobby Scoggins on the horse — and Marian Brewer. This is Cindy Blanchard." Cindy was the overweight teenager.

During the next twenty minutes Hack drank two cups of awful coffee, said nice things about babies, and asked a few questions. Mostly he just listened. After a slow start the women accepted him, and the dam burst. What he learned was:

Hope Springs — from "hope springs eternal" — was a shelter for homeless women. No men were taken in, ever. Violet Turner was a "permanent." She lived there and helped Gerry. The three other women around the table were the only ones at the shelter at present, though they sometimes had as many as twelve, most with babies or small children.

Even with Gerry Smith working herself to death, Hope Springs was in debt. The society that had started the shelter had gone bankrupt or something. At least they didn't send any more money. Last month Gerry had gotten a surprise check from somewhere that paid the bills, but that had all run out. Now with her hurt they'd have to close for sure. Then where could they go? What would they *do?* Cindy Blanchard began to sob again.

Hack's beeper, which he reluctantly wore when he thought of it, sounded. He went to the pickup and called Melba on the truck's radio. He had thus far successfully resisted carrying a mobile phone.

"Sam called," Melba said. "Gerry Smith's awake. He wants to know if he should question her?"

"No." Sam could handle drunks and stop knife fights, but victim-questioning was not among Hack's oldest detective's talents. His approach would be the same as he'd use for a knife fight.

"That's what I told him," Melba said.

"I'll be at the hospital in ten minutes. Tell Sam to wait — outside the room."

CHAPTER 6

Hack watched the slow rise and fall of the sleeping woman's chest then stepped to the bed and looked down at her face. The death-mask of the recovery room had softened but an almost transparent pallor remained. Her eyes were closed. A few freckles peppered her cheeks, and short-cut ash blond hair brushed back from her forehead showed a thin white scar at the hairline above her right eye. Hack began to rub the scar on his own cheek then realized what he was doing and lowered his hand.

"She'll be dozy for a while," the doctor said. "She's been drifting in and out. You want me to call you when she's alert?"

"I'll wait here. She doesn't look like a geranium, does she?"

The doctor laughed. "Hardly. Is there such a thing as a snow flower? Or . . . ah, she's awake."

The patient moaned, raised a trembling hand to the bandage that covered the right side of her chest, and opened blue-tinged gray eyes. After a few blank seconds the eyes focused on the doctor.

"I'm thirsty," she said. Her voice was lower than Hack would have expected, and a little hoarse. "I . . . what happened?" She looked around the room. "Where am I?"

"You're doing fine," the doctor said.

"What happened? I . . . there was a bus. I . . ." She squeezed her eyes shut. Frown lines creased her forehead. "There was fog. It was dark. I was on my bike. Oh, I remember now. I was . . ." She stopped talking, opened her eyes wide and stared at the ceiling.

Hack touched the doctor's arm. "Okay for questions?"

"I guess so, Chief. Be brief though." He turned to his patient. "Chief Hackett has some questions for you, Ms. Smith. I'll be right here."

The gray eyes looked up at him then shifted to Hack, then closed again.

"What happened?" Hack asked.

The woman's lower lip began to quiver. Her face crumpled. A repressed sob shook the bandaged shoulder and brought a grimace of pain. She moaned and, obviously trying not to, began to cry. Tears squeezed from under closed lids and rolled among the freckles. She turned her face toward the wall.

"Try to remember," Hack said. "We need to know what happened."

The doctor shook his head and nodded toward the door. Hack followed him from the room.

"Shock," the doctor said in the hallway. "It has different effects on people. I don't know when she'll be able to talk about it. Maybe never. Her mind might simply refuse to remember. Don't talk to her again until I tell you, okay?"

"Okay, doctor."

Hack watched the young surgeon walk — doctors, particularly surgeons, never bustled — down the hall, then called Melba from the nurse's station. He arranged for Louanne McLeod to come to the hospital with a tape recorder, then went to wait in a small visitor's alcove near Gerry Smith's room. Five minutes later an elevator across the hall dinged and well-greased doors slid open. Two pink-clad hospital volunteers stepped out, then Allie McLeod, Louanne's mother. She saw Hack and came to where he was.

"How is she, Jim?" she said. "I was downstairs and heard what happened."

"Hello, Allie. She woke up but won't talk. The doctor says she'll be okay. Here, sit down. I'm waiting for Louanne." Allie took a chair that faced him. "My niece just had a baby," she said. "I stopped in to see her. A little boy. Everything's fine, everybody's happy." She paused a moment then looked directly at Hack.

"Do you know I volunteer out at Hope Springs once a week?" she said. "I work in the kitchen. It's not happy out there. Who in the world would want to shoot Gerry Smith?"

"Dunno yet."

They sat for several minutes without further talk. Hack thought of the difference between the woman facing him and the wounded woman in the room across the hall. The contrast between Allie's neat dark hair, fresh-air complexion and ready smile, and Gerry Smith's fragile, pale, scared look was profound.

He knew Allie's age, forty-seven; Louanne, who thought that her new boss and her mother were just *made* for each other, had told him as part of a match-making campaign last year. Forty-seven was the same age Mary would have been if she had lived. In some ways Allie resembled Mary, but the resemblance hadn't helped Louanne's cause. In fact, it had been her biggest obstacle.

Allie broke the silence. "Have you ever been out to Hope Springs?"

"Yeah, this morning."

"It's depressing. Gerry Smith is — was — carrying the whole operation, really, all by herself. We volunteers help a little, but we go home after our two hours and forget. Not Gerry. It's her whole life. From what I hear, they're out of money, completely. She's afraid they'll have to close. And now . . ."

"Somebody told me she's a man-hater."

"No, that's not right. But from some comments she's made, I know she's had a hard life. Probably some bad things happened to her." Allie raised her blue eyes. "Bad things do happen. You and I both know that."

Allie's husband, Louanne's father, had been killed a dozen years earlier in a farm accident. From what Louanne had said, Hack knew just how much that missing husband still accompanied Allie wherever she went, whatever she did, whatever she tried to do.

The elevator opened again and Blue Ridge's first-ever female detective emerged, tape recorder and notebook in hand, brown eyes, as always, intent. Hack stood up.

"Hi, Mom," Louanne said. "Are you here about Gerry Smith?"

"No, I was downstairs with Marge and her baby and heard what happened. Terrible." Allie looked at her watch. "I've got to get back to work. Good luck with the . . . uh . . . patient, Jim. See you tonight, Louanne." She went to the elevator and disappeared when the doors opened. Hack told Louanne what he knew of the morning's shooting then gave instructions.

"You wait in her room," he said, "but don't ask any questions until the doctor says it's okay. Then just ask her to tell you what happened. Tape whatever she says. If anything. Be nice. She was scared of me."

"Okay, Chief. Mother likes Gerry, by the way, a lot."

"Good. Call Melba if anything happens here. I'll talk to you later."

Hack left the hospital, retrieved his pickup from the no-parking zone in front of the emergency room, and headed toward town. Instead of going in to the station where Melba and duty waited, however, he turned east, toward Whiteoak Mountain and Sky Valley College. After the events of the morning the urge to be quiet and let his mind sort itself out had become imperative, and the best way to be quiet was, for him, to ramble in his truck. Rambling had over the years become an indispensable part of his work, his mental reset button. Without conscious goal, with his mind in neutral, he would wander town streets or deserted mountain roads and timber trails, pausing often at high overlooks and on bridges, where he'd search the streams for glimpses of trout. In his rambles around the town he usually wound up at the college.

Today he drove into the campus and stopped in a spot of sunshine beside the World War I memorial. He sat, hands on the steering wheel, no clear thoughts in his head, and watched the passers by. At this time of morning they were mostly joggers, and most of the joggers were coeds. Not many years before, jogging coeds had been the main reason for his campus visits; today they were just parts of the overall scene of youth, energy and immaturity. The most appealing parts, to be sure, but . . .

Two jogging girls approached on the sidewalk, ponytails bouncing in rhythm. They stared at Hack; then when opposite the truck, one of the girls looked directly at him through the open window, smiled broadly, and said, "Hi." The other kept a straight face. Hack watched them in the rearview mirror. Straight-face nudged the smiler hard with an elbow, then both glanced back at the truck and grinned at each other. Hack could almost hear the giggles.

He sighed audibly, cranked up, and was about to head into town when the radio came to life.

"Sheriff wants you, Chief," Melba said, "right now. He told me to find you. Hold on."

Thomas Rutledge Black, the elected law in Cherokee County for even longer than Hack had been a cop in the county's largest town, came on the line. "Hack?"

"Yeah. What you got, Tom?"

"Couple of dead women. From your town. Fell off the Parkway."

"Drove off?"

"No, fell off. Woman and her daughter. Doreen Atkins and Corliss Pell, the daughter. The daughter's husband reported it. Harold Pell, you know him. Little short guy, thin sandy hair, a photographer. He's in the other office now, all broken up, shaking and blubbing all over the furniture."

"They fell off? How can you —"

"At Bear Wallow overlook, just off the main road. Unfortunately it's outside Park Service land, in the county, so it's all mine. You know the cliff there."

"Yeah, but how —"

"How? Hell, it's obvious. The husband pushed 'em. I asked him if they were insured. He *thinks* his wife was. Thinks. I'll bet."

"How does he claim it happened?"

"He was getting ready to take their picture, with them standing on the wall. They tripped or something when he wasn't looking and fell. Crap. He pushed them, no question, but I'm damned if I can see what to do about it. That's why I'm asking for your help, buddy."

"What can I do? I've got a shooting to worry about, and it looks like somebody's trying to burn down the damn college. We've even got a damn cat killer. What with the drunks and traffic, I'm not going to have —"

"Those two women lived in your town, Hack. You don't want to see the bastard get away with it, do you? The least you can do is help me squeeze the little scrunt."

"What you want me to do?"

"I'm going to keep him here all day, let him sweat. You go to his place this evening after he's had a chance to relax. Make him tell you how it happened all over again. We'll compare notes."

"Okay, I'll call you."

"Thanks, good buddy. And while you're out there, get down real close and give him one of your best grins. Try real hard to look friendly . . . Hawg. That just might scare him into confessing."

Hack switched off the truck engine and sat for a time, his unseeing eyes staring at the bayonet-carrying doughboy on the pedestal, his thoughts a swirling boil of dead faces, babies, mountain cliffs and crying women.

He kept seeing his wife — and the falling-down-drunk driver of the car that had killed her — and the woman named Geranium. They were both victims. And those women in the shelter were victims too. And now two women pushed off a mountain, more victims. What about the giggling coeds? Were they just victims waiting to happen? Were all victims women? Or were all women victims?

Stop thinking nonsense.

He pictured little Hattie Mae in the dark Rocking Chair parking lot that morning and her look of concern when he'd felt faint at the sight of Gerry Smith on the bloody ground. He thought of Aunt Ola. And of Melba and her never-ending efforts to get him married. And Louanne and Allie. He was surrounded by women, many of whom cared about him.

And he cared about *them*. *All* of them. Even the Yankee do-gooder with the gray eyes and angel hair.

Then why, with all this caring on both sides, did he live alone like he did, in a messy little cave of a condo? Why did he read himself to sleep every night? Why didn't he listen to Melba, to Hattie Mae? Why did he come over here and ogle coeds? Mary had been gone three years. It was time. Why didn't he just get up and *do* something.

Hattie Mae had talked about a church supper, a "singles' supper." Aunt Ola had too. That was a *something*. He usually avoided church affairs like he'd avoid cholera, even though Melba kept trying to get him to go to one. He vaguely remembered she'd talked recently about some kind of supper at the Methodist church, her church, but he hadn't paid any attention. He never paid attention to things like that.

Yeah, well, *pay* attention. Go to the damn supper and quit feeling sorry for yourself. Go ask Allie to go to the supper with you. Go on, do it now. *Right* now!

CHAPTER 7

When Hack got to the post office four people were in line at the window. He waited, reading wanted posters on the wall, until only old Harm Jacobs was left, then got in line behind him. If Allie realized he was there she didn't show it.

She wore a blue blouse today, with a little gold butterfly pinned to the collar. Hack hadn't noticed the blouse at the hospital; he wondered if she had picked it out to match her eyes, so different from the brown ones of her daughter. Her glasses were old-fashioned, with thick frames. Hack caught a flash of Louanne in the smile Allie gave Harm Jacobs.

"I like them ones with the flowers," the old man said.

"Oh, we have a whole series of flower stamps, Mr. Jacobs. What kind of flowers do you like?"

"Red ones. How you like workin' in Blue Ridge?"

"I like it fine." Allie reached into a drawer and took out a sheet of stamps. "Here are some pretty red roses. How about them?" Harm Jacobs took the stamps and frowned at them.

Allie had moved to Blue Ridge six months earlier when an opening occurred at the post office, and now shared her daughter's apartment. Louanne, after her attempt to play cupid last year, had just about given up trying to convince her boss and her mother that they ought to like one another, though Hack was sure she still thought they should.

And of course they *did*. But nothing had *happened*. He'd been interested, but Mary — and Allie's husband — was always there, between them, and the interest had just faded away, like a fire started with paper under wet wood. He could imagine Louanne's thoughts on the subject: All you could do with a horse — or a mule, or even a hickory stump — is lead him to water. If he's too stubborn to drink, and too big to push in the pond, go on to something else.

The old man looked up from the stamps. "I'm sending my great-granddaughter a birthday card."

"I'll bet she likes roses."

"Roses make me sneeze."

"Oh well."

"She's three. Her name's Desiree. Blue Ridge's better than Waynesville. More modern."

"Oh, they're both nice towns. I'm sure Desiree will like rose stamps."

Another customer joined the line. Hack considered stepping back and rereading posters until he could be alone with Allie, but kept his place. Whatever he did, the whole town would somehow know about it within hours, whether he tried to keep it quiet or not. He could of course wait and call Allie at home after work, but that just wasn't the way he did things.

"No, she won't like it," Mr. Jacobs said. "Roses make me sneeze. Lemme see them others over there."

"They're birds, not flowers."

"That's okay, I like birds."

"Fine. How many do you want?"

"One."

The line, which had grown to five by then, didn't seem to mind that it took Mr. Jacobs two minutes to read his stamp, turn it over and look at the back, lick it and place it in exactly the right spot on his envelope. He thumped it with his fist to make sure the glue stuck before handing it across the counter.

Hack took the great-grandfather's place when he left. Allie presented him the same smile she'd given the old man, but accompanied it with a barely perceptible wink.

"You want flowers or birds, Chief?"

Somebody at the back of the line called out, "How about bees?"

Hack ignored him. "Would you like to go to the church supper with me Sunday?"

"Yes."

"Okay. I'll pick you up."

That was it. He turned around and left the building. One of the things Hack liked about Allie McLeod was that she never fluttered.

Allie watched him make his way past the seven people in line. His usual misleading, scar-drawn frown gave him a sort of stormy Beethoven look, but each one of the waiting stamp-buyers and package-mailers smiled as he passed. Old Mrs. West reached out and patted his arm, and two men made grinning comments — probably extensions of birds and bees. They all liked him. Or maybe loved him is more accurate. Louanne thought he was some kind of god, and Melba would jump in front of a train to save him from getting hurt. Probably even the people he locked up liked him.

And it was clear why. He was exactly what he seemed to be, without a political bone in his body. The citizens also realized he was strong enough to take care of them, like a stern-but-fair father. Or maybe like a feudal lord, the kind who could raise an army just by lifting his sword.

Oh, come on, Allie, don't go all medieval. He's just a big old country boy, still only half grown. It was a wonder he got up nerve to ask for a date, in front of all these people to boot. Anybody else would have called.

Mrs. West tapped on the counter. "Hey, you still there?" She held out an envelope. "Do I need two stamps for this letter, or will one do?"

"Sorry. Daydreaming." Allie took the letter and weighed it. "It'll take two, Mrs. West," she said. "That'll be sixty-four cents." With her mind still detached from her actions, she accepted the old woman's change then smiled mechanically at the next customer.

What did she really know about her date-to-be? Well, she knew she had winked at him, for one thing, without even realizing she was going to do it. You didn't wink at men unless you knew they'd understand. Understand what?

Was Louanne going out Sunday night? Allie couldn't come right out and ask her own daughter to let her have the apartment for a while, but she'd bet Louanne would do it anyway, and manage in the process to let Allie know that she wouldn't be home until late, without coming right out and saying it.

Did feudal lords have wives or just mistresses?

When Hack got to the station, he found Honey Dewhurst, the county's most successful real estate agent and Blue Ridge's most eligible divorcee, in the visitor's chair by Melba's desk. With bright green blouse and full white skirt, several gold bracelets on each wrist, large gold hoop earrings, and a shiny Doris Day haircut, Melba's best friend stood out in Blue Ridge like a five-bedroom executive villa in a bunch of doublewides. Her lipstick today was what Hack might have called fuschia if somebody had asked. She started to get up when he came in, but Melba reached over and touched her arm.

"Don't go, Honey. Stay awhile."

"Oh, you're busy, I'll —"

"No, keep me company. I need it today. Chief, Louanne just called from the hospital. Gerry Smith is awake and the doctor okayed questions. Louanne tried to get her to talk, but she won't say anything. Not a single word, Louanne says. Not even 'hello.'"

"Tell her to stay there until I come. Hi, Honey." Hack had known Ms. Dewhurst for two decades, since before her marriage. She was on, as they say, his wavelength, one of the very few people in town that he could really talk to.

"Morning, Jim," she said. "I've really got to go, Melba. Clients, you know." She looked at her watch and stood up. "In eight minutes. Retired banker and spouse from Philadelphia, with plenty of what it takes." She rubbed thumb and fingers together. "They want to move down here and escape all that big city crime. I mustn't keep them waiting."

She went to the door, gave Hack a little finger-wiggle wave and left the building. Dewhurst Realty was three doors down the street from the station.

After a moment Melba, avoiding eye contact with her boss, spoke to the calendar on the wall. "Honey's bought a new dress.

She said it's your color, sort of off-grayish, maroonish brown, you know. She hopes you'll like it."

"Oh. Did Louanne —"

"She'll probably wear it to the singles' supper."

"Good. Did Louanne —"

"With you."

"With *me?* I didn't ask her to go to any church supper."

"Yes you did. Back in July, you asked her."

"I *did?*"

"Well, as good as. I told you about the supper and asked if you were planning to take Honey, and you plainly nodded yes. So I told her. I assumed you would . . . and now she's bought a new dress. Oh, you *men!*"

Hack pictured himself entering the church social hall with Allie on one arm and Honeydew on the other. He opened his mouth then closed it again, self-preservation being a very strong instinct. He was trying to retrieve his I-love-all-women mood when Melba relented.

"Anyway," she said, "no problem. Just go on and call Honey and arrange to pick her up. You'll have a good time at the supper."

Melba took his silence as acquiescence, and he let her.

"The hardware called," she continued, apparently satisfied with his social life for the moment. "There *was* another cat last night. They found it out back, cut up just like the others. Sam's over there now. There's blood all over everything. Horrible! *Sick!*"

"Yeah."

Hack walked over to the window and looked at Huskey Hardware across the square. The usual bags of fertilizer and animal feed were stacked on the sidewalk in front of the store beside flats of yellow and blue winter pansies, but the worn wooden bench by the door was unoccupied. Usually at this time of day it was full. The old men must all be around back.

"I don't know, Chief," Melba said. "These days I just don't know. What's going on in town? What's wrong with people? And I heard about those poor women on the Parkway. How in the *world* —"

"I don't know anything about that."

"Oh, and I almost forgot, Professor Taylor came by to see you half-an-hour ago. He said to tell you to come on over to Buford's. He'll buy you a cup of coffee. I think he wants to talk about the fires up at the college. At least Lurleen *hopes* he'll talk to you about them, but with that man you never know what he's thinking. The fires, that's *another* thing, Chief. How many crazy people have we *got* in this town?"

CHAPTER 8

Chez Pierre is on the south side of the square, opposite the police station, just across Main Street from the Confederate statue, next to Huskey Hardware. It's Blue Ridge's only authentic French restaurant, or as authentically French as a restaurant can get if it's run by a man named Buford Watkins. Buford started it three years ago as Buford's Country Barbecue, but soon found he couldn't compete with Jimmy's out by the golf course. Jimmy roasts his pigs in a pit behind the restaurant, and the aroma attracts customers from ten miles away. Buford bought his barbecue already cooked down in South Carolina somewhere. He didn't have a chance.

Realizing he was going broke, he went away to a cooking school in Atlanta, came back two months later with a certificate in French cuisine. He opened Chez Pierre, with sidewalk tables, wine racks, watercolors of Paris street scenes, the whole bit. He even talked old Milton Prickett into coming down and playing his violin on weekend nights. Now the best mountain fiddle in the county strolls around playing "Plaisir d'Amour" and "Always" and things like that. Every so often he bursts out with "She'll be Coming Around the Mountain." The tourists love it.

Buford attempted a French accent for a while but abandoned it after three different tourist couples laughed at him one night. He keeps two tables reserved for the town's dignitaries, one inside and one out on the sidewalk. He gives the dignitaries free coffee.

From his office window Hack could see Buford's. A few minutes after eleven Hack's best friend — and heaviest responsibility — sat down at a dignitary table. Hack told Melba where he was going and, despite a feeling that he should be out doing *something* about the Gerry Smith shooting, crossed the square.

Dr. Arthur Henry Taylor, philosophy professor and, for the past year, reluctant president of Sky Valley College, looked up but didn't speak when Hack pulled out a chair and sat down. Between the two friends, the usual "Hi, how ya' doin'?" wasn't necessary. It was only after Buford had brought Hack a steaming Eiffel-towered mug and gone back inside that the philosopher broke the silence.

"Buford said you had a shooting this morning."

"Woman named Gerry Smith." Hack glanced at his mug, decided he had already drunk too much of the stuff and pushed it away. "You know her?"

"The one who runs that Hope Springs Shelter place? Never met her. How bad's she hurt?"

"She'll live. Shotgun, right shoulder. Barely clipped her but she lost a bucket of blood. She was coming down off Jeter in the dark on her bicycle. Dumb thing to do."

"You know who shot her?"

"No. Wrong person got in the way, probably, part of some family feud going back a hundred years, you know how it is back in some of the coves. In the dark like that, the shooter couldn't tell who he was shooting at. I'll ask around, starting with Aunt Ola. She'll —"

"What does Smith say?"

"Nothing, yet. But it's clear from her expression that she doesn't like cops."

"What'd you do, get down close and try to look sympathetic? That'd be enough to scare her to death."

"*Art.* You're the *second* person this morning to tell me I'm ugly enough to scare people into telling the truth. Hell, man, I'm not ugly, I'm . . . I'm 'rugged.' Yeah, 'rugged,' that's what I am. Or maybe 'rock-hewn.' You're an author, how you like 'rock-hewn'? Or maybe 'brooding.' Or —"

"What *is* Hope Springs Shelter, by the way? What does the victim do out there, Mr. Hewn?"

"Hell, I don't know. She's probably just another one of the damn holier-than-thous that comes down to save us benighted hillbillies. These days, it could even be the animals they're here to save, and next year it'll probably be *insects*. They arrive, get things all agitated, then vanish. And they never once smile in the process."

"Oh, I don't know," Art said. "A lot of people these days need help. They —"

"Crap." Hack changed his mind and drank some of his coffee, which was cold. He made a face.

"Helping, hell," he continued. "You help people enough and pretty soon they'll forget how to take care of themselves. Won't be long until they'll need somebody to help 'em dress in the morning."

He pushed his mug away again, crossed his legs, and leaned back. "Damn traffic gets worse every day. That's the fourth time that gray Lincoln's gone around the square since I've been here."

"It's all this wonderful progress that's coming our way," Art said. "Includes traffic. Enjoy it."

For several minutes they watched an unbroken stream of cars and pickups creep around the square. Again it was Art who spoke. "Our phantom firebug struck again last night."

"I heard. And our phantom cat-cutter did his thing again over there back of Huskey's." Hack nodded in the direction of the hardware store. "Busy night for phantoms. Where was the fire?"

"Auditorium, on the stage. Another wastebasket, out in the open, not pushed up against the curtain as it could have been. Turns out nobody had locked the basement door, or at least it wasn't locked when the watchman checked it after the fire. We never used to have to worry about things like that."

"Yeah? Well times change."

"Some homesick mama's boy, probably, begging to be caught, careful not to cause real damage. Not a big deal, but Lurleen is all up in the air. She insists I get you involved."

"Okay then, involve me," Hack said. "You don't want Lurleen upset."

Lurleen Morgan, secretary to Sky Valley's presidents since people still used slide rules, had for many years kept the day-to-day operations of the college on track. Now, with a philosopher who didn't even *want* to be president behind the big walnut desk in the corner office, Lurleen pretty much ran everything.

Buford came out from the dining room and was making a little project of refilling Art's mug when another town dignitary, Blue Ridge's mayor, Charles Lee Jackson, waddled up to the table and sat down. Buford brought him a mug.

"Thanks, Bufe. Mornin' boys. Who shot poor little ol' Gerry Smith, Hack?"

"Don't know."

"Bet you don't know what 'Gerry' stands for, do you? It's —"

"Geranium."

"Oh. Well, what about Art's firebug? You know who he is?"

"No."

"You think it's a student, Art?"

"Don't know, Charlie." The philosopher smoothed his gray moustache.

"Hell, I know you get a bunch of squirrel food for students these days. No telling what they might think is fun. Like burning things down. Or killin' cats. What you doing about *that*, Chief?"

Hack glanced at his watch, then raised his eyes and looked directly at the mayor. "Nothing."

"A shooting this morning and fires at the college. Cut-up cats everywhere. Women falling off mountains, drunks sleeping all over the town, car wrecks. All that sounds kind of serious, don't you think? Like maybe you ought to be doing *something*?"

"Yeah, probably."

"Then, why aren't you —"

"Don't know what to do."

"Oh."

They watched the gray Lincoln complete its fifth circuit of the square and double-park in front of the bank two doors down from the restaurant. A tall, lanky man got out and went inside. A woman stayed in the car.

A rusty red pickup, loaded to the tipping-over point with rectangular hay bales, rattled around the Lincoln and parked next to a fireplug in front of the hardware. An old man in overalls got out, spit a long brown stream of tobacco juice on the street and went into the store.

"Parking around here is just getting *impossible,*" the mayor said. "And ol' Broadus Jenkins knows better than to spit on the damn street. You got any ideas about improving our parking situation, Hack?"

"No."

"Well, you going to do something about spitting?"

"Not as long as they don't spit on me."

"Well, what *do* you have ideas about?"

"Fishing. Women. Clemson football."

"You know what, *Chief?* It's a good damn thing you don't have to get elected by the people of this town like I do. And don't you think it might be nice if you'd wear your uniform once in a while? Particularly now that we're having a damn crime wave? See you, Art."

"Take care, Charlie."

The mayor arranged his elect-me smile and started his daily press-the-flesh-and-kiss-the-babies stroll around the square. They watched him until the morning's first mayoral handshake and back-slap occurred, then Art turned to Hack.

"Fishing, women and football, eh? You give up on free will and consciousness? What've you got against Charlie, anyway?"

"I don't know, but whatever it is, I've had it a long time. It's nice that the town doesn't actually *need* a mayor."

"It's also a good thing Charlie isn't the one who decides on rehiring you every year. And why *don't* you wear your uniform? It makes you look pretty, Mr. Brooding. Or is it still Mr. Hewn? Makes you look distinguished."

Hack glanced at his watch again. "I've got to go. About your firebug, make me a list of possibles — students, faculty, janitors, whoever, just some place to start. I'll send Louanne McLeod up to poke around the campus. She's good at that, still acts like a coed herself most of the time." He pushed back his chair and stood up. "And you keep your wastebaskets empty. That's what he seems to like to burn. Why don't I wear my uniform? Too much army. Tell old Bufe I said 'Mercy boo-coo.'"

Hack started to leave the little flowerpot-bounded area, then went back and leaned over the philosopher.

"Am I still interested in free will, so-called, and consciousness?" he said. "Yes. And what 'happy' means. And 'progress.' Why don't you *answer* some of my questions sometimes, instead of just sitting there trying to look like Solomon smoking a damn pipe?"

Art laughed out loud. "Hey, having a shooting in town really gets your hormones sizzling, doesn't it? Good for you. See you at Bertha's."

Hack walked from the restaurant over to the double-parked Lincoln, which had New Jersey plates. He met the driver returning from the bank.

"Plenty of parking around back, folks," he said. "You get in people's way when you stop in the street like this."

The man looked from Hack's plaid shirt to his khaki pants to his brown high-top shoes, then back to the badge pinned on his shirt.

"Are you the police?"

"Yessir."

The man stuck out his hand, gave his name and flashed a smile. "We just moved here. Sorry about blocking traffic."

Hack shook the hand. "Glad to meet you. Welcome to Blue Ridge."

He watched the Lincoln drive away, then stepped into the dimly lit, eighty-year-old, animal feed-smelling interior of Huskey Hardware. Broadus Jenkins was leaning on a stack of 10-10-10 talking to three other overall-wearers. He gave Hack a big three-teeth-missing, tobacco-stained grin.

"Hey, Hawg, how ya doin', good buddy?"

"Broadus, move your damn wreck out there," Hack said, "or I'll haul it off to the junkyard where it belongs. And stop spitting on the street where the mayor can see you."

"What you mean 'wreck,' Hawg? That's my Maisie-Belle, a genu-ine antique, man. Hell, my great granddaddy's Uncle Perkins used to plow tobacco with that pickup back in 1875. And tell Big Fat Charlie to come over here, I'll spit on *him*. Who was it shot that poor woman this morning, Chief? Same one that's carvin' up all the cats?"

"Don't know yet."

"You *don't*? Chief, you really ought to be doing something about all these crazy maniacs you got in this town. You just go out back there in the alley and look at what one of 'em done here last night. Hell, man, I tell you —"

"You got fifteen minutes, Broadus, then Maisie-Belle gets towed. And I'll tell the mayor you send him your love."

That brought a burst of coarse laughter, but the red pickup would be moved, and it wouldn't take fifteen minutes to happen. Hack was about to leave the store when Broadus yelled to him again.

"Hey, Hawg, I hear you're goin' to the church supper Sunday, *really* goin'. *Two* of 'em at the same time! We're impressed, man, but you better be careful. You ain't as young as you used to be, you know."

The farmers laughed so hard that one of them began to choke. Probably swallowed his damn chew, Hack thought. Good.

Outside, Hack checked the time. If he went back to his office now, he'd have to get past Melba, and then he'd just sit at his desk and stew. Melba would have surely been told about his little two-women church supper problem, and would have decided between icy silence and her responsibility lecture as his punishment. Or this time she might use both.

Deciding it really wasn't *too* early for lunch, he went to his pickup and drove across town to Hardee's. With a definite pang of dietary guilt he ordered two bacon cheeseburgers and a vanilla milkshake, items right up at the very top of Melba's "things you shouldn't eat, Chief" list. He carried his forbidden fruit to the hospital and ate it in the parking lot, then took the elevator to the third floor. Louanne, who was waiting on a folding chair outside Gerry Smith's room, stood up when she saw him.

A hundred and sixteen pounds of brown-eyed, single-minded intensity, officer McLeod was the prettiest brunette this side of Forge Mountain and — Hack had to admit it — the brightest person in his department. Bright and pretty, yes, but a cop? After more than a year, he still wasn't sure.

She obviously knew she was pretty and made a point of keeping herself that way. That was okay, but she was also tenderhearted, to the point of shooing flies out of her office rather than swatting them. Even though she wore a gun and was the department's best shot on the pistol range, could somebody who wouldn't kill a fly be a *cop*?

"No change, Chief," she said. "She seems to be feeling okay, but she won't even look at me when I ask questions. She's scared of me too, I think, but —"

"I've got another job for you. Let's go over there where we can talk."

Hack led the way to an empty patient room across the hall. He sat on the windowsill. Louanne stood in the middle of the room, tucked a loose wisp of hair behind her ear and waited. "There was another fire at the college last night," Hack said.

"I heard."

"I want you to spend some time up there and find out what's going on."

"Undercover?"

"No, you're too well known for that. Just wander around and talk. You know the sort of thing. Talk to the guard that spotted the last fire. Could well be he's the one set it. Start this afternoon. I'll take over here."

"Uh . . . Chief, I wonder. Wouldn't somebody else maybe be better for the college? I've just got started with Gerry."

"No. For the next two days, go back to college. Art Taylor knows what you're doing. I asked him to give you some names to start with, but don't let them know they're on a list. Report to me Friday morning. Sooner if you learn anything."

Hack could tell from the downturn of Louanne's mouth that she wasn't happy, but he could handle that. It was when her cheeks paled and her eyes started sparking that he knew he'd stepped over a line and better be ready to duck.

"Okay, Chief, if you say so." She left.

Hack stepped across the hall, tapped lightly on the half-open door of the shooting victim's room, and went in. Gerry Smith was asleep, or at least seemed to be asleep. He sat down in the room's one easy chair to wait. A nurse bustled in, nodded to him, checked the slow drip of clear fluid from an intravenous feeding bag, then left without speaking.

Hack leaned back, stretched out his legs so that his feet were in a bright patch of September sun. He tried to arrange in his mind the jumbled events of the day, but couldn't get past Allie, Honeydew and Melba. Frowning, he deliberately pushed those thoughts aside and turned his attention to the pallid woman on the bed who, except for the very slow rise and fall of her chest, could well have been lying on white satin surrounded by gardenias and low organ music. After a few minutes, to better concentrate his thoughts, he closed his own eyes and evened out his breathing.

The sunspot had left his feet and crept to the base of the wall when he woke up, and Gerry Smith was staring at him. Her gray eyes, pale cheeks, pale lips, and wreath of almost white hair gave her an unreal look. Like a ghost. Or a movie star. Or a hard-eyed angel.

"Feeling better?" he asked.

She turned away. For the next several minutes he talked to the back of her head but got no response. At 4:30 he gave up, left the hospital and climbed into his pickup, intending to go to the station and face reality . . . Melba. But, as he had done earlier that morning, he turned left on Buncombe Street, toward the mountains, instead of right toward the square.

For the next two hours, with the pickup in a low gear and his mind in neutral, he rambled, creeping along familiar old mountain timber lanes and farm roads, on gravel, dirt or crumbling pavement, on trails that often ended at the base of a steep slope in the head of a cove. In some low places kudzu vines had grown all the way across the road. At high points where there was a view he stopped and stared at the ridges to the west, or down into the valley below him. His thoughts, as they always did when he wandered the hills, smoothed themselves out and separated into recognizable pieces.

Unfortunately, ordered or not, one of the pieces was still the church supper.

Damn the church supper! He didn't have time to be worrying about that now, in the middle of a crime wave.

He could always just ignore the whole mess, go fishing Sunday afternoon, spend the night up along the creek, and let things just dabble along whatever path they chose. And then apologize the next day. Melba would fuss, but if he looked contrite and little-boy at her she'd forgive him.

But he'd done that too many times before. And he really liked Melba and Allie, and Honeydew too. They were all his friends. He didn't want to hurt any of their feelings.

Hell.

He cranked up and continued his ramble. When the sun was about to slide down behind Pisgah and his gas gauge was hovering over empty, Melba called on the radio. She connected him with the sheriff.

"Hack," the sheriff said, "the film in Pell's camera. I should have grabbed it first thing, of course, but it just never occurred to me till now. Get it from him, will you?"

Hack, who had completely forgotten his promised visit to the photographer, drove down the mountain and across town to where Pell had his studio.

CHAPTER 9

Harold had spent the afternoon in a bare room off the sheriff's office, in a wing of the county jail a mile beyond the town limits on the Waynesville highway. From the room's only window he could see the ten-foot-high, razor-wired fence of the deserted exercise yard of the jail, and beyond the fence, the mountains, the same mountains where . . .

No. Don't think of it.

He had learned long ago how to avoid unpleasant thoughts. He squeezed his eyes shut and deliberately looked at an array of kitchen objects. He arranged and rearranged a pitcher, a bowl and some fruit for a still-life shot. The pitcher and bowl were always old pewter, the fruit often reddish-gold apples with blemishes, and the surface on which they were arranged, a scarred oak table. His escape system usually worked. Today the apples kept dissolving into faces. Bloody faces.

In late afternoon the sheriff had finally told him he could go. He drove out of the jail parking lot, but instead of going home, wandered around town for half an hour, his eyes on the rearview mirror.

Of course it didn't really *matter* if they followed him, but whether they followed or not, Harold didn't trust them, not a bit. The half-sneer that the sheriff kept trying to disguise gave him away. He didn't believe what Harold had told him. They might try to trick him.

Well, he'd be ready.

He'd had to relate the events of the morning to different sets of people, over and over, all day long. It was obvious, of course, what they were trying to do. They were trying to make him contradict himself. But he'd been prepared for that. He simply told what had happened, *exactly* what had happened. He just left out some things.

He'd told about the mother-daughter series he'd been working on for the last three months, about the planned mountaintop shots, about the fog, about the women being cold, about the wall being damp. Yes, he'd admitted, the wall was rough and dangerous to stand on. He realized that now, and would never forgive himself.

Why did they fall? He didn't know. He'd finished one roll of film and gone back to the car to reload the camera. His back was to the women. Maybe a yellow jacket? There had been some flying around. When he'd turned around, Corliss and Doreen were simply gone.

No, he hadn't heard anything. He'd called, gotten no answer, then climbed down and found them both dead. It was terrible, terrible, tragic.

It *was* tragic. Harold's telling had brought it all back, and he'd begun to cry again. Corliss sprawled on the rocks, head downhill, arms spread out, eyes closed. Dead, thank the lord. Doreen must have rolled when she hit, she was further down. The bloody rocks . . .

No! Forget them! And forget all the things that happened next. Just forget! Wipe it out of your mind. Think about apples, or you'll go crazy.

Insurance? Every questioner wanted to know about insurance.

Yes, there was a policy on Corliss and one just like it on himself. None on Doreen that he knew of. How much? Fifty thousand dollars. Why had they taken out the policies? Corliss had wanted to. It had seemed a good idea at the time.

Over and over the questions came, until he was shaking. The cup of tea they gave him sloshed on his pants when he tried to drink it. They were always polite, no pressure, no intimidation, just the same questions repeated time and time again.

Well, he'd told his story, and would tell it ten thousand more times if he had to.

When Harold was sure nobody was following, he drove out Eamon Road and turned in at the long gravel driveway that led through woods to his studio. He stopped in his usual parking place at the edge of the clearing and sat in the car for a long time, his eyes seeing nothing, his ears hearing nothing, his rebellious mind refusing to stop picturing forbidden scenes. He kept re-seeing the shots he'd taken that morning.

The last picture had been a mistake. He had planned to leave the camera empty after the first roll, just let the flash do . . . it. The last shot wasn't necessary, and if anybody ever saw it . . .

But the idea of the last picture, the *last* picture, had gripped him. The last moment of life, the instant when they knew. He'd had to take it, he couldn't waste the opportunity.

". . . then burn it, print and negative. Burn it, immediately. Don't talk to yourself."

He got out of the car. The sight of his studio arrested him again as it had that morning. The little building wasn't a crouching beast in the fog now, it was more like a . . . a . . . dwarf, maybe, a happy dwarf. Contented, smiling, settled back, resting. Warm colors. The moss on the roof was soft, like green mouse fur. If he shot from the left he could get that stalk of yellow daisies in the foreground. Then tomorrow, in the fog, he could contrast the evening dwarf with the morning beast.

He took the camera from its case and moved into the woods beyond the sunlit daisies. During the next half-hour, totally absorbed in the changing shades of color of the stucco — from tawny, almost orange, to blue-gray as the sunlight faded and shadows advanced — he finished the second roll from the morning. The last shots were in full shade, really too dark, but they would fit in a series about the personality of a house, how it changed from morning gloom to evening peace. Maybe a whole book. With poetry. He could find plenty of house poems. Or just a long photo piece, without poetry.

He stepped into the studio. The events of the day returned like icy water in the face, and he started to shake. Willing himself still, he reached into his jacket pocket for the morning's film roll. He'd been sitting in the sheriff's office ready to hand over that film — it was part of his plan — when he suddenly realized that the sheriff might ask for his *camera* as well as the film in his pocket. He'd almost fainted at the thought. That was when they had brought him the tea.

His hands quivering badly, he rewound the film in the camera, took out the roll, went into the darkroom, and proceeded through the mechanical steps of developing and printing both rolls.

How could he *possibly* have forgotten that they might want the camera too? After what he'd told them, the last picture, the only one in the camera at the time, would have . . . sent him to the electric chair.

He must really be losing his mind.

He'd decided to just refuse to give them the camera if they asked. Of course that wouldn't have helped for long, but they hadn't even *asked!*

Over the years Harold had learned to process film without really looking at it. He always postponed *seeing* until the prints had dried. Then he would clear all other thoughts from his mind and deliberately, slowly, critically — deliciously — review what he had achieved. With the prints from the day's two rolls still slightly damp he began his "seeing" with the shots he'd just taken of the studio.

He'd caught it! The building was alive. In the sunlight it smiled! It breathed. It beckoned. Not a dwarf, a leprechaun. No, leprechauns were skinny. Maybe a troll, whatever they were. No matter, it lived. Tomorrow, early, before sunrise, in the fog, he'd repeat the same set of shots. But now . . .

Heart racing and breath shallow he pushed the troll shots aside and spread out the morning's pictures, the ones from the first film roll. Discarding the idiot client studies that had been in the camera when he started, he lined up the morning's shots of Corliss and Doreen — all of them except the last one. That would come later, with the desk clean, his mind wiped blank.

He adjusted the desk lamp angle and studied his work. Corliss and Doreen standing by the red-streaked boulder had worked well. Doreen's expression wasn't natural, not shrewish enough, but if you hadn't known her it would do. The sitting-on-the-wall shots were excellent, with just the right amount of sober awe in the women's eyes, the result of cold bottoms, probably. The sense of nothingness behind the wall came through powerfully. Then the standing-on-the-wall pose really grabbed. Their expressions . . . intense, uneasy, but no real fear. And they were holding hands, a nice touch.

He looked for ways the pictures might have been improved — different angle, sharper expressions, but he was satisfied. It was good work. Now . . .

He cleared the desk of everything and put the last picture, face down, in the center of the space. He closed his eyes, waited several seconds then opened them, turned the picture over and looked.

His breath stopped and his face became hot. A shivering thrill began at the base of his neck and spread up and down through his whole body. The two women's eyes reached out to him. Not to the camera, not to the sky, to *him!* Terror and shock. Disbelief. Dread. And, in Corliss's eyes, something else. What?

Love. There was love in his wife's eyes. She had loved him to the end. He broke down in a convulsion of sobs. Delicious sobs, wonderful sobs. Sweet sadness. Love and death, the essence. He could crop a bit from the left, move Corliss almost to the center, Doreen to the side — there was no love in *her* eyes.

Title? Something that combined love and death. Something simple.

"But I should burn it. Now. Oh, no. NO!"

How could he destroy his best work? No, impossible! He would hide it. Then in years to come, after he was dead, the world would know.

". . . where? Hide it where? They might search. In the woods?"

Harold heard the crunch of gravel. A car was coming up the driveway. It stopped. A door slammed.

CHAPTER 10

Before he switched off the pickup's headlights, Hack studied the small stucco building that was Pell's studio. It had one bare window on either side of a dark-painted door. A crack in the stucco started at the upper left corner of the doorframe and traced a zigzag pattern up to the slightly sagging roof. A short path, cluttered with leaves and woods debris, led from the driveway to the door. A mildewed sign on the wall to the left of the door read STUDIO. Lights were on in the building. Hack was about to go to the door when his radio came to life.

"Chief, Gerry Smith's doctor called from the hospital," Melba said. "She remembers what happened now and wants to talk with us. You want me to send Billy?"

"No, I'll go when I finish here. Tell the doctor I'll be there in half an hour. Ask him to wait for me. What do you know about Harold Pell, the photographer? I'm outside his studio right now."

"He took my niece's wedding pictures. I never met him, or his wife. I'm hearing rumors that he actually pushed those women off . . . did he?"

"Don't know. You working late?"

"Yes," Melba said, "there's so much going on."

"If you get a chance, look through the files for anything on Pell. I don't remember anything, but it won't hurt to check."

"All right." After a short pause, Melba added, "I know about your visit to the post office this afternoon. My cousin was in line and heard you ask Allie. Now everybody in town knows you're taking her to the singles' supper."

"Oh."

"Chief, why didn't you just *tell* Honey when she was here this afternoon? Now she'll hear about it from everybody. And Allie, how do you think *she'll* feel? What are you going to do?"

"Yeah, that's a problem, isn't it? I just didn't remember ever asking Honey. My mistake. I'll straighten it out. Talk to you tomorrow."

Without waiting for comment, Hack switched off the radio, brushed away thoughts of Allie, Honey and church suppers, and began to pull his mind into the proper shape for questioning a likely double murderer.

As her boss thought about murder, Melba fumed. She knew very well how he would "straighten it out." He'd just ignore everything and go off somewhere on Sunday, fishing probably, then claim he'd forgotten the supper. He'd apologize, be contrite, smile his I'm-*really*-sorry little smile, then probably go to Bertha's and laugh about it with Art Taylor and Moon Gulledge and the rest of Bertha's animals. He'd done it before.

And, of course, everybody, even the women involved, would wind up feeling sorry for him. "Poor man, lost his wife, you know." It was that little-boy grin of his. It let him get away with *anything!*

That man! He ought to get married again. He was lonely. She *knew* it. And he knew it too. He was just stubborn. His wife had been dead for three years now. It was time. And Honey was just right for him. Or Allie, she would be right for him, too. They were totally different, but either one would make him happy. It didn't matter which one. But he had to choose. *He* had to do it. She couldn't choose for him. She resolutely ignored a faint little voice that kept whispering: "It's *his* business, Melba. You should just go on home and put your own boys to bed and leave him alone. You know it's not really that important, not even to Honey and Allie. Just to you."

But it was that important! He just didn't realize it.

Hack knocked on the studio door and tried the knob, which turned. He entered the room without waiting for a response. A faint unpleasant odor, chemicals mixed with mildew and lilac, met him. The little photographer, seated at a well-lighted desk in the middle of the room, raised red, puffy eyes. Several photographs were spread on the desktop.

"Mr. Pell?"

"Yes."

"I'm James Hackett, Blue Ridge police."

"I know."

"A few questions if you have a minute."

Harold nodded.

Hack, who had no idea how to proceed or even exactly what he was trying to accomplish, pulled a wooden chair up to the desk, sat down, and looked around the busy room. Photographs, mostly in color, covered the walls. There were brides in long dresses, chins up, eyes filled with hope; sober older couples; beautiful children; cats and dogs; a few landscapes, including a particularly striking sunset that showed Pisgah peak in the foreground, then a sea of clouds, then the setting sun and the Great Smokies in the distance.

Four metal file cabinets against the back wall were piled with papers and envelopes. At the end of the room a full-length mirror hung beside a closed door labeled DARKROOM. The studio seemed well-used, not quite tidy. Hack leaned over the desk and looked at the pictures spread there, all of which were shots of the studio.

"I heard about the accident on the Parkway this morning," he said. "Tell me about it."

The photographer gave an audible sigh and rubbed his temples. "I spent the whole day telling the sheriff. Do I really have to —"

"Yes."

"Okay." Harold sighed again, long, drawn-out and shuddering. "I was doing a mother-daughter series, been working on it for months. The shots today were to be the climax. We left here around eight, filled up the gas tank at Dean's, then drove up to the Parkway and spent about an hour looking for the right spot. I wanted full sun with fog in the background. The fog from up there looked like whipped cream, you know, as far as you could see. We drove almost to Waynesville then turned around."

Harold had begun his story in a low monotone, but jerky little sobs began to shake his voice when he reached their arrival at Bear Wallow overlook. Tears came to his eyes. At the standing-on-the-wall shots and the disappearance of the women he broke down and had to stop. Hack waited without speaking.

After a minute of sobbing and eye-dabbing, the photographer took a deep breath, cleared his throat and resumed the story. He told of going down and finding both women dead, of climbing back up to the road. He had hated to leave Corliss and Doreen, but . . . He drove down to the ranger station at Pisgah Forest, then rode with the ranger back up the mountain and waited in the car while the rescue people brought up the bodies.

"I spent the rest of the day at the sheriff's office, until they said I could go. When I got here I took these pictures of the studio and developed them, I don't know why. My mind . . . I really don't know what to do now. About the bodies, you know, and the funerals. You want to see the pictures I took before they fell?"

"They're already developed?"

"Yes, I . . . I had to keep doing something, couldn't just sit here."

"The sheriff asked me to pick up any pictures you took this morning."

Harold opened the desk drawer and handed Hack a thin stack of photographs. The first several were of two women standing in bright sun before a tan and red boulder, with endless fog and brilliant blue sky in the background. The women, unmistakably mother and daughter, would have been pleased with the result. Alert, attractive and appealing — even "glamorous" seemed to fit. They certainly showed no hint of fear.

The next two shots were of them sitting on a rock wall, then one with them standing on the wall holding hands. In the standing picture they squinted toward the camera, tense, not smiling.

"They were nervous there," Harold said. "I didn't realize how dangerous the wall was. I was out of film so I went to the car to reload. When I turned around they were gone. No sound, no call, nothing, or at least I didn't hear anything. Just gone." He raised tear-filled eyes.

"Chief, you know, I realize now what I should have done then. I should have just climbed up on that wall and jumped off after them."

At the hospital Hack found Gerry Smith sitting up in bed, her lips and cheeks still pale but her eyes now definitely alive. At first glance something about her face — a mixture of fragility and toughness — brought to Hack's mind a particular wildflower, a painted trillium. With its three white petals bright against the coarse brown forest floor of early spring, a trillium called out for care and protection.

Not wanting to tower over her, he pulled up the visitor chair and sat down by the bed. "You look better," he said. "What happened this morning?"

"A man shot me." Unblinking gray eyes stared straight at him.

"Who was it?"

"I don't know, I couldn't see him."

"How do you know it was a man?"

"I just know." Gerry Smith's hard look wavered. "Well, I guess I don't really know," she said.

"Tell me what happened."

"I was coming down the mountain. It was dark and foggy. I was using my bike light. All of a sudden headlights came on, right in front of me, in the middle of the road. I stopped. He — somebody — shot me. I fell down. I heard him get back in the pickup. I thought he was going to run over me, but he drove past and went on up the mountain. The pickup was red. The back fender, the left one, was dented. I guess he thought I was dead. So did I for a while, but I managed to get back on and ride down to the Rocking Chair. A bus almost ran over me. That's all I remember."

"How could you tell it was a pickup and see the dent in the fender?"

"My bike light was still on. He drove right by my head, I could see. I'm tired. I want to rest now. That's all I'm going to say." She closed her eyes and turned her head toward the wall.

Hack stood up. Rubbing his scar and frowning, he watched the regular breathing of feigned sleep. He wondered what would happen if he pinched her toe.

Whatever, it wouldn't be good.

He left the hospital and drove back to town. On the way he remembered he hadn't had dinner, hadn't even thought about it. When was the last time he'd done *that*? What about lunch? Had he even . . . oh, yes, cheeseburgers and milkshake . . . two months ago, it felt like.

He drove to Hardee's, repeated his lunch order to the disembodied take-out voice, added french fries and apple pie for completeness, then drove aimlessly around town until he had absorbed the last mustard drop and the last greasy crumb.

At the hospital, when Gerry Smith heard her inquisitor leave the room, she opened her eyes and lay staring at the ceiling. With the passing minutes the hard lines of her face softened and her eyes slowly filled with tears. They spilled over, made little wet tracks down her cheeks and dropped onto the pillow. She tried to stifle a sob but it emerged as a strangled hiccough. Then she stopped struggling and lay there weeping.

Melba had decided to stay at her desk until her boss arrived, even if it took all night. She owed it to Honey to . . . to do what? At four minutes after ten the chief entered through the back door and came to her desk.

"You still here?" he said. "Anything happen?"

"No."

Melba noticed that he looked her right in the eye as he spoke, just like a little boy who knew he was going to get a well-deserved spanking and wanted to go on and get it over with.

"Where's Ferguson?" Hack asked.

"At the diner. I told him to go have a snack."

"Good. Gerry Smith told me what happened to her."

"What?"

"She says a man shot her. He was driving a red pickup."

"Huh. Why would somebody —"

"She didn't know. Anything on Pell in the files?"

"No. Chief, about the singles' supper. You really have to —"

"I will."

"Will what?"

"See about it. Now you go home and get ready for tomorrow. Good night."

From his office window Hack watched Melba back her little Chevy out of a reserved space and drive away, to home and family. The thought came to him that if he were married he'd also have someone to go home to. Someone who'd fix him a snack, then sit with him while he rehashed the confusions and frustrations of the day. He could even allow himself to whine a little. She'd listen and she'd care and, for a while, he wouldn't have to be the chief.

He pictured the scene. Allie McLeod was the snack-fixer and frustration-listener. He hadn't consciously put her there, she'd just slipped in unbidden. But she seemed to fit. He tried to imagine Honeydew in place of Allie but his imagination wouldn't cooperate. Maybe it was the big earrings.

At 10:30 he breathed a great sigh, went to his desk, spread out all of Harold Pell's pictures and called the sheriff on their direct line. There was no need for protocol.

"Tom?"

"Yeah. What you got?"

"I talked to your boy. He'd already developed the film from this morning. I have the pictures and the negatives."

"What you think?"

"I don't know. He got all emotional, real tears, when he was telling about it. And you'll see from the pictures that the women weren't expecting to be pushed." Hack held the standing-on-the-wall photo up to the light. "I'm looking at them right now."

"You think he's nuts?"

"Depends on your definition. After you let him go this afternoon he used up a whole roll of film taking shots of the little dump he uses for a studio. Seems like a nutty thing to do. I picked up those pictures too."

"You think he pushed 'em?"

"Yeah, probably. Been planning it for months. What are you going to do about it?"

"Oh, we'll go over the scene with a microscope, and Doc Porter will do the same with the bodies. Maybe Pell drugged them or something. I'll look for possible witnesses, use the newspaper and TV, but the chances of finding any are zilch, unless somebody in the valley with a damn telescope just happened to be looking up. But even then it would have to be a telescope that could see through fog. I'll talk to the insurance people, but nothing they could possibly say would prove anything."

"Yeah, without a witness who actually *saw* him push them off . . ."

"Hack, I'm certain he killed them. I'm going to keep squeezing till he'll wish he'd never even seen a mountain. Maybe he'll crack and confess. Fat chance, but I can at least make his life miserable for a while. You can help."

"Don't see how," Hack said. "My plate's so full already that I'm dripping gravy all over the damn tablecloth. Take the Smith shooting . . . I just got back from the hospital on that, by the way. You happen to know of any red pickups in the county with a dented left rear fender?"

"Red pickups?" The sheriff paused a moment. "Offhand I can't think of but about fifty, all with dented fenders. Or maybe it's a hundred. That help?"

"Thanks."

"There wasn't any robbery with Smith? Or assault?"

"Not that she told me about."

"Well, hell, Hack, that'll be easy. Just find out who had a reason to shoot her. Can't be all that many."

"Aunt Ola thinks Gerry Smith wasn't the real target, she just got in the way."

"Well, all I can say is I'm glad it happened on your side of the town line. Or at least that's where you found her. And, friend, some advice for you."

"Yeah?"

"You really ought to go on and catch that cat lover I been hearing about, you know. People like that sometimes decide what they *really* want to slice up is people. And 'people' is usually women or children. Just trying to be helpful." The sheriff hung up.

Hack put down the phone. As the Presbyterian church clock began to bong eleven he stood up and stretched until he heard joints crack, then locked his desk and left the building. It had been a long, long day and he was dusty-brain tired. He should knock off and get some sleep, but he still wasn't ready to face going "home" to his condo. Besides, Art was waiting for him at Bertha's. He climbed into his pickup and drove out of the station parking lot onto the square.

The buildings around the square were mostly dark — even Chez Pierre had closed up shop — but a light still burned in the office at Dewhurst Realty. Hack tried to ignore his conscience and drive by, but at the last instant he succumbed and pulled into a parking place across the sidewalk from the realty. He went to the glass front door and found it locked, but he could see Honey's brightly lit office to the left of the dark reception area. He knocked. Honey came out and let him in. There was no need for a lot of talk between friends.

"Hi," Honey said.

"Need to talk."

"Okay." She went into the office and sat down behind her desk. Hack took one of the plush client chairs. They regarded each other.

Honey's I've-got-*just*-the-house-for-you working look had been ground away during the day and replaced by the drooping sag of bone-deep, forty-three-year-old fatigue. She reached up, unscrewed a clamp and took a golden hoop from an unpierced right ear, then repeated the process on the left. She turned sparkly-eyes-gone-dull toward her visitor.

"I sometimes wish all the retirees in America would go to Montana," she said, "or any other place so long as it's not here. Right now they could all even go to hell as far as I'm concerned."

Hack looked around the bright, cheerful room. A vase of fully opened yellow roses on the window sill behind the desk had shed a few petals. House pictures covered one office wall. Another wall featured mountain activities: a gray-haired smiling couple hiking a leafy trail, a trout fisherman in a stream that Hack recognized as Bradley Creek, rock climbers hanging from Jumpoff Rock, a photographer shooting an autumn scene. Hack stood up and went to the wall to see if the man with the camera was Harold Pell. It wasn't. Several pictures of rock collectors were grouped together below the photographer. In one a broadly smiling, younger Honey held a greenish rock toward the camera. Hack stooped and looked at it closely.

"That's my emerald," Honey said. "My ex was a rock-hunting nut. I tried to be one too, but he found somebody who obviously tried harder. Anyway, he ran off with her. Thank god. My emerald was worth $85, we were told."

Hack went back to his chair and after a moment said, "I didn't remember asking you to go to the church thing. I've asked Allie."

"I know, I know, I've heard. It's okay. It was just Melba trying to play cupid. Besides, I couldn't have gone anyway. I've got too much work to do." She gestured to the cluttered desk.

"I really am sorry," Hack said.

Honey abruptly stood up. "Sorry about what? Look, it's late and I've got three more listings to finish. Just go away, will you, so I can get back to work. Go on, go."

Hack left before the tears that were damming up behind Honey's eyes spilled over.

CHAPTER 11

Hack drove into the unlighted gravel parking lot of Bertha's and stopped well away from the eight vehicles — seven pickups and Art Taylor's yellow-and-rust 1971 Ford Pinto — clustered around the door of the low, brown-painted wooden building. The only light showing in the club was a red neon Coors sign in the one unshuttered window. A black plywood board with orange letters nailed above the door was barely visible. It read:

BERTHA'S PRIVATE CLUB AND LOUNGE
MEMBERS ONLY

Before getting out of his own pickup Hack took time to study the parked ones, experience having taught him that he should know who was in the club before he joined them. Tonight, as usual, he recognized all the trucks. Six belonged to Bertha's regulars and were to be found in the parking lot most nights. The seventh, originally red but now mud-colored, was Jakey Boatwright's, and Jakey was bad news.

Hack had long ago decided that the youngest and meanest of the Boatwright clan — or swarm, or nest, or plague — would be one of the very first to go if the state ever instituted shoot-undesirables-on-sight as a crime prevention technique. Jakey had stopped coming to Bertha's a year earlier when, one Saturday night, the broad-shouldered proprietress stopped a drunken melee by rearranging his scalp with her sawed-off pool cue. But tonight he was back.

Forewarned, Hack reached under the seat for his just-in-case handcuffs and stepped down from his cab. He was about to leave the shadows and go into the building when the heavy black door burst open and hit the wall with a bang, followed by a low, throaty shout. "Get out and stay out! Damn rotbirds, all of you!"

Bertha was using her "move-your-ass-right-now" voice, the one that no one ever argued with twice. Three men crowded through the door, Jakey Boatwright first, then Purvis Morrel and Hunch Huggins. When the latter hesitated a moment on the threshold, Bertha gave him a neck-jerking shove then stood in the empty door, square, glaring, pool cue at the ready. After an unchallenged half minute she went inside and slammed the door hard enough to rattle the sign on the roof. During the one-sided battle no one had seen Hack standing in the shadows.

Jakey Boatwright took a step toward Morrel. "You goddamn stealin' son of a bitch!"

"You touch me again, Boatwright," Morrel said, "and I'll —"

Hunch Huggins pushed between them, then jumped back. "Watch out, Purvis! He's got a knife!"

Hack, still unobserved, stepped up to the trio, grabbed Boatwright's arm and wrenched it backwards. A thick-bladed folding knife fell to the ground. Hack kicked it away and threw its owner face down on the gravel, where he lay still.

"Jesus, Chief, where'd you come from?" Morrel said.

Hack pulled Boatwright's unprotesting hands behind his back and clicked on handcuffs. He picked up the knife before turning to the other two men.

"What's this all about?"

"Hell, Chief, I dunno," Morrel said. "Boatwright just come storming in and started givin' me a hard time. I dunno why. He was talkin' about me *stealin'* from him. Hell, I wouldn't even *touch* anything of his, much less steal."

"Jakey's insane," Hunch Huggins said. "All them damn Boatwrights are. The whole bunch of 'em ought to be castrated! That's what, *castrated!*"

"Okay, you two go back inside," Hack said. "I want to talk to you some more. Wait for me." He helped his handcuffed prisoner to stand up, got him into the pickup's passenger seat, took him to the station, and turned him over to Ferguson.

The youngest Boatwright, twenty-two years old, greasy, dirty, stringy, and possum-faced, customarily spent one or two nights a month in the lockup as a drunk and disorderly. Tonight he didn't have anything to say, but then he never had anything to say. Hack couldn't remember having ever heard him use a sentence that contained more than half a dozen words, and whenever they questioned him at the station, even *that* language reverted to unintelligible grunts.

Feeling a little guilty for passing off his unsavory prize, Hack returned to Bertha's. It was after midnight and he was mumble-stumble tired, but he really should find out more about Jakey's outburst. It had to have been caused by *something*. Besides, if he didn't go to Bertha's, he'd have to go home.

The same vehicles as earlier were in the lot. Leaving the handcuffs under the seat this time, he went to the building, pulled open the black door and entered the dark, whiskey-smelling cave. Instead of hearing the usual comfortable murmur and laughter of a late-night roadhouse, he was met by dead silence.

Three tables near Bertha's bar were occupied. The one dedicated to cardplaying was illuminated by a suspended lamp, the others only by the faint flickering reddish electric candles that Bertha put on all the tables. In the back of the room a red, blue and yellow 1950s jukebox, quiet at the moment, glowed like the county fair on Saturday night. Art Taylor slumped at a table next to it.

After the frozen moment that followed Hack's entrance, Bertha called out, "Come on in, Chief. Thought maybe you was the rat snake coming back. Good thing for you, you ain't."

The room relaxed. The snick of a deck of cards being tapped on the table was followed by the riffle of shuffling. Someone called from one of the dark tables. Hack recognized Moon Gulledge's controlled bellow.

"Hey, Hawg, you done good, boy! But whyn't you just shoot the son of a bitch while you had him? Hell, *somebody's* gonna have to shoot him one of these —"

"Ah, Moon, Hawg ain't gonna shoot nobody, you know that," somebody else said. "Ol' Hawg, he's too *nice*. Ain't you too nice, Hawg? Real purty, too, ain't you? Haw, haw."

Hack grinned despite himself. As long as the tobacco-spitters at Bertha's called him by his old high school nickname, he'd get along okay. If they ever started saying "Chief Hackett" to him, his cop days would be numbered. Ignoring Moon and his buddies, he looked at Purvis Morrel, Hunch Huggins and two others at the card table, then turned to Bertha, a question in his eyes.

"Oh, it was Jakey was the problem," she said, "not my boys there. Sometimes I lose my temper a little bit, you know, but I get over it. I let 'em back in. And apologized, didn't I, boys? You want —"

"Damn good thing it was just a little bit you lost your temper," Morrel said. "If it'd been a lot, hell, you wouldn't even of had to bury what was left of me. I wouldn't of been nothing but red juice and some teeth. I'd of just soaked away in the damn dirt. Haw. Ain't that right, Hunch?"

Bertha made a snorting sound that Hack recognized as a laugh, then said: "You want your Mountain Dew, Chief? Doc's drinkin' Old Bushmill's back there, of course. He's been waiting for you, ain't played a single record. Don't know what kind of music we're gonna have tonight."

"Yeah, and bring us some peanuts." Hack went to the card table and waited beside it until Purvis Morrel put down his cards and looked at him.

"Okay Purvis, now tell me, what was all that about with Jakey? He wouldn't just come in here for nothing."

"Chief, I really don't know, honest. As far as I can tell, the Boatwrights are pissed off at me because I like to hunt squirrels up on Jeter. Hell, it's public land. I never go near their place, believe me, but they think I *stole* something of theirs, I don't even know *what*. But, really, Chief, I think they're all completely over the ridge. Probably drink antifreeze or something."

"Well, just stay away from them."

"Hey, no problem with *that*."

Hack walked back to Art Taylor's jukebox table and sat down. Bertha brought a sweating silver can of Mountain Dew and a wooden bowl of peanuts and put them in front of him. Without a word Art reached over and dropped a quarter into the jukebox slot. Everyone in the room looked up, waiting to hear what "Doc Taylor's" mood was tonight.

The mechanism jerked and, with a grinding sound, deposited a little 45 record on the turntable. The needle dropped onto the record and a plaintive operatic soprano filled the room. The poker players grinned at each other and resumed play. Moon Gulledge yelled, "Hey, hey, music! Way to go, Doc." Bertha sat back in her chair, a rare smile on her face.

Over the years that the philosopher had been a Bertha's regular, a system had developed. The jukebox became his private music source. He furnished the records for it and, after a session with Old Bushmill's, would select the music that suited him at the moment. Some nights cold, clear Bach organ fugues shook the walls. Other nights there would be heart-tugging arias, or Stephen Foster, or 50s pop songs. These were all good. It was when Tennessee Ernie Ford began to sing hymns and sad songs, and when Art began to drink straight from the bottle and ignore his glass, that the worry started.

In particular, when Tennessee Ernie started walking all by himself down that famous lonesome valley, Art would often drink himself unconscious. But before he laid his head on the table he'd talk of suicide. That was when Bertha called Hack. For her and her patrons the gray-haired philosopher, who looked like William Faulkner, was a window on that other world, the one they scorned but were in awe of, the arrogant world of privilege, education and high places. Art connected them with that world. They teased him, feared him, and loved him.

On the other hand, Bertha's was Art's anchor, something rough and solid to hold on to in a world of posturing and slush. As Art had told Hack often over the years, his favorite literature was *The Emperor's New Clothes*. He had decided that, of the people he knew, the ones most likely to see the king naked were those at Bertha's.

Hack sipped from his can, listened to the music, and waited. After a minute Art said, "Joan Sutherland."

"Oh?"

"The greatest voice. Listen."

"What's she singing about? Why doesn't she sing in English?"

"Why not, indeed? It's the mad scene from *Lucia di Lammermoor*."

"Oh."

The short record ended. There were four quarters on the table but Art left them there. He took a swallow from his glass. "What got into Boatwright tonight?"

"Don't know. Hallucinations, maybe."

"Your brown-eyed beauty queen was on campus upsetting the boys today. I'm not going to give her any fire-suspect names."

Conversations with the philosopher were often a series of subject lurches. It took Hack a few seconds to catch up.

"Why not? You don't care if he burns the place down?"

"Hope Springs Shelter," Art said. "I looked into that. You shouldn't curl your lip at what they're doing out there. They're honest, they're trying, they're not hypocrites. They're *helping*."

"Geranium Smith is a damn do-gooder snob, and you're drunk."

"Yes. Also, it's not possible that those women fell off the Parkway. They jumped."

It took Hack another couple of seconds to connect. "He pushed 'em."

"Huh."

Hack finished the peanuts and dabbed up the salt with his thumb. Over the next ten minutes of comfortable silence the whiskey level in Art's bottle fell half-an-inch, Bertha brought another Mountain Dew and more peanuts, and two more poker players came in and joined the game. Moon Gulledge, as he often did, put his head on the table and began to emit a gurgling snore. Somebody shook him and he stopped.

Hack scratched his chin and looked across the table at his companion. "Art," he said, "there's something I've been wondering about. Been wondering since I was a little boy. I was talking to Aunt Ola about it this morning."

"Ah, the question of the day," Art said, his words slurred. "I was wondering when —"

"Back in pioneer days," Hack said, "back when there were still wolves in the woods, were people happy? As happy as we are? As —"

"Happy? How could anybody *possibly* be happier than we are?"

"Women in particular. I spent an hour out at Hope Springs this morning, in the kitchen, just listening to those poor women. They're all victims of something, usually men, and now their boss is a victim too, almost a dead one. Half the crimes I see wind up with some woman being a victim. And I wonder, weren't we better off — happier — back when . . ."

"Happier than in today's wonder world? Why, man, with modern computers you can have the Encyclopedia Britannica on a rice grain. All the knowledge of mankind right there, you could tape it to the end of your nose. Why, you talk about *happy* —"

"You're drunk. Why won't you give Louanne some firebug names?"

"Because I know little Mr. Arsonist. He's a nice little boy, maybe five-foot-two, jumpy, extra polite, talks low, afraid somebody'll notice him, likes poetry, likes girls but is scared they'll say boo at him, loves Mama but is terrified of Daddy. He's just a little boy needing help, not you cops. He's the kind of boy your mother would have said was sweet. So, no name list."

"Well, hell, Art —"

"Your Miss Brown-eyes would terrify him if she started asking him questions. If she smiled at him, he'd probably die."

CHAPTER 12

Smiling yellow kangaroos and little red teddy bears decorated the dusty, faded brown curtains. By opening them all the way and leaning forward he could see most of the quadrangle, where the girl was talking to three boys outside the snack bar. He couldn't hear the conversation, but he could see the boys laughing, showing off, the way they always did around girls like her.

Goddamned idiots.

She wasn't even trying to hide who she was or what she was doing. He'd been in the snack bar, sitting by himself at a table next to the candy machine, when she came in. Even before he saw her his fists had begun to clinch and his legs to make jerky little movements that he couldn't control. Since early morning the tensions in him had been rebuilding — so soon — but the pains hadn't started yet and he could still, by concentrating, keep his face its usual blank mask. He waited for the girl to come to him. He wanted to see her up close.

She bought a coke and started moving around the room, going up to students, giving a little half-apologetic grin to get their attention, then asking her question: "You have any ideas about these fires?"

What did she hope to find out like that? Nobody *could* have any "ideas." He'd known the night watchman's schedule, of course, and he'd been careful. Nobody had seen him. He wasn't stupid.

She'd looked right at him once, clearly making eye contact. He'd met her glance and even tried to smile, but she'd turned away without speaking. Deliberately.

His face had begun to twitch, and he couldn't stop it. He'd left the snack bar then and come up to the room where, alone, he could quit pretending. Gritting his teeth he watched the group in the quadrangle. Without warning, hated memories began to bubble up in his mind in a swirling jumble. Again, so soon. They came every time, a warning of what would follow. He always tried to blot out the scenes, but never could. The more he tried, the sharper the images grew. One memory dominated the others.

He saw his gentle grandfather, white shirt red with blood, twisted face unrecognizable, hands clawing the air. Three men half-dragged him, struggling and shrieking, from the house. Then he saw himself in blurry, unspeakable scenes from his own time in the . . . the hospital. He also saw kittens. And girls.

Earlier, in the snack bar, the cop-girl had handed out cards. "I don't want names," she'd said, "just anything out of the ordinary that you saw, anything that seemed even a little bit suspicious. Think about it. Give me a call."

He'd held out his hand and she had to give him a card, but she hadn't *looked* at him when she did it. The dirty, nasty, stinking bitch!

He hated her.

A voice from somewhere in the churning flux that was his mind whispered, *You're insane.*

He slapped his forehead hard, twice, then pushed away from the window and crossed the hall to the room they called the study. Opening the bottom drawer of the desk, he reached far back into it and took out a knife, a long, thin-bladed, folding stiletto he had found in a Charlotte pawn shop and paid eighteen dollars for.

Just holding the polished bone handle and looking at the blade made his face hot. His breath came in jerks. A low, rhythmic, rasping started deep in his throat. It rose and fell as he breathed in and out. The knife had a name, Sammy. For Samurai. He never used water on Sammy. A dry cloth always made the blade gleam again. He closed his eyes, pressed the cool steel against his cheek and tried to call up images, but the dark-eyed girl kept pushing her way in. He recrossed the hall and looked down again at the quadrangle. She was still there, still surrounded by boys. She turned toward one of them and smiled. Smiled!

He took her card from his pocket, put it on the windowsill and slammed Sammy down on it, driving the knife deep into the wood. After working the blade loose he pulled the pierced card off and began to stroke the knife's cutting edge with his index finger, his eyes fixed on the girl. The purring inside him intensified.

CHAPTER 13

At four o'clock that afternoon the entire detective division of the Blue Ridge police force arranged itself in a half-circle before the chief's desk. Billy Holloway was on the left, then Ferguson Jenkins, then Sam Bailey, chewing as usual on a toothpick. On the far right Louanne, the unofficial recording secretary of the group, had moved her chair as far away from Billy as she could. She opened her notebook and uncapped a ballpoint.

Hack turned away from the window where he had been standing with his foot in its usual worn place on the low sill, staring out at the square. He didn't sit down. He never sat down during meetings in his office. No point. They never lasted long enough to warrant it.

"Okay," he said, "with all that's going on, I just want to make sure everybody knows what everybody else is doing. No details, just an overview. What you doing, Sam?"

"Huh?"

Hack's oldest detective, whose near-bald, gray head had already begun to sag toward his chest, loved all meetings, the longer the better. Since he was hardly ever asked his opinion about anything, he dozed through them. He took the frayed toothpick from his mouth before responding.

"Me? Billy said for me to see about the dead cats."

"What you got?"

"Three of them, young ones, kittens. There was the one the other night and two last week. Messy. All cut up the same way. Real ugly. I —"

"Where?"

"On the square. The last one back of the hardware and the other two behind Buford's — there's always stray cats back there. I guess whoever's doing it can only catch little ones. People find them next morning, blood and stuff all over. Damn maniac. I'm looking for witnesses, but there ain't gonna be none."

"What else you doing, besides the cats?"

"Pot. We've sort of staked out that little patch over by Wildcat Creek, but, hell, Chief, we can't watch all the time. I checked it again this morning. Far as I could tell, hadn't been nobody there since last time. Bushes still growing. But of course there's little patches like that all over the place. We tear up one, they just start another. What can we —"

"Just try to know what's going on, and not let it get out of hand."

"Yeah, well, knowing some of the damn lazy, dog-mange bastards that plant the stuff, they're soon gonna start raiding each other's patches. Probably already doing it. Less work than planting it themselves. Some people are gonna probably get their damn asses shot off. Good riddance, I say."

"Just don't get yourself shot, Sam." Hack turned to the department's only black member, who sat up even a little straighter than he had been.

"What about you, Ferguson? What you doing?"

"The Gerry Smith shooting mainly. Billy said for me to go over the road again looking for where she got shot, with my nose rubbing asphalt this time. I found a little bit of blood about halfway up Jeter, on the pavement. We took pictures and got samples. I —"

"I looked for tire tracks but the road's too clean there," Billy said. "Nothing but the few drops of blood. Don't see how it could be where she was shot. There ought to be more blood. The lab'll tell if it's hers. I got everybody in three states watching for your red pickup with the dented fender, but . . ."

"Yeah, too many of them," Hack said. "I'll keep talking to Geranium. Something about that whole setup doesn't sit right with me."

"And we're gonna be up to our eyeballs in traffic, Chief," Billy said. "I know we're supposed to be detectives, but with the leaf-peepers starting to show up — the ninety-year-old Florida ones in the five-mile-an-hour Cadillacs — we're gonna have to . . . for the next couple months they'll be blocking roads and —"

Hack held up his hand. "Okay, okay. Louanne, what you got?"

"You asked me to try to find the firebug at the college," she said. "I talked to students up there all morning. I don't think I learned anything useful, but I'll keep trying. Nobody but Lurleen seems very concerned."

"Yeah, well I'd put *my* bet on Lurleen," Billy said. "The rest of that damn bunch of nose-in-the-airs up there wouldn't recognize their own belly buttons."

"And after lunch I spent a little time with the women out at Hope Springs, trying to learn about their husbands or boyfriends and their pickups. It's a depressing place." Louanne frowned pointedly at Billy.

"Hey, don't look at *me*," he said. "*My* wife's not —"

Hack held up his hand again. "Don't start, Billy. What do the women say?"

For the third time since the meeting began, Louanne pushed an uncooperative strand of dark hair back behind her ear. She gave Billy a quick "gotcha" look.

Hack sometimes wondered what it would be like to have an adult police force.

"At first they don't want to talk," Louanne said. "Ashamed, I guess, but once they get started they're desperate to tell somebody. Then I can't make them stop. I've got some names, but nothing stands out. None of the husbands or boyfriends drives a red pickup as far as the women know, assuming they're telling me the truth. You never know. But of course pickups change hands all the time. I didn't learn anything solid, Chief, just that it's a real sad place."

They all pondered that for a moment.

"Okay," Hack said, "nothing we can do about that. Let's go back to the college. You must have gotten some impressions, *something*. What do the students think about the fires?"

"Oh, you know students," Louanne said. "They think it's cute. Hope the chemistry department will burn next, or history, or sociology. Or the administration building. I don't really think they know anything about the fires. They —"

"Bunch o' damn snotty, longhaired goof-offs," Billy said. "They ought to draft the lot of 'em and skin their heads. They think —"

"You talk to Art Taylor?" Hack had found that ignoring Billy was usually the best course.

"He didn't have any names for me and I don't think he intends to give me any," Louanne said. "And I don't think I blame him. It could be *anybody*, and putting names on a list . . . I spent almost an hour in the snack bar. Drank a lot of Coke, talked to students and faculty. But, like I said, I didn't really learn anything. Maybe just a police presence —"

"Riiight," Billy said. "I'm sure you put the fear of god in 'em. What'd you do, look up at the boys and bat your eyes? Maybe wiggle your —"

"*Billy*, if you don't quit."

"All right, *stop* that." Hack spaced his words. "And don't start it again." He looked from Billy to Louanne, then back to Billy, then continued. "Art thinks the firebug's some harmless mama's boy who needs attention. He sets fires, hopes we'll catch him."

Louanne, who had been trying to burn the smug look from Billy's face with a black glare, sighed and turned back to her boss.

"If the fires keep on happening, maybe we can set some kind of trap or something," she said. "I talked to each of the guards, but I don't think they know anything. I left a bunch of cards with students and faculty and told people to call me."

Hack nodded then turned around and looked out the window again. No one spoke. Louanne poised her pen. A minute passed. Sam's eyes closed, his toothpick drooped. Billy yawned and crossed his legs. Ferguson felt the knot of his tie. When a soft half-snore escaped Sam, Hack turned around, went to his desk, sat down, scratched his neck, fiddled with a pencil and gave Sam a sour look.

"Okay," he said, "I guess we'll just leave things like they are for now, I don't see anything else to do. But keep your heads up and your eyes open, what with cat murderers and shotgun ambushers and fire starters out there, not to mention women falling off cliffs. Just be thankful *that* one's not ours. Bad things always seem to come in bunches. Billy, forget about traffic, we'll call in part-timers to do that. All of you keep me in touch, come see me if —"

Melba opened the door without knocking.

"Chief, two bodies, out in Pisgah Estates. Man and woman, dead, in their kitchen, shot."

CHAPTER 14

A mailbox decorated with a mountain scene and a huge emerald marked the driveway that led up through woods to the Winoskis' house. "THE WINOSKIS, PAUL AND FRANCES" was painted in black letters above the emerald. As he turned onto the drive, Hack had the fleeting thought that it was good to live in a place where such a mailbox could remain unbashed. Then he remembered that — pretty mailbox or not — the people who lived there were dead, probably murdered.

At the top of the driveway a man in white tee shirt and faded jeans stood beside a nondescript red Ford pickup parked in a turn space carved from the hillside, next to a one-story, brick, ranch-style house. Oaks, poplars and hemlocks formed a green canopy over most of the roof. A row of overgrown yews ranged along the front wall of the house. There was no lawn. An open double garage door faced the turn space. Hack parked beside the pickup and got out. The waiting man pointed to the house.

"In the kitchen," he said.

Billy's cruiser, blue light flashing, came up the drive. Sam and Louanne were with him. The rescue squad siren sounded from the direction of town. Hack told the man to wait where he was, then went into the garage.

A muddy, four-wheel-drive Subaru, dark blue, was parked in a small open space surrounded by tables and shelves, all piled with rocks of different sizes. The rocks ranged in color from glossy black through various shades of red and brown to pale green. A shelf at the back of the garage held a selection of bottles, some glass-stoppered, and assorted beakers and racked test tubes. A counter below the shelf was clear except for three one-gallon solvent cans, a stained brown notebook, and a half-dozen small stones.

The air in that part of the garage smelled faintly of chemicals, an odor Hack remembered from long-ago high school labs. Two short-handled picks hung from nails in the wall next to an open door that led to a kitchen trimmed in bright yellow. He went to the door.

The body of a gray-haired woman wearing a faded light blue man's shirt not tucked into her belt lay face down on the floor in the middle of the room. Behind her a man lay on his back, one arm stretched out, the other across his chest, his eyes half-open. Blood on the white-and-yellow vinyl floor beside both bodies had dried.

A quick look around the room revealed no gun. On the yellow formica counter beside the sink were an unopened can of vegetable soup, a clear plastic cutting board, an unsliced loaf of bread and a long knife. Little notes and cards held by magnets almost covered the door of the brown refrigerator.

Hack knelt beside the woman and felt her wrist, which was cold, then moved to the man. He recognized him as a Rocking Chair regular, but didn't know his name. Billy and Louanne came into the room. Hack stood up.

"Billy, you and Sam check the outside," he said. "Tell that guy out there to wait."

The rescue squad, three men and a young woman, a different crew from the one yesterday morning in the fog at the Rocking Chair, appeared at the door and crowded into the kitchen. One of the men said, "Jesus."

Hack raised his hand. "They're cold, nothing you can do for them. Don't mess around with the bodies until Dr. Porter gets here. Wait in the garage. Louanne, you stay here, I'll check the house."

He walked quickly through each room. There was modest clutter and dust everywhere, but nothing seemed to have been disturbed. Only the kitchen, the main bedroom and what must have been intended as the den, looked lived-in. The latter, a dark-paneled room with stone fireplace and hardwood floor, was, like the garage, filled with rocks. Big and small, labeled and unlabeled, formless and crystalline, bright colored and dull, rocks were everywhere. On a table three rectangular boxes with glass covers held labeled specimens in little square compartments.

Hack returned to the kitchen, where Ferguson had arrived with the department's camera and was taking pictures. Louanne was in the garage talking to the EMT crew. Hack went out through the garage to where the man in the white tee shirt was still leaning against the hood of his truck.

"Your name?" Hack said.

"Uh . . . Redding. John Redding."

"What happened?"

"I came up here a little after four o'clock. The garage was open, so was the kitchen door. I went in and found them like . . . like you saw them. I used the phone in there to call you."

"You knew them? They're the Winoskis?"

"Oh yes, we're — were — good friends. I can't understand who would —"

"Why did you come here?"

"We normally meet for lunch at the Rocking Chair on Wednesdays, been doing it for a couple of years. They didn't show up yesterday, so I called the house, no answer. I called again this morning, then again this afternoon. Still no answer, so I just came by."

"How'd you know they weren't off in the hills somewhere?"

"Oh, it wasn't like them to go off without letting me know."

The sound of a car crunching gravel interrupted the interrogation. A new, black Chevrolet crept up the driveway and stopped behind the ambulance. Dr. Starke Porter, examiner of the town's and county's corpses since Eisenhower was president, got out and made his way slowly up the slight slope to where Hack and Redding stood. The doctor put his black bag on the ground, took an unlit cigar from his mouth, leaned on the pickup and panted.

"Too damn old for this," he said.

"Aw, Doc, you been saying that for twenty years. Hell, you're not even ninety yet, so stop whining." Hack pointed to the house. "In there."

The old man nodded, picked up his bag, and went into the garage. Hack turned back to his witness.

"What do you know about the Winoskis? Any problems?"

"No, not that I knew of anyway. There didn't seem to be money problems, and they got along fine together."

"How long had they lived here?"

"Uh . . . eight or nine years. Paul owned a furniture store up in New Jersey some place. They sold out when they could afford to and came down here. They loved the mountains."

"They collect rocks?"

"It was their life, Paul's anyway. Frances's too, just not quite as much. Paul was president of our club last year, very dedicated. They spend — spent — most of their time in the field."

"Children? Family?"

"No children. A few relatives in New Jersey, I think, but none close. It was pretty much just Paul and Frances."

Dr. Porter came to the garage door and motioned for Hack, who followed him into the kitchen.

The bodies didn't appear to have been touched. The doctor leaned against the refrigerator and took the well-masticated cigar from his mouth.

"They're dead," he said.

"Thanks, Doc. I guess I sort of already knew that. Time?"

"Hours ago. Last night, yesterday. Tell you more later. Two shots in each. One of the shots in each body was from close range. In the heart. Powder burns on the cloth. With the woman, the close shot was from the back. You find a gun?"

"No," Hack said. "Looks like the killer must have come to the door. The woman opened it, he shot her. Her husband came in the kitchen. The killer shot him, then went back and shot each one again to make sure. *Coup de grace?* That how it look to you?"

"I only see what I see. You're the one who has to see the ghosts. You got all the pictures you want?"

"Yeah, you can take 'em away."

Hack watched the EMTs move the bodies to stretchers, leaving only the blood spots and Ferguson's chalk outlines, formless sketches somehow even more pathetic than the bodies. The doctor followed the EMTs from the room.

Billy and Sam came in and reported having found nothing of interest outside. Hack called for John Redding to come into the kitchen. In the doorway he looked once at the blood spots and chalk outlines, grimaced, then deliberately looked away.

"Do you know the house well enough to tell if anything is missing?" Hack said.

"Not really, I've only been in the kitchen and the rock room. I didn't know them *that* well. But, Chief . . . there is one thing."

"What's that?"

"Paul's ruby. I don't know if it's important or not, but he'd found — or thought he'd found — a ruby."

"How big? Where?"

"He didn't say how big, but from the way he talked . . . he was pretty excited about it. And I don't know where. That's the kind of thing people keep to themselves, you know. It's bad form to even ask."

"When did he find it?"

"Last week. He told me — just couldn't keep it completely to himself— but he didn't tell the club. He didn't give any details."

"Could the ruby be valuable?"

"It's possible. Every now and then somebody'll find a monster. A few years ago a young guy found a 59-carat emerald up at Hiddenite. Part of it made the first page of the Tiffany catalog the next year. It's the kind of thing that keeps us digging, you know."

CHAPTER 15

Hack and his detectives stayed at the murder scene for the next two hours doing all the obvious things. Louanne, Billy and Ferguson went through the neighborhood. Most of the houses, built twenty years earlier when Blue Ridge was just becoming known as a retirement place, were isolated from the road on large wooded lots. None of the neighbors had heard shots or seen anything suspicious. All were shocked. The Winoskis had apparently been universally considered good neighbors.

A methodical second search of the house and grounds showed no evidence of robbery, no evidence of anything of interest. Louanne found a little wooden box labeled RUBIES in a kitchen drawer, but inside were only three tiny grains the color of dried blood.

Hack had John Redding examine all the rocks in the house and garage. If the Winoskis had discovered a large ruby, Redding didn't find it, or at least didn't admit to having found it. He made Hack a list of the fourteen members of the local mineral club, "The Scrabblers," then was sent home with instructions not to leave town.

Hack walked through the house again, alone, slowly, then went back into the garage and poked around among the rocks there. He leafed through the notebook on the counter that held the chemicals. Stained and acid-eaten throughout, it contained nothing but barely readable scribbles and lists of numbers, with the last entry dating from a month earlier. He opened all the doors of the Subaru and looked for the kind of clues — folded notes, cigarette butts, stains — that private eyes in books always seemed to find. He even got down and looked under the automobile. Nothing.

Just before nine o'clock he collected his troops in the kitchen for a wrap-up and instructions. After reviewing the little that they had learned, he told Billy, Louanne and Ferguson to meet him in his office at 7:30 the next morning — with ideas — and told Sam to spend the night in the murder house, after first blocking the driveway.

Driving slowly toward town, Hack searched his memory for anything he might know about the murdered couple. He had often seen them around the square, just two more retirees-to-the-mountains, but had neither spoken to them nor, that he could recall, heard anything about them. He knew they ate sometimes at the Rocking Chair. Redding said he'd been supposed to meet them there.

But, wait a minute, hadn't they been there for breakfast yesterday?

He'd been talking with Aunt Ola and wasn't paying any attention, but was pretty sure he remembered the Winoskis coming down the serving line. They'd talked to Hattie Mae then sat down at a table over by the window.

Instead of going to the station, he drove across town to the Rocking Chair. It was closed, but he could see Hattie Mae inside emptying steam table pans. She peered hard when he knocked on the window, then came to the door and opened it.

"Hello, Chief."

"Need to talk to you a minute. Now okay?"

"I reckon. Come on in, sit down."

She turned to the nearest cleared table, pulled out a chair, collapsed in it, stuck her legs out straight and sighed deeply. "Lord, I get so tired."

Hack looked around the room. Most of the tables were still covered with dirty dishes. The busboy's cart, empty, stood at the end of the serving line, a white cloth draped over its push-bar. Dish clatter came from the kitchen.

"Where's your busboy?" he said.

"He didn't show up. Didn't call neither."

"Where's Maureen?" Maureen Hatcher, who owned the café and worked as hard as Hattie Mae did, was usually the last to leave in the evening.

"At her nephew's wedding. It's just Sally and me to clean up and get ready for breakfast, so we'll be here a while. I heard about the poor Winoskis."

"I remember they were in here for breakfast yesterday," Hack said. "Then later in the day somebody killed them. They didn't just happen to tell you where they were going, did they? Or anything?"

"I been thinking about that."

Hack stood up. "Well, think about it some more. What did they say? Take your time." He went to the bus cart and began to load dishes from the nearest table.

"Ah, Chief, you don't have to do that. I can —"

"Where were the Winoskis going? How were they dressed? You want a cup of coffee?"

"Coffee . . . me? Yeah. I do. Why not?" She leaned back in her chair and lifted her feet onto another one. "I'll take decaf, thank you, black."

Hack brought a cup from the kitchen, then continued clearing tables. Hattie Mae sagged in her chair, sipped coffee, and stared at her feet for several minutes.

"We kidded around a little about them going rock collecting, I remember," she said. "I asked them to bring me back a diamond, but Frances said I'd have to go to Arkansas for that. I didn't know they had diamonds in Arkansas."

"What about rubies?"

"Yeah. Frances said *something* about rubies. I been sitting here trying to think what, but I wasn't really paying attention. Just chitchat, you know. I heard this evening about the ruby they found, though. Heard it from about fifteen different people. It was big as a baseball, somebody said, the color of fresh blood."

"Who said that?"

"Oh, I don't know, everybody was talking about it. They say John Redding told somebody something. One guy in here said the ruby was big as a *softball.* You know how news travels in this town. And grows."

"Well, when it gets as big as a basketball, you let me know, hear?"

Hack pushed the last cartload to the kitchen, where he told Sally — thin-haired, skinny and seventy-four — that she was looking younger and prettier every day.

"Pshaw, you! You get on out of here or *I'll* put you to work." She tried to growl, but a grin got in the way.

Hack went back to Hattie Mae. "Okay, finish up and go on to bed. And hire a new busboy tomorrow, a better one. I'll see you at breakfast."

Hattie Mae drained her cup and swung her legs off the chair. "Chief," she said, "you're always kidding about wanting me to elope with you. Well let me tell you, mister, any time, any time you say. Like right now."

At the station Hack called each of the "Scrabblers" on Redding's list. He spoke directly to ten of them, none of whom claimed to know anything about a big ruby, though they had all heard the current rumors. It was *possible* Paul had found one, they reckoned, but where in the world? Every place they knew to look had been so picked over.

No one claimed to know where the Winoskis had gone yesterday and, like the Winoskis' neighbors, all the Scrabblers were shocked. Paul and Frances? Why would *anybody* want to kill them? Unless there really *was* a ruby the size of a goose egg.

Of the four members that Hack did not reach, he learned that two were in the middle of a Caribbean cruise and a third was in the hospital recovering from last week's heart bypass. That left only Miss Janet Benjamin, whose phone was busy the four times he tried it. He left the office and drove out to Pinnacle Mountain Estates, Blue Ridge's newest almost-retirement-home development, the kind with a never-manned guard gate and a pretty flowerbed at the entrance.

The porch light at the Benjamin condo came on when he rang the doorbell. When the door didn't open right away, Hack smiled and nodded at the little hole in the front door. A moment later the door opened. A large, formless woman with short gray hair and sunburned cheeks blocked the way. She wore too-big jeans and brown, mud-stained farm shoes, and had hearing aids in both ears. She peered hard at him.

"You're the police." Her deep voice boomed. "You've come about the Winoskis. Why don't you wear a uniform?"

"Miss Benjamin?"

"Yes."

"A few questions. May I come in?"

"Okay."

She led him to a cramped, untidy living room and gestured to the small sofa, half of which held a cardboard box filled with gray-green rocks. Red mud stains marred the room's beige carpet. Hack sat down, leaned back, crossed his legs, and said nothing. He had once estimated that during his career as a cop he had questioned about twenty thousand people. In the course of those twenty thousand strained conversations he'd evolved a technique with two central principles: never ask an expected question, and never hurry.

"Well?" the big woman said after a silent minute.

"How big is the ruby the Winoskis found?"

"Huh. Frances didn't say and, apparently, I was the only Scrabbler she told *anything* about it. I've been on the phone all evening talking to the others. Frances shouldn't have mentioned it in the first place if she wasn't going to *tell* me anything."

"What did she say, exactly?"

"Oh, just that Paul had found this great ruby source. 'But don't mention a *word* to anybody,' she said. 'Paul would be furious, but I just *had* to tell somebody.' She was all excited. We talked a few minutes but she didn't really say anything."

"Where —"

"She would have eventually told me more, I'm sure, but one of the women came in then with a squalling baby. Nothing serious, poor little thing, just diaper rash. Anyway, Frances and I didn't get to talk any more. She went home before we had a chance, said she was getting up early in the morning."

"When was this?"

"Monday night."

"Where were you? Where did the conversation take place?"

"Out at Hope Springs Shelter. Monday was our night. We worked in the kitchen. Most of the Scrabbler women volunteer at Hope Springs. Poor Gerry Smith needs all the help she can get out there. You found out who shot her yet? Probably one of the . . . the . . . rotten, rotten *snakes* that sent the women to the shelter in the first place. What are you doing about *them*?"

Another of Hack's interviewing principles was never to answer a question.

"When you were talking about the ruby," he said, "were there other people in the room?"

"Oh, yes, the Hope Springs kitchen is where everybody collects, you know."

"How many women were there that night? Could anyone have overheard the conversation?"

"Seven or eight, about average. No, nobody could have heard us. We were whispering," thundered the hard-of-hearing rock hound.

At a few minutes past midnight, Hack, having learned vastly more than he wanted to know about the intricacies of rock collecting, left Janet Benjamin and drove out of town toward Hope Springs. The moon was high in the cloudless sky and night fog had begun to form in low places. There was no traffic on the road.

If there had been lights on at Hope Springs he would have stopped and knocked, but except for a single bulb over the front door, the building was dark. As he drove past the parking lot he noticed a pickup with someone sitting in it. Hack made a U-turn and went back and pulled in — driver's window to driver's window — beside the rust-eaten relic which he recognized as Jimmy Mayhew's. He shined his spotlight briefly into the cab then switched it off.

"What you doing here, Jimmy?"

"Nothin'."

"Why don't you go home?"

Hack waited a long time but got no response. From the direction of the river a bullfrog with a voice lower than the lowest pipe on the big organ at the Lutheran church added his bass to the thousand other sounds of the late summer night. In the heavy warm air the perfume of unknown flowers blended with the scent of pine. Somewhere in the distance a whippoorwill chanted his monotonous song. The sound of a baby tuning up came from the shelter. No light appeared in the building, but the baby abruptly hushed. Probably a lot of anxious eyes were watching the two pickups from the dark windows.

"Minnie Lee in there?" Hack asked.

"Yeah."

"What happened?"

"Violet Turner run me off, made me leave. She call you?"

"No. I mean why is Minnie Lee in the shelter?"

"Her and the boy."

"Why?"

"I dunno."

"What do you mean, you don't know?"

"I got drunk."

"You hit them?"

"I don't *never* hit 'em . . . only when I'm drunk. Minnie Lee call you?"

"You know anything about a ruby?"

After a pause long enough for the bullfrog to thrumb twice, Jimmy said, "Ruby who? I don't know no Ruby."

"What happened with you and Minnie Lee?"

"Ah, hell . . . a bunch of us got laid off at the chicken plant down at Forest City, and I started drinkin'. I come home early. She was setting in front of the TV watching that . . . that hog slop they watch. The boy was on the floor whining, looking like he hadn't had a bath in five years. There wasn't no supper cookin'. I . . . I hit her."

"Why don't you just go on home?"

"I hit Minnie Lee, I'm telling you! You gonna take me in? I don't care if you do."

"Not unless she complains. You got another job lined up?"

"Naw, nobody don't want me. Maybe the chicken plant'll take me back when they get busy again. Stinkin' work, but I don't care."

"Go on home, Jimmy."

"I don't want to go back to the trailer, ain't nobody there. I'd just get drunk again." He turned, and for the first time looked directly at Hack. "Chief, you know, anymore . . . I just don't know what to do."

It was too dark for Hack to see Jimmy's eyes, but he didn't have to. He saw them over and over in his work, every day.

They were the eyes of people who lived in sagging mobile homes in nameless trailer parks that squatted just beyond the town limits, just beyond the golf courses. Or they lived at the end of unmarked, rutted red lanes scattered here and there among the rich pastures, orchards and cornfields of the valley. They lived in trailers that had taken on the color of the dirt they sat on, in yards cluttered with red, yellow and blue plastic toys, where long-dead vehicles gradually sank in weeds on one side of the trailer and a scratched-out potato patch struggled on the other, where children with dragging, dirty clothes stared open-mouthed at visitors, where dogs barked. They lived in trailers where the inside smelled of cabbage and the TV was always on. Always.

Hack wished for words that would solve Jimmy Mayhew's problems, for nice crisp bright words full of wisdom and hope. But there were no such words.

Some problems don't *have* solutions.

"I don't know what you should do either, Jimmy, but right now you've got to do it someplace else. You can't stay here. If you do, those women over there watching us'll just call me to come get you. And I don't want you."

"I'll go."

The rusted-out pickup's starter ground for a long time before the engine caught.

"Wait a minute," Hack called.

The truck engine slowed and stalled.

"You want a job?" Hack said.

"Yeah."

"Go by the Rocking Chair in the morning. Be there at six o'clock. Shave first. Tell Hattie Mae I sent you."

Hack watched the pickup rattle away in the direction of Blue Ridge. Then, after staring a long time at the dark windows of the shelter, he cranked up, drove out of the parking lot, and turned toward his own "ain't-nobody-there" place.

As he passed the entrance to the development where Louanne — and now Allie — lived, he turned in without really intending to and crept at five miles an hour through the manicured condo community. Louanne's unit was the last in a row of five in a building carved into the steep slope at the base of Jeter Mountain. Tall pines grew in the front of the building and thick brush of the forest's edge crowded up against the rear. There was no light in the windows. He slowed to a crawl and stopped, his thoughts a disordered jumble.

He remembered the little wink Allie had given him yesterday in the post office when he was about to ask her for a date. A wink, if you knew how to read it, could say more than a whole conversation of polite words, but right now what he wanted was words. He wanted to talk to her, not about anything in particular, just talk. Talk about the weather . . . or the church supper even. Anything, it didn't matter.

He'd call her tomorrow and talk. Should have done it today. Or, hell, why not call her *now*. He had a mobile phone in the truck tonight. He could dial Louanne's number from where he sat and watch the light come on in the condo.

And say what?

He didn't know what, but he did know that if he hung around where he was much longer somebody behind one of those dark windows would call the station and report a suspicious pickup. Then Billy, who was on the desk, might just call him . . . to report *him*. Feeling lower than a squashed toad in the bottom of a pothole he drove on across town to the place he had to call home.

Next morning Jimmy Mayhew, shaved and out-of-place-looking, was unloading a dishwasher in the kitchen when Hack passed down the line at the Rocking Chair. Hack nodded when Jimmy looked at him, but got no response.

A night's sleep had transformed Hattie Mae. She was again as bright and cheerful as one of the yellow table daisies, and she didn't even mention elopement.

* * *

An hour later, in his office, Hack tried to put himself in the proper frame of mind for the 7:30 staff meeting he had called, a meeting he now, in the bright light of day, wished he had never thought of. Meetings were so predictable. And so fruitless.

Sam would doze, Billy and Louanne would jab and pick at each other, and Ferguson would look earnest. Nothing useful would be said, and the morning, or the best part of it, would be shot. And after all the blabber and fuss, he'd just wind up telling everybody what to do, the same things he would have told them without the damn meeting. The older he got the less tolerant he was of boredom. But he'd called the damn thing himself, so he might as well get it over with.

CHAPTER 16

Although Louanne was always ready ten minutes early for meetings, she made it a point never to be the first to go into the chief's office. From her desk she could watch his door without appearing to look. After more than a year as detective she was still a little afraid of him. Even when she knew he was smiling, the scar on his cheek made him look like a hailstorm about to happen.

But, though she might be a bit in awe of her boss, she had *definitely* gotten over being scared of Billy Holloway, that chauvinist caveman throwback.

When Ferguson knocked on the chief's door and went in, she gathered her notes, all typed and arranged. Then, just before leaving her office, she undid the top button of her blouse. Billy would see it immediately and start throwing her his women-don't-belong-here looks. She'd smile sweetly at him. None of the other men ever even noticed her button. She knew she was being childish, but Billy asked for it.

The chief always wanted her report first, for obvious reasons. The others, except for Ferguson, wouldn't have thoughts arranged well enough for anything much but, "Duh . . ."

At the chief's door she met Ferguson coming out.

"No meeting," he said. "He canceled it, looks like he's got the fidgets this morning."

Deflated, Louanne went back to her desk. She was trying to decide how to spend the unplanned-for time when, a few minutes later, the chief leaned in at her door.

"Come on," he said. "You drive."

She caught up with him at her cruiser, where he took the passenger seat. She got behind the wheel.

"Okay, where to?"

"Hope Springs. And you can button your blouse, Billy's not coming."

Louanne felt her face begin to burn. Her cheeks must look like beet slices, she thought. The chief didn't seem to notice her blushing, but then earlier he hadn't seemed to notice her undone button either. So much for teasing Billy.

Eyes straight ahead, she pulled into the line of traffic circling the square. The next several minutes passed in silence. They had reached the woods beyond the town limits when the chief spoke again.

"I called the hospital," he said. "Gerry Smith checked out this morning, against the doctor's advice. Maybe her memory'll improve once she's back on home ground. Also, though it's hard to imagine a connection, it turns out she might have known about the ruby the Winoskis found. Frances Winoski worked — look out!"

Louanne had braked hard when a squirrel, one of the white ones the region is famous for, shot onto the pavement in front of them. The car skidded off the road and bumped to a stop on the rough shoulder two feet from a steep drop-off.

After a deep breath, Louanne loosened her grip on the steering wheel. The squirrel shook its tail twice at them and scampered back into the woods.

"I'm sorry." Louanne kept her eyes straight ahead. "It jumped right out."

"You shouldn't have stopped."

"I think it's a young one. I couldn't just . . . just run over the poor little thing."

"You shouldn't have stopped."

"But, Chief, I . . . you're right, I know. I didn't have time to think."

"A guy, a young one, comes at you with a weapon. What're you going to do?"

"That's different."

"Yeah, different. One's a squirrel and the other's a human being. Come on, let's go. Fill me in again on what's happening with the firebug." Louanne got the car back on the road and, with difficulty, turned her thoughts to the college assignment. They had driven a half-mile before she responded.

"Uh, not much. Like I said yesterday, I talked to a bunch of students and faculty but didn't learn anything. It could be anybody — anybody crazy, that is, or part crazy, at least. But they're not going to be wearing a sign saying, 'I'm crazy.'"

Another white bundle obeyed the universal squirrel-ish compulsion to jump under car wheels, but Louanne saw it in time and only had to slow down. The chief didn't comment.

"There weren't any fires last night," she continued, "so maybe just me being there . . . I made an appointment with Professor Taylor for this afternoon to talk about it. Two o'clock." They drove the rest of the way in silence.

The only vehicle at Hope Springs was the shelter's gray Dodge van parked at the rear of the building. Louanne stopped beside it, and they went up two steps to the back door. The overgrown lawn around the building, still glistening with last night's dew, looked like a weedy hay field ready for harvest. Violet Turner opened the back door before the chief knocked.

"Morning, Violet," he said. "Gerry Smith here? We need to talk to her."

"She don't feel too good, still real weak. Hi, Louanne."

"We won't upset her," the chief said.

"Okay . . . I guess. Come on in." Violet stepped aside.

Louanne followed her boss into the room, where four women, three of them fat and one a skeleton, a different group from the ones who were there on her last visit, sat around the table. Three babies in high chairs were being fed. A thin-faced, dark-haired boy of six or seven was on the floor playing with little toy cars at the back of the room. The old wooden rocking horse was resting.

Gerry Smith, bundled in a gray blanket, lay back in a long folding lawn chair by a window, her face pallid and drawn. Her big gray eyes, so light in color they seemed almost transparent, watched the chief. The small forehead scar stood out where her almost-white hair had been pulled back in a bun, and her faded green quilted housecoat, fastened at the neck, showed a bulge over the right shoulder.

Louanne saw that the slightly dazed look Gerry had worn in the hospital had been replaced by . . . what? Defiance? Probably. And no wonder, after what she'd just been through. But it wasn't just defiance in those eyes, there was something else. What?

In the silence that followed their entry Violet Turner went to the long chair and stood behind it like a bodyguard. Everyone, babies included, stared at the chief until Gerry Smith finally motioned toward the table.

"Go on, go on, go on, eat your breakfast," she said. Her low-pitched voice was hoarse.

The scene unfroze. One of the babies banged on her tray with a metal spoon, and the women at the table relaxed a little. Violet went to the stove and stirred a pot.

"You all want some coffee, Chief?"

Gerry Smith said, "No coffee."

"Oh."

The women at the table all looked down, and the spoon scrapings and baby noises stopped. The invalid's eyes, open wide, locked with the chief's. He matched her stare.

After a long tense moment, Gerry said, "Well, what do you want?"

For an answer the chief pointedly turned his back to her and spoke to one of the women, the bony one, at the table.

"Minnie Lee, Jimmy's working at the Rocking Chair. What happened with you two? When you going home?"

"He's got a job? We'll go home whenever he comes to get us, I reckon. We had a little fuss is all, nothing much. It's just he drinks sometimes."

"He hit you?"

"It's okay. I'll call him at the Rocking Chair. We got to get on home, Ricky and me." She gestured to the boy at the back of the room.

One of the babies pushed her plastic bowl off the high chair tray. It landed upside down and splattered oatmeal on the worn linoleum.

"Here, I'll get that," Louanne said. She stooped and picked up the bowl. "You got a rag, Violet?"

Violet handed her a cloth.

The chief turned back to Gerry. "Why don't you get somebody to mow your lawn?"

"Tractor won't run," Violet said quickly. "We were mowing it ourselves, but now the tractor won't run. We know the yard looks terrible. We —"

"We're looking for your red pickup," the chief said to Gerry. "Why were you riding in the dark like that? Why'd you decide to come to work so early that morning?"

"I can start work whenever I want to."

"Have you had any threats?" He nodded toward the women at the table. "From husbands or whatever?"

"No."

"Where do you get the money to operate this place?"

In the long silence that followed that question, Louanne watched Gerry, whose eyes never left the chief's face. Louanne thought she saw her lower lip begin, barely perceptibly, to quiver.

When a baby suddenly began to wail, the chief turned to Louanne, who was still wiping up oatmeal. "Finish that up and come outside," he said, then left the room by the back door.

Louanne followed two minutes later. He wasn't in sight but the door of the outbuilding was open, and she found him looking at the engine of a small green John Deere tractor.

"Probably the plug," he said. "You see a wrench anywhere?"

She looked around the cluttered space. The floor was covered with miscellaneous cardboard boxes, many with split sides that leaked old clothes and magazines — income-tax-reducing donations from charitable souls, she assumed. There were no tools. A door that apparently led to a back room was locked.

The chief found a rusty pair of pliers under a bench.

He unscrewed the plug, examined it, said, "Fouled," wrapped the greasy object in a scrap of cloth and put it in his shirt pocket, then turned to Louanne.

"Go back in the kitchen," he said. "Spend the rest of the morning there, more if you need to. My being there just scares the babies. And their mamas. And dear, sweet, precious little Geranium would probably chew my nose off if I asked her any more questions."

"What will I be looking for?"

"Oh, I don't know. Like you were doing yesterday, look for boyfriends and husbands who didn't like Gerry Smith, to start with. Probably a lot of *them*. Just keep your eyes open. And your ears."

"Okay."

"And listen for anything about the Winoski ruby, but don't mention it. Frances Winoski was a volunteer here, you can ask about her. She talked about the ruby to one of the other volunteers in the kitchen the night before she was killed, which was also the night before Gerry Smith was shot. Maybe somebody overheard and got excited. Hell, maybe it was Geranium who heard the word 'ruby,' though I don't see how that would have gotten her shot."

"You don't think Gerry —"

"I don't think anything. Just get 'em talking, you're good at that. Who knows? Ask for a cup of coffee and see if Geranium relents. I'll send somebody to pick you up in time for your meeting with Art Taylor."

"Okay, Chief."

Louanne went back in the kitchen, where all the women except the patient started talking at once.

"What does he want? What's he after? Is he as mean as he looks? Has he got a girlfriend?"

At 1:45 Sam arrived at Hope Springs in Louanne's cruiser. She drove him back to the station, then continued across town to Sky Valley College, where she parked in a visitor's space, went into the administration building and climbed the poorly lighted, wide wooden staircase to the second floor. Lurleen Watkins looked up from her secretary's desk in the hall outside the president's office. Voices came through the open office door.

"Hi, Louanne, have a seat." Lurleen motioned to a straight-backed chair beside her desk. "They won't be long."

"Thanks. Who're they?"

"Some students. They got together a committee to complain about all the fires we're having. There's even a reporter from *Sky Talk* with them. No telling what they'll put in the next issue of that . . . rag. Students . . . huh! If it weren't for them, the college would be a pretty nice place."

Louanne laughed. "Aw, Lurleen, you know you really love 'em all. You're —"

"One thing I know is that students shouldn't come to the president with their silly complaints, but they do. They'd stay in there all afternoon if we let 'em, but Professor Taylor told me to interrupt at two o'clock."

A girl's voice rose above the murmur in the office. "But we're *afraid!*"

"That's Heather Holmes," Lurleen said. "She wants the college to schedule karate classes for all females. Last month she wanted more modern dance courses. The month before that it was something else, I forget."

After a short pause a man said, in the hollow tones of a funeral director closing a ceremony, "Cost too much, much too much. Anyway, not feasible."

Lurleen lowered her voice to a whisper. "Do you know Mr. McFee? That was him."

"The comptroller? No, I've seen him but never met him."

"He's also in charge of security, and absolutely the tightest man with a dollar I ever met. The students won't get a nickel from him, and I imagine they know it. That's why they came to Professor Taylor in the first place, to get around Mr. McFee. They even brought Brent — that's the McFee's son. They probably hope he can get around his dad. Fat chance."

"Just *one* lesson would help," Heather Holmes cried. "*That* wouldn't cost much."

"Impossible," the comptroller responded.

"Mr. McFee sounds like a bear with a bellyache," Lurleen whispered in the extended silence that followed. "But we know better."

"We do? What do we know?"

"He's so henpecked he probably lays eggs. Takes it out on everybody else. It's really strange. When *she's* around, he just absolutely changes to another person."

"He doesn't sound like a wimp."

"She's a professor, child psychology, and you know how *they* are. Marie. *Doctor* — and don't you forget it — Marie McFee. It rhymes. She leads him around like a . . . a . . . I don't know what. He had a nervous breakdown or something awhile back. With her for a wife, it's easy to understand why. She —"

"How long have the McFees been here?"

"Oh, ages. Since Brent was a baby. Poor Brent. He's really strange, I mean *odd.* All that child-psychologizing, I guess. They say he's in what they call, you know, 'therapy' or whatever. He looks like a . . . a . . . lump of uncooked dough. With about the same personality. Except for his eyes. They . . . I don't know, but I can tell you one thing, Brent's the kind of guy I wouldn't want to meet in a dark alley. Or even in a bright alley, if you want to know the truth."

"What does he do?" Louanne said.

"Oh, I don't know, nothing, I suppose. It's just the way he looks at you, but I'm prejudiced. Child psychology, huh. I'm sure Brent'd be okay if he could ever get away from mama."

"What do the students think of . . . Marie?" Louanne said.

"Oh, they all hate her." The secretary reached across the desk and nudged a flip-page calendar to make it line up with the desk edge.

"Then why does the college keep her?"

"She's got tenure, and apparently she has some kind of reputation in her field. All child psychologists are probably just like her, if you can imagine that. She spends most of her time going to 'meetings' and giving 'papers.'"

The clock in the chapel tower chimed twice. Lurleen gave Louanne a "watch this" look, rolled her chair to the left and leaned in the doorway. "Louanne McLeod is here, Professor Taylor."

"Send her in," Art said. "We're finished."

The seven people in the room — three boys and two girls on one side, the college president and a small, almost bald, dark-suited man on the other — stared in silence as Louanne crossed the thick carpet to the only vacant chair. The pistol on her belt felt huge, like a ham hanging from her hip. She sat down next to a thin-faced boy holding an open notebook and pencil. When she nodded to him he dropped his eyes and blushed.

What *was* it with boys? Couldn't she even *look* at them without them having a stroke or something?

One of the girls — dark-eyed, dancer's figure, Barbra Streisand haircut, no makeup, no bra — leaned forward in her chair.

"I don't think it's *fair*," she said, then turned to a large, formless boy next to her. "What do you think, Brent?"

Lurleen's don't-meet-him-in-the-alley looked up from the carpet and murmured, "Yeah, not fair."

He glanced at Louanne then turned in his chair and stared directly at her, his gray-green eyes, absolutely devoid of any expression Louanne could read, seeming to focus somewhere behind her head. After a moment he blinked several times and turned toward his father. The dough of his face seemed to reshape itself. Louanne saw a sudden brief flash of intense, unreadable emotion.

What emotion? Fear? Hate? Despair? She didn't know, but she wouldn't soon forget those pale blank eyes.

She'd noticed Brent in her campus questioning but hadn't spoken to him, thinking at the time that she knew his type, which seemed these days to accumulate on college campuses.

Always visibly bored and above-it-all, the type who would stand apart from a group, smoking intensely, eyes narrowed in contemplation of far-off truths unrecognized by the unfortunates around him or her. Boy-types usually wore ponytails and nose rings; girl-types, outlandish clothes. They seldom actually showed up in class. Though Brent didn't fit the image visually — his dark hair was cut in a bristle crewcut and his nose and ears were ringless — Louanne had thought that she had him pegged. But now, seeing him up close, she wasn't sure.

She looked around the room, which had obviously been redone recently. New carpet aroma dominated the usual musty old-wooden-building smell. The colors reminded her of mushroom soup and dried tomato. The only bright spot in the room, other than Heather's sequined blue tee shirt, was a tall vase of bronze chrysanthemums on the huge walnut desk. Not a bad effect overall.

Art Taylor — Louanne had heard the chief call the college president "Art" so many times that that was how she thought of him — slouched in his chair behind the desk, his philosopher's worn tweed coat unbuttoned, his soft thick brownish tie carefully knotted. The collar tips of his light blue shirt showed white where the fabric had frayed from too many washings.

He yawned deeply without trying to hide it and blinked several times, then swiveled his chair toward the window. Hammond McFee cleared his throat and gave an emphatic little nod. The meeting was over. The students stood up after an awkward moment and filed out of the room, Heather first, Brent next. The thin-faced reporter stopped in the doorway and turned back to the president.

"Uh, Dr. Taylor, do you think the arsonist is a student? Or . . ."

Without even a glance, the philosopher waved him out of the room.

"Art," Hammond McFee said when the journalist had left, "I've hired two extra watchmen, but karate lessons are too much. The students —"

"It's up to you, Hammond. Do whatever you want. Thanks. Close the door when you leave."

After a narrow look at Louanne, the comptroller did as asked. When the door clicked behind him, Art used his heels to pull his chair across the carpet to the desk.

"I've decided what meetings are," he said. "Meetings are hell. Just imagine sitting through a meeting that lasted for all eternity. Say with coffee breaks every two hundred years. If that's not hell . . ."

Louanne laughed. "I apologize for starting another one, but the chief is still hoping you'll give me some names, firebug possibles."

"But, you know, if the devil were there, maybe it wouldn't be so bad. We could have . . . oh, I don't know, politicians and lawyers maybe, and college professors, and make them sit there without talking for a hundred years. Now, that would be real torture. Jab 'em with pitchforks every decade or so. Maybe the devil could . . . I don't have any names for you."

"Oh. Uh, will you?"

"No. Not a good idea. None of the fires was a real danger. Some pathetic lonely sick child. We'll find him and kiss him to make him feel wanted. Sorry I bothered you with it. How do you like working for Hack?"

"I love it. He's a good boss. Scares me, though, sometimes. Is it okay if I keep interviewing students on campus? The chief wants me to."

"Sure. Give the boys something to talk about. Make 'em blush like you just did our intrepid young reporter. The girls will talk about you too, but they won't blush, they'll grit their teeth. You say Hack scares you? Well, he scares me too, sometimes."

Art sat for a moment frowning at his fingertips, then turned back to the window. Louanne decided she'd been forgotten and stood up to leave.

"Give Hack a message from me, will you," Art said without looking at her. "Tell him that happiness is jumping out of bed in the morning, whistling, to go fight somebody. In a good cause. Tell him that happiness is having something bad to fight against. Sometimes people have to *invent* bad things to fight, if they want to be happy."

Louanne closed the door behind her, nodded to Lurleen, and walked to the head of the stairs that led down to the lobby. Hammond McFee and a thin woman of medium height and man-cut black hair stood at the bottom almost blocking the way. Brent had draped himself over the corner rail post. A suitcase, one of the modern walking kind with its retractable handle extended, was on the floor beside the woman, who carried a thick, stuffed, old-style briefcase in her left hand. Louanne edged around them. The woman was speaking.

". . . and don't forget to feed the cats, like you did last time."

"But Marie . . ." Hammond McFee's funereal voice had become a thin bleat.

Louanne looked to see if it really was him speaking. It was, but he had been transformed. His shoulders drooped and his mouth and eyes had become those of a hurt puppy. Fascinated, she paused and made a little project of referring to her notebook.

"And I told you yesterday to talk to sociology about Brent's last test grade," Dr. Marie continued. "He says you haven't done it yet. The way they graded it was *positively indecent*. And prejudiced."

"But Marie . . ."

Louanne glanced up from her notebook. Mrs. Doctor Professor, glaring, jaw stuck out, reminded her of pictures of General MacArthur in the Philippines. A pipe in Marie's mouth wouldn't have seemed out of place.

"Hammond, do you realize there's a spot on your tie?" she said. "Let's go, Brent. Bring my bag."

Her son, who had been regarding the back of his mother's head with another unreadable expression, turned toward Louanne and stared at her again, unblinking.

CHAPTER 17

Hack turned from the window where he had been watching four sixty-ish tourists in the park across from the station lay out a picnic on the table nearest the Confederate statue. He went to his desk, took a pencil and a no-nonsense sheet of blue-lined school notebook paper from the drawer, wrote PLANS across the top of the sheet, then wrote a 1 on the first line. Encouraged, he wrote 2, 3, 4, and 5 below that, skipping four lines between numbers. After a moment he added a 6 at the bottom. He couldn't recall at the moment just what his sixth problem was, but he knew he'd counted that many earlier.

After scowling at the paper for about a minute, he put the pencil down and went back to the window. On Whiteoak Mountain, up beyond the college, maples and poplars had begun to make early autumn splashes of red and yellow in the solid green matte of oaks. Here and there in a crease in the mountain's side he could pick out the sparkle of Bradley Creek, where two years earlier he had caught a twenty-six-inch rainbow in the deep pool below Bradley Falls. In his mind he recaught the trout, for maybe the hundredth time, then sighed and went back to the pristine white-and-blue challenge on his desk. Fifteen minutes later the page looked like this:

PLANS

1. Hope Springs. Geranium?? Get tractor plug.
2. Winoski murders. Ruby. Geranium??
3. Firebug. Call Art.

4. Women off cliff. Help sheriff.
5. Cat killer. Sam.
6.

He was scowling at the last number when Sam stuck his head in the open office door. "Need to talk to you, Chief."

"Come on in, sit down. What you got?"

Sam ignored the offered chair. "That pot patch out by Wildcat Creek. You gotta come look."

"Oh, yeah . . . pot. I almost forgot that." Hack scribbled the word next to 6, then looked up at his oldest detective. "What's at Wildcat?"

"You need to see it."

"You catch somebody hoeing his garden?"

"No. You need to see."

"What you got on our cat killer?"

"Nothin'. You need to come out to Wildcat to see what I found."

Hack knew that when good Officer Bailey made up his mind, there was no budging him. Besides, there were brown trout in Wildcat that could *eat* the rainbow he'd caught in Bradley Creek. He'd finish his plans later. When he stood up to go with Sam, Louanne appeared in the doorway, notebook in hand.

"You want me to come back later, Chief?" she said.

"No, come on in. What you got? Sit down, Sam."

"Not a whole lot," Louanne said. "I just came from the college. Professor Taylor isn't going to give me a list of suspects. He's not worried about the fires."

"Yeah? Well, he ought to be."

"He also said to tell you that happiness is when you jump out of bed and go fight somebody bad."

"He have any suggestions as to who's good and who's bad?"

"You're supposed to just make up bad things if you need to."

Yeah, that was Art. He'd pick up the theme at Bertha's and philosophize about it until Hack had forgotten what the original question was. "Wonderful. Did he say anything else?"

"He said it's okay if I keep talking to people on campus, though I'm not completely sure what I'll be looking for."

"What did you find out at Hope Springs after I left?"

It took a moment for Louanne to shift scenes. "Well, to start with, you were right. All of them, even Gerry, talked to me. Couldn't wait. And Violet fixed me a cup of coffee. It's pathetic."

"What's pathetic?"

"The whole place, Chief. They haven't got *any* money, and no hopes of getting any as far as I can see. I don't think they know what they're going to have for supper tonight, it's that bad. And the poor women there — like Minnie Lee Mayhew — they'll just have to go back to wherever it was they came from. And the children . . . it's just pathetic. I'm going out there tonight. As a volunteer. I'll take them some supper."

"Anything about who shot Geranium?"

"Nobody's got a clue, I think. Some of the husbands or boyfriends might shoot their own women — or the other way around — but from what I heard there's no real reason to think they'd shoot Gerry. I'm sure they don't *like* her, but . . ."

"What about Frances Winoski?"

"Oh, they seem to think she was okay. Some of the volunteers act condescending to them, you know, and the women pick up on that real quick, but Frances wasn't that way. She hadn't made much of an impression one way or the other, actually."

"Had they heard about the ruby?"

"Only the town rumors. Nobody's very interested. When you're worrying about your next meal . . ."

Hack got up from his desk and went back to the window. The picnickers had progressed from drumsticks to what looked like apple pie. In the small playground across the square a young couple sat on a bench watching three children on the swings. Hack knew the family. *They* weren't worried about their next meal. He went back to his desk, took a checkbook from a drawer, quickly scribbled a check, tore it out of the book and gave it to Louanne.

"Cash this and give Geranium the money when you go back out there. I've got a special fund. Just say it's a contribution, not where it came from. Anonymous."

"Okay, Chief. Believe me, they'll appreciate it."

Hack's "special fund" — known by everybody in the department to be his personal checking account — was never talked about. If the subject ever came up in his presence he quickly scowled it away.

"Uh, what do you want me to do now, Chief? Should I go back up to the college?"

"Put that aside for now. Maybe Art's right, maybe it's over. We've got to find out about the damn Winoski ruby, assuming it actually exists. Well, there *must* be one, I guess, or they wouldn't have told John Redding. So, let's find it." He took a slip of paper from the desk drawer and held it out to Louanne.

"Here, this is a list of gem dealers in the area. Redding gave it to me. There aren't many. I want you to visit all of them, unannounced. See what turns up."

"Okay, but I don't know anything about the subject, nothing. Never even thought about it."

"Go to the library, read about it, but don't ask John Redding."

"You think he —"

"Don't know. Maybe the ruby was stolen earlier than he said, maybe before Geranium was shot. Maybe . . . look, carry pictures of the Winoskis — there's one in their bedroom — and one of Redding. And Gerry Smith too. See if the gem dealers recognize anybody."

Louanne looked doubtful. "Where can I get pictures of Redding? And Gerry?"

"Hell, ask 'em. You don't have to say why."

"Well, I guess."

"Give it a try. You never know what kind of fish you might catch until you put your little bug in the water. So go fishing." When Hack realized that Louanne was peering down at the PLANS on his desk he turned the sheet over and stood up.

"Come on, Sam, wake up. Let's go."

Officer Bailey, toothpick half-chewed, pulled off the pavement onto an old logging road, drove a couple hundred yards and stopped in a clearing in thick woods.

"Maybe I shouldn't have left it, but I wanted you to see, Chief."

"Left what?"

"You'll see. It's not far."

Sam entered an almost invisible path that led downhill from the road. Hack followed. Beyond the thick underbrush at the edge of the woods, widely spaced huge trees, mostly oak, formed a green ceiling high above. The path they followed, an ancient one with no signs of recent use, was clear. He heard the rush of Wildcat Creek somewhere ahead.

After a quarter-mile they reached the creek, where piles of rotting leaves, broken tree limbs and bent saplings showed the effects of the last flood. Lush weeds and bushes grew in the flood plain.

Sam stopped. "See it?"

"See what?"

"You don't see it. Watch."

Sam picked up a long stick and probed the surface of the path before him. With a loud whoosh a small tree that had been bent in a U jerked upright, leaving a rope noose dangling over the path.

"Using goddamn old Indian tricks," Sam said. "Could of broke somebody's goddamn neck. That's what I wanted you to see. Come on."

A dozen yards further was a small cleared area. Five-foot-high marijuana plants, weed-free and cultivated, were evenly spaced in the clearing.

"Like the newspapers say, street value of a zillion million dollars, at least," Sam said. "Bastard's probably out there somewhere watching us now. Saw my car. I don't normally drive to places like this. What you want me to do?"

"Dig 'em up and burn 'em. You stay here. I'll send Billy and some guys with shovels. If anybody bothers you, shoot 'em."

On his way back to town in Sam's cruiser, Hack got a radio call from Melba. "The sheriff's here looking for you, Chief. He decided to wait in your office."

A few minutes later Hack found his friend of many years seated at his desk, chair tilted back, smoking a cigar.

"Where the hell you been, Hawg-boy?" the Sheriff said, waving his cigar. He stood up. "Come on, let's go agitate my murdering little creep."

CHAPTER 18

Harold had always wondered about eyes. A single glance at a pair of them could tell you what was in a person's mind. But what *was* it about eyes? How could there be so much information when there was so little about them that could change. The pupils could contract or expand, the eyelids and eyebrows move up or down a millimeter or so, and the skin around the eyes could scrunch up, but that was all. How could those tiny features show love, happiness, boredom, terror, all emotions?

He moved the picture closer to the light. In Corliss's eyes were love *and* terror, together. How could that *be*?

He'd often wondered if dead eyes showed expression, the last living expression. The quick answer was no, dead faces couldn't *have* expressions. But, if so, what was it that actually changed about the eyes when a person died? Did eye colors fade with death, like the colors of fish. He wished now that he had taken shots of the women's bodies. Then he could compare live eyes with dead ones.

Actually, he couldn't remember for sure now if their eyes had been open or closed when he found them on the rocks. How could he possibly forget that?

If their eyes were closed, it wouldn't have mattered. He could have opened them. Closeups of dead eyes to put beside those same eyes alive, what a study that would have made!

". . . could never have published it, though, except maybe with false names, maybe in some other country. Too bad. Stop talking to yourself."

He got up and put the picture back in its hiding place, then wandered aimlessly around the studio looking at this photo and that, straightening things, puttering. After two rounds of the room he sat back down at the desk and let his mind drift.

Soon he was lost in his favorite fantasy, one he'd feasted on for years, a photography club for boys. Or even girls. Or possibly both. It didn't matter a whole lot to him which. Nine to twelve was the right age, or maybe just up to eleven. It would take time, but that didn't matter, he had time. A lot of little steps, a little farther every time they got together. They would learn to trust him. To love him.

Harold turned toward the wall mirror and smiled his sweet, innocent smile, the one in which his blue eyes positively begged to be loved.

There they were again, eyes. How was he able to make his own eyes look so . . . so nice? He leaned toward the mirror to better see his eyebrows and pupils, but when he did the sweetness left his expression. He laughed.

"You can't look at your own expression, idiot. Looking changes it. Maybe if I took a surprise picture of *me.* How could I do that?"

The sound of a car on the gravel broke his reverie. He went to the window. It was the sheriff's gray, gold-star-painted cruiser, and the police chief was with him. Harold realized he was glad to see them. He was lonely. No clients had shown up at the studio since the . . . accident, not even the ones with appointments.

The sheriff would make him go over the whole affair again, but that was good. The question sessions had become a game, a sparring match, little ol' Harold versus the big bad sheriff. The game was fun, and he was winning.

He arranged his face in its most likeable expression and opened the door before his visitors reached it. "Come in, Sheriff, come in. And Chief Hackett. Pretty evening, isn't it? I just *love* this time of day in summer."

The sheriff scowled and strode into the room. Harold went back to the desk and sat down. The sheriff took the chair beside the desk and began, without preamble, to ask the same questions that Harold had now answered how many times? A hundred? It was funny. Harold's sweet smile became a grin at the thought.

While the sheriff talked, the chief walked around the studio, poking here and there, looking at things. Sometimes he was only inches away from the picture. Harold felt like calling out, "Now you're getting warmer," or, "You're getting cold."

". . . they fell, how long did you wait before you climbed down?" the sheriff said. "Why didn't you go right then?"

"Oh, sorry, Sheriff, my mind drifted. How long before I climbed down? Two minutes, three maybe." Harold had to restrain an urge to giggle.

The sheriff went through his insurance and inheritance questions, then seemed to run out of things to ask. Maybe he would decide to start at the top again. It was fun to watch the big man's eyes, washed-out blue set in deep wrinkles. He always kept a poker face, but couldn't control his eyes.

What they said was that the sheriff would really *like* to just reach over the desk and kill Harold. He'd grab him around the neck and squeeze until Harold's eyes popped out and his tongue turned black.

The image made Harold grin again.

"How much land you got here?" the chief said from the back of the room.

"Eighty-two acres. Corliss's grandfather was a farmer."

"How much of it is inside the town limits?"

"Just this little corner where the studio is. The rest is county."

"You grow pot out there?"

Grow marijuana? Him? This was new. Harold chuckled. "Hardly."

"Tom, if I were you, I'd check that out." The chief talked over Harold's head as though he weren't present. "There could be a damn plantation of the stuff along the creeks. This guy looks to me like the type that would grow it. Hell, maybe his wife found out and . . ."

"Good idea," the sheriff said. "I'll get a crew in here tomorrow."

Ah! Another phase of the game. They wanted to make him mad. Wonderful. "Yes, please check it out for me," Harold said.

"Somebody could be using my land. I never go out there, and I would certainly *hate* to be breaking the law, even if I wasn't aware of doing it. You just never know what some people will do."

The sour look the sheriff gave him then was just precious. Like a piece of pecan pie after a good dinner. Harold thought of a way to add whipped cream to the pie.

"By the way sheriff, there's something I've been wondering. Would you men let me take your picture? A study, you know. 'Intrepid lawman at his task,' or some such title. You both have such strong faces. There would be no charge for the pictures, of course."

CHAPTER 19

The sheriff drove away from the studio in silence. Just after passing Deal's Exxon he reached out and slapped the dashboard with the flat of his hand. "I'm not going to run next election."

"You said that last time," Hack replied. "But you —"

"When you get so you want to kill your suspects — slowly — it's time to quit. That guy knows we know he killed the women. He's laughing at us."

"Yeah."

"Your marijuana search idea is good. Maybe we can give him something else to laugh at. I'll fly over and spot something suspicious, enough to justify looking. We'll drag it out, stomp over every square inch of his woods. Hell, maybe we'll be lucky and find a few plants, it wouldn't matter whether he put them there or not. We find anything, I'll yank him back in my jail and keep him there till his butt grows moss."

"You going to search his studio? Ever been up in the house?"

"No, I thought of it, but it'd be hard to justify a warrant unless we get something more. Anyway, the studio's in your jurisdiction, remember. If there'd been a weapon or something... Maybe we'll actually find some pot. I got half a mind to plant some in his woods myself, just so we can find it. *Then* we'd see who does the goddamn laughing. He —"

"Turn here and let's go by the Rocking Chair," Hack said. "And quit feeling sorry for yourself. A piece of pie'll get your mind off little pink-cheeks back there. Besides, I want you to tell me all about rubies. And then I want to tell you all *my* troubles. I'm tired of listening to yours."

* * *

The Rocking Chair was in full supper swing. Wednesday night was Rotary night, and the eight tables at the back of the room, kept a little apart from the rest to serve as a town meeting place, were occupied by late-middle-aged men in suits and ties. Laughter, dish clatter, and tobacco smoke filled the bright room. In the serving line Hattie Mae's only response to Hack's suggestion that they elope was to say "Pshaw!" and add another spoonful of ice cream to his pie. He and the sheriff carried their trays to a shunned table by the cigarette machine and sat with their backs to the Rotarians.

"Okay, now tell me about rubies," Hack said.

The sheriff didn't know, or care, anything about rubies. And he couldn't get his mind off Harold Pell long enough to pay much attention to Hack's subsequent recital of double murders, firebugs, dead cats, booby-trapped pot gardens, cops who primped and would run in the ditch rather than hit a squirrel, and women's shelters going broke. But the pie lived up to its reputation, and both men felt better when they'd finished eating. On the way out of the café Hack noticed Jimmy Mayhew in the kitchen. The sight of Minnie Lee's husband, shaved, haircut, working, was one little plus in what had been a very minus day.

After the sheriff dropped him off at the station a little after ten, the supreme strategy-maker and order-giver of the Blue Ridge constabulary retired to his office. He took out his planning sheet, laid it on the desk and scowled blackly at it. With a sigh, he reached in the desk drawer for a pencil. Close inspection showed the pencil point to be a bit blunt, so he went out to the sharpener on the dispatcher's desk. Ferguson looked up from the calculus book he was studying as part of his take-courses-when-you-can program at the community college, but he didn't put the book down.

"Quiet night?" Hack asked.

"So far."

"How's the math coming?"

"Okay, I guess. But there's this one problem, a differential equation. I don't . . ." Ferguson looked down at a notebook page covered with math scribbles. "Say, maybe you can help me, Chief. I'm not sure what to do with the x-cubed here. Do you think —"

"No, I definitely don't think. Afraid I can't help you with x-anything. I'll go check on our prisoner."

Sharpened pencil in hand, Hack went downstairs to the two cells that constituted the town's jail, where Jakey Boatwright, the only occupant, was sprawled on a cot snoring. Hack stared for a minute, realized that waking Jakey and trying to get him to talk was an even worse prospect than strategizing, then went back upstairs to PLAN.

Ten minutes later he wrote "booby-trap" next to "pot." Then he added another big question mark by "Hope Springs." There was more to that story than he'd been told. He was positive. At least he was pretty sure he was positive. *Probably* sure he was positive, anyway.

Hell.

He moved up his list to "Winoskis." Their double murder was where he should be concentrating his effort. He doodled a lopsided, multifaceted jewel beside the name. The missing — or maybe mythical — ruby was his only real lead, unless the couple had been shot as part of a random burglary gone bad.

No, a burglary just didn't fit the facts. They hadn't been killed randomly, they'd been executed. Why?

Well, of course, a valuable gem would have been reason enough for somebody to kill them. But had the Winoskis *really* found one, or was it just a typical town rumor gone wild? Of course it wasn't necessary that the ruby actually existed. All that was required was for someone to *believe* it existed.

Okay. For now, just assume the ruby's real, and worth a bundle. Take it from there. Or, no, don't do that. Start by assuming there *isn't* a ruby, or that, if there is one, it's not worth much. Isn't that more likely? He'd never heard of anybody else ever finding a damn ruby.

Maybe the Winoskis hadn't been able to convince the thief, who would almost surely have been known to them, that the rumor wasn't true, and he'd shot them in a rage. Or maybe he killed them in cold blood, since they'd recognized him.

Unless he wore a mask.

He? Why not she? Or a gang? Or a space alien? Or a trained monkey, like Edgar Allen Poe's?

When a picture of a pistol-toting gorilla at the Winoskis' kitchen door popped into his mind, Hack shook his head and grunted. He should stop daydreaming like a damned idiot and get back to facts. Two people were dead, and he should be doing something about it. He should find the damn ruby. If it actually existed. And if it didn't, he should find that out too. Somehow.

The brooding, rock-hewn boss-of-it-all rubbed the scar on his cheek, which had begun to itch as it always did when he was frustrated, and closed the planning session with a decision. He would go with Louanne next morning to visit the Asheville gem shops. At least that would be doing *something*. He put planning sheet and pencil back in the drawer, slammed it shut, and sat back, a sour look on his face.

What the hell did he think he was trying to do? His brain was about as useful as one of those kudzu-covered junk cars in Moon Gulledge's front yard. He ought to quit trying to act like a damn detective. Maybe he could still handle drunks and wife beaters, but crime waves? Hell, why didn't he just go back home and grow tobacco for Mama? She still loved him. He ought to just quit right now.

Oh, stop whining. If he were to quit, Billy was next in line to be chief. The town deserved better than that.

What he needed right now was a jukebox session with Art. Actually, most of Hack's days now ended in front of Bertha's jukebox. Without a bit of "what-*is*-happiness" talk with his favorite philosopher, the day seemed somehow incomplete. Art would probably be about eight-tenths drunk by now, mumble-philosophy drunk, have-to-be-driven-home drunk. But he'd be Art at his conversational best, and Hack didn't mind ferrying him home.

The ancient yellow Ford wasn't in Bertha's parking lot, so Hack didn't stop, a talk session with Moon Gulledge and his buddies, whose pickups were in their usual places, not being high on his list of priorities. He thought of going by Art's house on Faculty Row, decided against it, and turned in the direction of his condo. Halfway there, still not ready to face unmade bed and dirty cereal bowl, he changed his mind and began to ramble aimlessly through town. He considered going by Louanne's place and talking to Allie. But, as last night, it was clearly too late to just drop in. And besides, Louanne, who wasn't on duty, would probably be there. Not that that really ought to matter — if he ever actually married Allie, Louanne would be his *stepdaughter*. They might all live in the same house. That would be okay, he supposed, but not tonight.

Anyway . . . what was he thinking about? Marry Allie? Hell, he'd never even had a date with her. If he actually were to come out and propose, she'd probably giggle in his face. No, Allie was too polite. She'd giggle later, in private.

But, hell, he'd been giggled at before and it hadn't killed him. He ought to go on and ask her. At least Louanne thought he should.

He was idling along beside the college about to give up and go home when an unexpected thought came to him. He realized there *was* something other than talk to Allie that he wanted to do right now. He'd like to talk with Gerry Smith. With hard-eyed, frozen-faced Geranium.

Why should he want to do that? He considered the question.

He didn't want to interrogate her, just *talk*. He wanted to see those lines around her mouth soften, maybe even coax out a little smile, and find out why her seeing cops, even Louanne, brought out a caged wildcat look. Geranium had become a puzzle for him, and he wanted to solve it.

Puzzle, hell. Don't kid yourself. You can't get the damn bedroom out of your mind, you know what you'd like to do.

His better judgment stepped right up in front of his face then and stamped its foot. Pretty little Geranium was a Yankee do-gooder. She'd get things all stirred up in town and then leave, just like all the do-gooders. And some person had come within a twitch of blowing her away the other night. She knew something about that that she wasn't saying. Geranium was trouble just waiting to happen.

But what about those poor women in the shelter? The clients, or residents, or whatever you called them. The ones like Minnie Lee Mayhew. *They* weren't foreign do-gooders, they were *his* people, the people he really cared about, the ones he grew up with back in tobacco land. They needed help. And Geranium was trying to help them, right? And somebody had tried to kill her, right? So what was he doing to keep it from happening again?

Hell.

He drove out to Hope Springs. There was a light on in the kitchen but the parking lot was empty. He pulled in and stopped but, once there, couldn't think of an even half-valid reason to knock on the door at ten minutes after midnight. He'd just scare people, wake up babies. The babies would cry.

Then he realized that Gerry Smith probably wouldn't be there anyway, she'd be back in her cabin up on Jeter. He considered for a moment driving up the mountain and knocking on *her* door, but that would be insane. With that thought he finally surrendered and went to his condo.

Still not sleepy, he ignored dirty dishes, got in bed and read one more time the section on "Free Will" in the philosophy encyclopedia Art had given him. As with each of the previous attempts, he fell asleep, this time in the middle of paragraph three. During the night he dreamed of gorillas and Jakey Boatwright. And Gerry Smith.

Next morning he skipped the Rocking Chair and his customary Aunt Ola briefing, picked up coffee and sausage biscuits at Hardee's, and was waiting in front of Louanne's apartment when she came out to go rock hunting in Asheville.

CHAPTER 20

The Asheville Gem and Mineral Company, Jack Lange, President, turned out to be a small moldy wooden building in the woods behind a modest brick house in a residential section north of Asheville. Poison ivy half-covered a little wooden sign that gave the company name and marked a short brick path that led from a two-car parking area up to the building. The whole setup reminded Hack of Harold Pell's studio.

Hack followed Louanne to the door, where she rang the bell. After a short wait someone called up to them from the house.

"Jack's not here today. Can I help you?" The speaker was a woman, middle-aged, wearing a long red housecoat. She had come out through the garage.

"Police," Hack said. "Are you Mrs. Lange?"

"Oh lord, is there a problem? Is Jack —"

"No, no, nothing like that," Louanne called back. "We just have a few questions. Maybe if we could sit down somewhere . . ."

"Go on in the office there, it's not locked. Let me get some shoes on. I'll be right up. I'm Valerie Lange."

Louanne opened the door and Hack followed her into the office. Rocks were everywhere — even books and stacks of papers were holders for rocks. It was worse than at the Winoskis'. A computer, its screen dark, took up half of a cluttered desk to the right of the door. A faint mildew smell in the room underlay a glue-like odor. In one corner, under its own burden of stones, was a small black safe.

Valerie Lange, forty-ish, substantial, unnaturally blond, open-faced, joined them.

"Pardon the mess," she said. "Actually, it's not a mess. Jack knows every pebble in here. I worry when he goes out in the field by himself, and I thought . . . I was afraid he'd . . ." She moved a tray of small brown-orange stones from one of three wooden chairs and pointed to another.

"Just move the box off that one," she said. "Have a seat. This is the first time the police have ever been to see us. What can I do for you?"

Louanne glanced at Hack, who gave a little nod, then turned back to the woman in the red housecoat. "Where is Mr. Lange?"

"Somewhere up on the other side of Craggy, looking for garnets. There was a rockslide up there last winter. A slide usually turns up something interesting. Sometimes I go with him, but not this time."

"How long has he been away?"

"He left Monday afternoon. He should be back today. When I saw your uniform I was afraid. You know, snakebite, fall . . ."

"We're interested in a ruby somebody found," Louanne said. "Possibly a big one. Is Mr. Lange where he can be reached?"

"No, he camps. No phone, no way to get in touch except to climb the mountain. That's the way he wants it. A big ruby? Nothing like that in a long time as far as I know, but Jack's the one. He runs the business. I really don't know details."

Louanne took an envelope from her coat pocket and held out several photographs.

"Do you recognize anybody?"

Valerie Lange studied each picture. "I know John Redding. He and Jack have gone in the field together a few times. Nice guy. And I've seen these two, but I don't know them." She handed Louanne the snapshot that had been in the Winoskis' bedroom. "Like I say, I don't have much to do with the business. If you want to know the truth, I don't think I even *like* rocks. But don't tell Jack."

"When did you see these people?" Louanne tapped the Winoskis' picture.

"I don't know, maybe last month. They came to see Jack. I just happened to be in the garage and noticed them drive up."

"You haven't seen them in, say, the last week?"

"No, but I wasn't looking. They could well have come to see Jack before he left for Craggy."

Hack began to feel a small wisp of optimism. His hunt for a maybe hypothetical ruby was becoming a hunt for a definitely real person. It was comforting. He walked over to a framed map of the region hanging on the wall.

"Mrs. Lange, could you show me where your husband is?"

She went to the map and, after a moment's contemplation, circled an area with her finger that included all of Craggy Mountain and part of Mount Mitchell, about a hundred square miles of woods. "Somewhere in here, I think," she said. "I really don't know the area. Sorry."

"That's okay. Could you describe your husband's car?"

"He took the Bronco, four-wheel drive, you know. It's dark red, kind of beat up." She even knew the license number without having to look it up.

"Well, sorry to have bothered you, Mrs. Lange," Hack said when Louanne had written down the car description. "Please have your husband call the Blue Ridge Police Department as soon as he gets home."

They rode in silence until they passed through Beaucatcher Tunnel, then Hack said:

"Okay, you're Jack Lange. The Winoskis come to see you. They show you a big ruby. They're all hush-hush about it. They may even leave it with you for appraisal. They trust you. You see that it's worth a lot of money. You put them off somehow, then go to their house while you're supposedly incommunicado up on the mountain. You kill them, steal the ruby — if you don't already have it — then go camp out on Craggy a few days. What's wrong with that?"

"Nothing that I can see."

"I want his fingerprints."

"Oh."

"Any ideas about how to get them?"

"Well, there were things on his desk," Louanne said after a moment. "Those smooth rocks, for instance. If we can think of a reason, I could go back right now and —"

"No. Not yet, anyway. We'll see what turns up under his name, see if he's got a record. I'll ask the Buncombe sheriff to look for his car. And we can ask the people around the Winoski house if they saw a red Bronco the day they —"

"Oh, look at that!"

A young deer, almost a fawn, was sprawled just off the pavement, its neck bent backwards and fresh blood showing at its mouth.

"Oh, the poor thing. It must have just happened."

"Too many deer these days. No way to keep them off the roads."

"But it's so . . . so . . . *terrible.* I hate to see the blood."

There were a couple of things Hack could have said to that, but didn't. They drove on, grim and tight-lipped for Louanne, dozing and head-nodding for Hack, until the radio squawked to life.

"Chief, accident on 64 east, just beyond the underpass," Melba said. "Apparently some people are hurt. Sam and Ferguson are on the way."

Hack took the mike. "They need me?"

"No, it didn't sound too bad from what the caller said. The wounded are all at least walking. Sam'll let me know if he needs help. Just thought you'd want to know."

At the station twenty minutes later Hack was giving Melba instructions for checking on Jack Lange when another call came in. She picked up the phone and listened briefly.

"Just a minute," she said, "here's the chief." She held her hand over the phone. "Another dead cat. The woman's very upset."

Hack took the phone and listened to a semi-hysterical description of a dismembered kitten in a child's sandbox. He waited until the woman paused for breath, then said in his calmest voice, "Your name and address, please." She told him and he scribbled it down. "Don't touch anything, Mrs. Archer. Someone will be there in a few minutes."

He turned and looked across the room to Louanne's cubbyhole, where she was standing in the door staring at him with big eyes. He'd go to the Archer house himself.

No. No, he wouldn't.

With Sam unavailable, this was Louanne's job. She was right there. She was a cop. At least she wanted to be a cop. If he started censoring assignments on the basis of feelings . . .

"Go see about it," he said. "Here's the address."

Without waiting for comment, he went into his office, shut the door, and looked out his window. Seventy-two seconds later, by his watch, Louanne came out of the building, got in her cruiser and left the parking lot. She wanted to be a cop. She *was* a cop.

Hack sighed, thought briefly once more about the advantages of tobacco farming over police chiefing, then took out the PLAN. In the space below "Winoski murder" he wrote:

Jack Lange. Find him. Check with Asheville cops and Buncombe sheriff.

He made the calls, spent several minutes in professional chitchat and learned that neither the Asheville police nor the Buncombe County sheriff had ever heard of Jack Lange. In making his request for the sheriff to look for Lange's Bronco, Hack managed not to say exactly why he was interested, just that he needed to talk to the gem dealer about rubies.

When the sheriff learned that the car was probably on some timber road up on the side of Craggy his only comment was, "Awful lot of woods up there, Hack, but we'll keep our eyes open. I'll have the helicopter swing over that way. But don't get your hopes up."

Twenty minutes later another call, a fire call, came in. A house on the college campus was burning.

CHAPTER 21

Hack switched on his pickup's rarely used siren and reached the fire scene in three-and-a-half minutes. Two pumper trucks, red lights flashing, were already there. He drove onto the patchy lawn of the second house on the street and jerked to a stop beside one of the trucks.

Black smoke poured from a basement window on the campus side of the house, one of the seven college-owned, turreted, Victorian monstrosities that made up the south end of Faculty Row. Some students who had gathered to watch cheered when Hack jumped out of his truck.

The fire crew turned on a hose just then and sent its hissing water-spike through the basement window. Hack stepped over the swollen tube and ran to the front of the house where, from the street, he had seen someone on the porch. He found Hammond McFee, the college comptroller, holding the screen door open and peering inside.

"Anybody in there?" Hack yelled as he ran up the porch steps.

"Marie's book!" McFee cried.

A woman in baggy jeans and gray sweatshirt came out from the house, one arm hugging a thick bundle of papers, the other a struggling gray cat. The cat wriggled loose and jumped off the porch, and the papers fell and scattered on the floor.

Hack pushed around her and went inside. He called, got no response, then ran upstairs to a landing. There were three doors, all closed. The first led to a bathroom, empty, the second to a bedroom, cluttered and messy. From the looks of the clothes scattered about, it was a man's room. Hack ignored a black cat with yellow eyes that slunk under the bed when he came into the room. He went back to the landing and tried the third door. It was locked. He banged on it but got no response.

Back downstairs, he checked the other rooms and found them all empty. He called to Hammond McFee, who was still standing in the doorway to the porch.

"The locked room upstairs, anybody in there?"

"No. It's the study."

Hack went back out to the porch. The woman — Hack recognized her as the formidable Dr. Marie McFee — was gathering up sheets of paper. Though Hack had never met her, he felt he knew the grim-faced professor well from some of Art's more memorable whiskey-sharpened descriptions at Bertha's.

The fire chief came striding around the corner of the house. "Fire's out," he said. "You're lucky, Mr. McFee. Good smoke alarm. Come see, Hack."

Hack followed him around the house to a side door that led into the basement. They entered an apparent storage room, now a soggy but uncharred mess. The air smelled like soot and something sharp and acrid, but was almost clear of smoke. A wisp of steam rose from a stack of wet, partly burned newspapers in the corner of the room next to stairs that led up into the house. "We usually say 'arson suspected' in a case like this," the fire chief said. "But not this time. There's no 'suspecting' about it. Somebody poured something on those papers and lit it. Smell it?"

"Gasoline?"

"No, we'd recognize that smell. Not kerosene either. We'll use our sniffer to tell us."

"How did, uh, he, I guess, get in?"

"Basement door was wide open when we got here."

"It wasn't a very big fire."

"No, and it was right under the smoke alarm. On the other hand, just a few minutes more — see where the wall over there had already started to smolder — and the whole place would have gone up like kindling. You figure it out."

A young fireman came into the basement. "This was in the bushes around on the other side of the house, Chief." He held out a gallon-sized red metal can with a handle and a spring-loaded closure. ACETONE was stenciled in yellow letters on the side.

"Put it down," Hack said. "There might be prints."

"Oh." The fireman set the can on the floor and jerked his hand back as from a snake.

Hack went to his pickup for a plastic bag, collected the can, and carried it around to the front porch. The McFees had gone inside and were sitting across from one another at the kitchen table. He put the bagged red can down between them.

"This was in the shrubbery," he said. "Looks like somebody used it to set the fire. Any ideas?"

The couple looked first at the can, then at each other. "No," the comptroller said. "It's the firebug again. I don't know . . ." His voice trailed off.

"What don't you know?" Hack said.

"Well, I'm the most hated man on campus. They probably —"

"Oh, Hammond, you're not *hated*," his wife said. "Don't be ridiculous. Just because you don't let the students waste money, that's no reason for them to burn down our house."

"But, Marie, you know —"

"What I know is, you let Arthur Taylor twist you around his little finger. If the students don't like you, it's because of him."

"But, Marie . . ." Hammond McFee's thin, almost singsong bleat was unpleasant to listen to.

"You know you ought to have an assistant," Marie said. "Maybe two. You won't even *ask*."

"But, Marie . . ."

"Where's your son?" Hack said.

Both McFees turned toward him. "Why?" Marie asked.

"Where is he?"

"How should I know? Off studying somewhere, probably." She deliberately moved in her chair so that her back was toward Hack and, with the fire remains in the basement of her house not yet cool, resumed her husband-lecture. Intrigued by her order of priorities, Hack kept quiet and listened.

Beyond the central fact that Hammond never got to complete a sentence, he learned several things: Marie had almost finished writing her third book (the rescued manuscript that she had placed on the table showed a title, *Television and the Rebellious Teen*); she had been away from home just *one* night, and look what happened; the firebug was obviously a disturbed adolescent in need of help; the police should quit twiddling their toes and put a stop to the fires; and the college's so-called president was an ineffectual dreamer in the first stages of Alzheimer's.

The noted psychologist was elaborating the last point when the so-called president himself came into the room. Her back toward the door, she didn't see him.

"Philosopher," she said, making the word sound like fish bait left in the sun too long. "If he spent half as much time doing his job as he does drinking whiskey with those red-necked Neanderthals at Bertha's —"

"Cromagnon, at least, Marie." Art stepped into her view. Hammond McFee slid down in his chair and emitted a barely perceptible groan.

"Oh," Marie said, then added, without sounding sorry at all, "I'm sorry."

"No, no, you're right," Art said. "Maybe we *are* Neanderthal. Maybe we should start drawing animal pictures on Bertha's walls, you think? What happened here?" He gestured toward the red can. "They use that kind of can in the chemistry labs."

Hack told what they had found in the basement and asked Art if he had any ideas — he hadn't — then told the McFees that Louanne McLeod would be up to see them. He pushed back from the table.

"Tonight," Art murmured. "Ten o'clock."

"Okay."

Good. A long session at Bertha's with his fellow cavemen was what Hack needed right now to get his damn thoughts in some kind of order. There was just too much going on in Blue Ridge. Hell, Big Fat Charlie had actually been right for once, they really were having a damn *crime wave.*

Hack turned to leave the room and stopped. A tall, overweight, pale-faced boy with dark crew-cut hair, nineteen or twenty years old, was standing, slump-shouldered, in the doorway. He met Hack's eyes for an instant, then looked down. Hack looked for the earrings that often went with such a face but there were none.

"What happened?" the boy said, his voice low.

Marie stood up. "Go to your room. It's over. Nothing happened. Go upstairs."

Louanne appeared at the front door and stepped into the crowded kitchen. Hack nodded to her, then called to the boy, who had started up the stairs.

"Wait a minute. What's your name?"

"That's Brent, of course, our son," Marie said.

"Where've you been, Brent?"

"In the library."

"All morning?"

"Yes."

"That's enough," Marie said. "Go to your room, Brent. You —"

"Stay here." Hack's seldom-heard command voice froze everybody, even Marie. In normal tones he added, "Officer McLeod will want to talk to you."

Then, with a vague feeling of deserting his troops in the face of hostile fire, he nodded again to Louanne and left the house.

CHAPTER 22

From a narrow window on the never-used third floor of the library, he watched the last pumper truck leave the fire scene. The knuckles of his fists, clenched on the windowsill, were white. He pictured the girl.

An hour earlier, when the chief left the house and she started asking questions, he could have reached out and touched her. She'd *had* to talk to him then, but he could read in her eyes what she was thinking about him. For her he was dirt. Less than dirt.

He hated her.

The other morning when she refused to talk to him in the snack bar, when she had looked right through him, she had become all the gray, formless, grabbing things that more and more each day filled his mind. Killing her had become all that really mattered to him, and it didn't even occur to him to wonder why.

You don't wonder about obvious things. Rational things.

You just did them.

One part of his mind still whispered at times and raised pictures of his bloody, screaming grandfather, but he'd learned to shut that part of his mind out. And even if its voice got through, he refused to listen. He knew what he was doing. And why.

Why? Because it was the right thing to do, that's why. He *had* to kill the girl.

Since the snack bar, he'd followed her several times. He knew where she lived, when she went to work in the morning and when she went to bed at night. From the bushes behind her condo he'd watched her through a gap in the bedroom curtains. He knew she didn't pick up her underclothes at night, just left them in a pile on the floor. The thought of her naked stopped his breath. He stepped back from the dusty library window, went to the old desk the library people let him use, unlocked a drawer and took out a long-haired blond wig. With breath now coming in little jerks, he fitted it on his head. Then he reached into the drawer and took out Sammy.

He began to rasp deep in his throat, the sound resonating throughout his body, rising and falling as he breathed in and out. He put his index finger on the knife blade and moved it along the cutting edge. Little drops of blood appeared. Holding his breath he watched them swell, then licked the blood from his finger and pressed the cut to make it bleed again.

The door of the elevator across the room opened with a whir and clash. A girl's voice called out, "Are you up here?"

He didn't respond. He couldn't breathe. It had never happened before. He had told them not to interrupt when he was working. He'd *told* them!

"You're back there, aren't you?"

He couldn't make his voice respond.

Sliding footsteps sounded on the bare wood floor. He snatched off his wig, jammed it in the drawer and covered Sammy with his right arm.

A girl — fat, dirty-haired, without makeup, library-solicitous — appeared at the end of his aisle. "I thought you were up here," she said. "There was somebody from the police downstairs a while back asking about you. I came up to get you but you weren't . . . oh, did you cut yourself?"

CHAPTER 23

Without removing the phone wedged between her neck and shoulder, Melba took a bite from the apple that was her late afternoon snack. She was talking to Lurleen, her second cousin, at the college. Lurleen would give her plenty of time to chew before she had to speak again.

"Everybody in town is scared to death, Melba. The McFee fire is just the last straw. And those two people, the Winoskis . . . murdered. Cold blood. I've been on the phone all morning. People are really terrified. And that Gerry Smith getting shot. They say it's the same guy. The cat killer, you know, shot Gerry Smith and killed the Winoskis. And he's the one set the fire too. Really, Melba, the police ought to —"

"Why do people think the fire setter killed the Winoskis?" Melba took another apple bite.

"Huh. Why not, who else? It's some maniac, and they say drugs are involved. All the pot growing in the woods. Maybe the Mafia . . . but it could be anybody. *Anybody.* They say the McFees' basement was a blazing inferno when the firemen got there." Lurleen paused for a quick breath, but hurried on before Melba finished chewing her last bite. "It's really unbelievable that the house didn't just burn right down to the ground, Melba. They say it was something from the chemistry labs that started it, some kind of acid or something. Somebody wanted to kill Hammond McFee. Or Marie. Or both. With her, I could see it, maybe."

"Why would the firebug want to kill them?"

"They say it wasn't the firebug, it was a copycat. Wants us to *think* it was the firebug."

"Why do they say that, and who's 'they'? Did the copycat kill the Winoskis?"

"Oh, I don't know. I saw the great Marie in the cafeteria at lunch. She *still* managed to look at the rest of us like we were bean beetles or something, even after her house burned down. Or practically. That woman! I just don't know. Say, I hear the chief is taking Allie McLeod to the singles' supper, not Honeydew. That right?"

"That's what he says, but I wouldn't put money on it. He'll probably wind up being 'busy' like the last time. If he does that again, I think I'll just grab him and *shake* him."

"Well, hang in there, don't get discouraged. The chief's like a big old block of ice. You just keep shining sunshine on it long enough, it'll melt and run all over the place. It reminds me of Henry Loftus. He's your third cousin once removed. Remember him?"

"Of course. He married Alma Jean Duncan last year, didn't he?"

"That's him. Almost everybody thought he was a confirmed bachelor, including him. But not your Aunt Margie. Not her *or* Alma Jean. Every time Henry thought he was safe, Margie would . . ."

Four minutes into the account of Henry Loftus's zigzag path to matrimony, Melba's other phone rang.

"I've got a call on the other line, Lurleen," she said. "I'll get back to you." She put down one phone and picked up the other. "Police department."

"Louanne McLeod." The voice was male, slow, not much above a whisper.

"She's not here at the moment," Melba said. "Can I take a message?"

Click.

Melba looked at the dead phone, put it down, and resumed her apple, a red-gold Gala, one of the first varieties to come each season from the county's many square miles of orchards. It was so juicy she had to wipe her chin.

A reporter for the *Times and Republican* called, for the fourth time in the last two hours. He wanted the chief.

"Still not here, Lonnie," Melba said.

"Well, where *is* he?"

"Dunno."

"Sure you know. Is he in his office? What's he doing? Worst crime wave in our history, and he's gone . . . incognito? Should I put that in the headlines? I'm coming over there and sit outside his —"

"Don't come, Lonnie," Melba said. Lonnie was her brother's youngest son. "You know I'll let you know as soon as there's anything. Please."

Ten minutes and three worried-citizen phone calls later Louanne came in. As she often did, she flopped down in one of the visitor chairs next to Melba's desk and stuck out her feet. She didn't speak, and her expression was glum.

"You got a call a few minutes ago," Melba said. "No message."

"Who was it?"

"Didn't say. Heavy-breathing-weirdo voice, one of those. Sort of whispered, you know."

"Oh. You mean the type with dog food for brains? I seem to attract 'em. Idiots."

"What did the McFees say?" Melba said.

"You ever meet Marie, the great professor? Unbelievable. I can see why both the males of the family disappeared pretty soon after I got there. Marie treated me like I was the septic tank pumper or something . . . or maybe something he found in the tank. I tell you I'd just *love* to stop *her* for speeding sometime."

"Did Mr. McFee know anything about the fire?"

"No, but what a wimp. Lurleen's got him pinned down just right. She says he's an egg-laying rooster."

"What about the son?"

"Brent? He's fat, won't meet your eyes, mumbles at the floor. But when you consider the mother he's got . . . he says he was in the library all morning."

"Was he?"

"The woman at the desk remembers seeing him, but that was early, well before the fire. He could have left and . . . I'm still checking. Chief here?"

"He hasn't been back since he ran out to go to the fire, after you went to see about . . . uh . . . Mrs. Archer's kitten. What did you find out there?"

"I don't want to talk about it. It was sickening."

"All right. Is your —"

"I mean sickening! Some maniac! Out behind the garage. He didn't just kill the poor little thing, he . . . I don't want to talk about it."

"Of course you don't. Is your mother —"

"I mean, really, could somebody like that actually be *human?* I buried it for her. Surely the chief wouldn't want to keep the evidence. Then I went from the cat scene to being spit on by the great child psychologist. What a day! I drove out to Hope Springs after I left the college, just to talk to some normal people."

"How're they getting along?"

"Oh, hanging on. Gerry Smith doesn't remember anything more about her shooting. I think they've all pretty much put it out of their minds. Actually, they had a little good news this morning for a change. A woman from the bank called and wanted some background on the place. She said they're going to make a contribution. Didn't say how much. I wonder if maybe the chief talked to somebody up at the bank."

"Probably. What's your mother think about the singles' supper? Does she —"

One of the phones rang. It was a tourist who had gotten a parking ticket. While Melba was telling him how to go about paying the fine, Billy and Sam came in. Billy spotted Louanne. Melba saw him grin and knew what was coming.

"Hey, Louanne, hear you demonstrated real good driving skills yesterday," Billy said. "The road crew out there saw it all. You missed that old squirrel. Good for you, girl! Almost wrecked the car and killed the chief, but we can always get replacements for them. A squashed squirrel now —"

"Shut up, Billy," Louanne said.

"But, you know, on the other hand, if you'd just save squirrel skins, they'd make a nice warm coat. Or, hell, why not a cat-squirrel mixture. You could save cat skins too. Ha. Ha."

Louanne jumped to her feet. "That's *sick!*"

"Stop that, Billy." Melba used her I'm-not-going-to-argue voice, the one she used when her own boys misbehaved. Billy laughed again but went into his office and shut the door. "I found another bent-tree booby trap," Sam said in an attempt to lighten the atmosphere. "It was sprung. Up on Jeter this time. Guess what got caught. A big old fat possum was hanging up in the air, mad as hell."

Both women turned and stared at him.

"Good for you," Louanne said. "You and Billy can start a possum-skin coat. It'd look good on Billy. What'd you do, cut its tail off to watch it bleed and leave it hanging there?"

"Naw, turned it loose. Louanne, Billy don't mean what he says. You know, the way he talks. He's thinks he's making jokes. Just don't pay him no attention."

Sam reached over and patted Louanne's shoulder. Melba thought that if Billy had done it, Louanne would have slapped him, but from the old man, the gesture was touching.

"Thanks, Sam," Louanne said. "But you can just tell Billy his jokes aren't funny."

"Naw, they ain't, but tellin' him won't do no good." Sam discarded a shredded toothpick in Melba's wastebasket and went downstairs to his cubicle in the basement.

Louanne slumped again in Melba's chair and frowned at the floor.

"So, is your mother ready for her big date Sunday?" Melba asked after a moment.

"Oh, yeah. She told me just this morning that —" She stopped when the chief came in from the street.

He sat down in the chair on the other side of Melba's desk, sagged, and stuck out *his* feet. Melba had long realized that the flopped-down, feet-out posture, whether it was Louanne, Billy or the boss, meant discouragement. She also knew that part of her job was to listen to the moans and groans that always followed.

"Anything come in?" Hack muttered.

"Nothing important. Lurleen called from the college. She says the town is getting into an uproar. They think we've got an insane killer on the loose . . . what with a shotgun ambush, double murder, dead cats, arson. Lurleen told me all about the McFee fire."

Hack looked across the desk at Louanne, "What'd you find with the cat?"

"Same as Sam found. Little thing cut up in pieces." Keeping her voice carefully neutral, she described the scene, ending with, "I didn't see anything helpful. No 'clues,' I mean, no footprints, nothing dropped. The house backs up on that patch of woods out beyond the college, so no witnesses likely. I buried the . . . uh . . . parts for the poor woman. She would never have —"

"Good. Give your notes to Sam and forget cats. What'd the McFees say?"

"Nothing, really. Strange bunch, to put it mildly, Chief. Hammond thinks it was some disgruntled student out to get him. Marie disagrees, no surprise there. She thinks it was the firebug, who just happened to find that they don't — or didn't — lock their basement door. If Brent has any thoughts about anything, he didn't let me in on them."

"Yeah, Brent. Fine young man. What do you think, he set the fire?"

Louanne studied her fingertips before replying. "I don't have any evidence that he did . . . but I'm looking. None of the neighbors saw anything suspicious, but nobody was home on either side of the McFees. Brent says he was in the library all morning, but it's just a two-minute walk from there to his house, and the library is usually crowded."

"Does he take chemistry courses?" Hack said.

"No. But I went by the chemistry labs after I talked to him. I just walked in — the doors weren't locked — and could have walked right back out with another solvent can, and nobody would have seen me."

"The crime lab will check for prints on the can, but it looked wiped. One way or the other, we're going to have to get a set of Brent's."

Louanne sat up straight. "Hey, don't you think maybe we need the *whole family's* prints? I could get them. And I'd start with the great psychologist herself. I can't wait. I'll —"

"Wait, don't get carried away," Hack said. "She could squawk pretty loud if she took a notion to."

"Okay, Chief, I promise," Louanne said, then after a moment added, "Uh, I went out to Hope Springs when I left the college."

"Yeah?"

"Gerry Smith's feeling better. The 'anonymous' donation helped everybody. I think she's put the shooting out of her mind, assumes she wasn't the real target."

"Huh," Hack said. "I still wonder why she was riding in the dark dressed in black."

"Gerry's just different, Chief," Louanne said. "Did you know she spends most of her free time hiking all over the mountains, all by herself, starting from that cabin she lives in up there? Sometimes she takes a blanket and spends the night, just lies down under a tree and goes to sleep, as I understand it."

"Good lord," Melba said. "There are bears out there. And worse, *Boatwrights*. How can she —"

"Like I say, she's different," Louanne said. "And Violet Turner says that every now and then Gerry'll just take off and leave town for a day or two, not tell anybody anything. Other times she'll come to the shelter at two or three o'clock in the morning and just putter around in the shed until daylight, probably sorting through those old clothes and stuff. And, according to Violet, she doesn't like answering *anybody's* questions, not just ours."

"Probably comes from being named Geranium," Hack said.

"They thought they had a prowler out there last night," Louanne continued. "Got 'em all excited. We almost got a call about it, Violet said."

"What happened?"

"There were noises in the basement about eleven o'clock. Violet wanted to call us but Gerry said no. She got a butcher knife and went down to check, hurt shoulder and all. She found a mother cat and two little kittens. The mother had knocked down some empty paint cans. Hunting mice, I guess, there must be plenty of them. I went down and checked the area for them. The room is full of junk, the women never go down there."

"How did the cat get in? *Could* there have been somebody there?"

"I doubt it. The door to the outside is warped so much a child could push it open, but it was still locked. I looked outside. The grass and weeds are practically up to my waist, even worse than in the front. Nobody's walked there for a long time."

Hack turned to Melba. "Nothing from the Asheville gem guy, I suppose?"

"No."

"Huh." Hack sagged a little further.

Melba saw that his earlier gloomy expression had progressed from dark gray to black. She knew the signs. Here they were in the middle of Blue Ridge's worst-ever crime spree, and the boss didn't know what to do next, on anything. She wished she could help.

A phone rang again. Melba picked it up. "Police Department."

"Melba? Tom Black. Hack there?"

"Oh, hello, Sheriff." Melba glanced at the chief, who was making I'm-not-here signs.

"He's not in right now," she said. "I don't know where he is."

"Oh. I'm going to talk to my favorite little killer. I wanted Hack along for moral support. Have him call me."

"Okay, I'll tell him as soon as he comes in." She hung up. "He wanted you to go out to Harold Pell's with him."

"I thought so. I haven't got time to mess with that fussy little lump of . . . of . . ." Hack looked at Melba. "I can't . . . I've gotta . . ."

He stood up, unclipped the beeper from his belt and put it on her desk. "Keep this damn thing," he said. "I'll see you later." Without another word, he turned and strode through the station door.

Through the front window, Melba and Louanne watched him get in his green pickup and drive away in the direction of the mountains. They looked at each other. The boss was obviously in a bad state. He'd said "damn" to Melba.

CHAPTER 24

Hack screwed a new spark plug into the tractor's engine with his fingers, then tried to get a grip on it with the rusty pliers. The pliers slipped. He banged a knuckle on the air cleaner.

"Goddamn it!"

He raised his arm to throw the pliers across the cluttered garage, then took a deep breath and managed to get the plug in tight enough so it wouldn't leak. The old tractor started with a loud pop followed by a clacking roar and cloud of blue exhaust. He noticed a pair of ear protectors hanging from a nail and put them on before backing the tractor out of the garage.

Gerry Smith and Violet Turner had come out to the back stoop and were watching. He didn't acknowledge their presence.

The lawn looked barely mowable, another week and it would take a bush-hog to cut it. He started at the front. With the tractor in lowest gear, not looking toward the building, he began to mow.

In the total mental silence created by noisy engine and earmuffs, he tried to order his thoughts. It was time he started earning his goddamn pay, instead of just going around wanting to kick somebody. He began with the double murder. Wasn't there *something* he could be doing besides waiting for a probably dopey rock collector to come down off the mountain and tell him about rubies? If there was, he didn't know what it might be.

And the gray-eyed, cop-hating, looks-like-a-movie-star over there on the porch watching him. Who'd shot her? Why? Was it really mistaken identity? Was somebody maybe waiting to try again, take better aim this time? Probably. Then why couldn't he think of some intelligent step to prevent it? Was he just going to sit around and fret until somebody succeeded in blowing her head off? Why couldn't he think?

At what age did Alzheimer's start? Maybe he *and* Art were both — *Whang!* The mower blade hit a rock.

"Goddamn it!"

The engine almost stalled but caught and struggled back to life.

And what about the lunatic up at the college? Now that he'd started burning houses — assuming the house-burner was the firebug — wouldn't he probably take a bigger step? Like a dorm?

Roast how many students? Fifty?

So what had the great white chief done to prevent *that?* He'd sent one girl "to talk to students." One girl who didn't weigh much more than the gun she carried and who would wreck a car before running over a squirrel. Was that going to prevent cooked students? Was he going to be the one to have to call fifty sets of parents and say he was sorry to tell them that there had been an accident?

Was the McFee boy the firebug? Or did he maybe just set fire to his own house, copycat? Maybe he didn't have anything to do with any of it. But didn't "Brent" actually mean "burn" or something like that in German? No, that was dumb.

The tractor chugged to a stop when he tried to mow through a patch of head-high ragweed growing in what had started as a flowerbed. A haze of pollen stirred up by his assault brought on a fit of sneezing.

"God . . . *damn* it!" he bellowed after the seventh sneeze. He backed up, shifted to a higher gear for momentum, then rammed through the weeds.

And he shouldn't forget the knuckle-dragging imbeciles growing pot in the woods and setting booby traps for each other. He'd shout "hallelujah!" if they all succeeded in mutually hanging themselves or blowing their brains out. All of them. But as a cop, he had to pretend to care. Sam was handling that, but if the old man wasn't careful, he'd stumble over one of the traps and . . . wasn't there something he should be doing about that?

And to top it off, another sick-sick-sicky was killing cats. How could a chief who bragged about knowing his town not have a goddamn *idea* of what to do about that one? After what? Four dead kittens? Five? He'd lost count.

He finished the front yard and began to mulch the weed tangle that grew outside the basement door behind the building. A movement in front of the mower made him stop. A yellow kitten emerged, then a gray one. They scurried to a hole in the ground-level window and disappeared. Hack crept ahead another foot then stopped again in case more fur balls were hidden in the grass. When none showed he continued along the edge of the building.

Hell, right now he probably couldn't manage to give a ticket to a 100-year-old Florida tourist for running over a fireplug. He should do everybody a favor and quit. And move all the way out of the mountains. Go back and live with Mama and grow tobacco. Or maybe he'd have to switch to peanuts these kill-the-smoker days.

As he turned the tractor to make the next pass, the engine stopped. He ground the starter but got no response, then looked down at the gas gauge. Empty. He was cursing silently and trying to decide where he could kick the tractor to hurt it most when Gerry Smith came from the garage with a gas can. Hack took off his earmuffs.

"Just sit still," she said.

He watched without speaking as she unscrewed the gas cap and, using the arm on her unwounded side and a knee to prop the can, emptied it into the tractor. Her cheeks had regained some color, and she had completely lost the scared-zombie look of the hospital. She raised her eyes, pushed pale hair back from her face and gave a little nod. But she didn't smile. Hack couldn't imagine her smiling.

"Thanks for mowing," she said. "I think maybe I can pay somebody to do it next time. We've gotten a little money."

"Good. How's your shoulder?"

"Better."

"You remember any more about what happened?"

"No."

Gerry's face clouded and the tension lines Hack had seen at the hospital reformed around her mouth. She turned away, carried the gas can to the back porch, and went inside. Hack could see several indistinct faces watching from the kitchen window.

The tractor caught after a long starter grind. He resumed mowing and thought-organizing, starting over with the Winoskis. He was on the second pass around the backyard when the sheriff stepped into view and held up his hand. Hack stopped and took off the earmuffs again.

"Happened to see your pickup," the county's number-one lawman said. "Melba didn't know where you were. Or that's what she said anyway. You running away?"

Hack glared but didn't speak.

"Don't see how you've got time to mow lawns, good buddy. I'd think with all the stuff going on in your town —"

"What the hell you want?"

"Come on out to Pell's place with me again."

"Damn it, Tom, I haven't got time to waste on that crap. You'll never get anywhere with him. Like you said, the little turd's laughing at us. You make his day when you go there. He's nuts. I got too much —"

"Yeah, too much, I can see that. What you working on right now? You helping that poor little ol' blond in there? You planning to help inside the house next time? You aiming to maybe help in the bedroom, down the road a piece?"

"Get out of here."

The sheriff turned and left without another word. Hack watched him drive away in the direction of the Pell house, then, feeling even more futile than he had earlier, resumed mowing. But he couldn't ignore the sheriff's taunts. Why *was* he wasting a couple of hours doing a job he could have paid somebody a few bucks to do better than he could? He hadn't really thought about it. It had just seemed like an unfrustrating thing to do, but . . .

Come on, man, don't try to kid your own damn self. You've thought plenty about her bedroom, up there in that little cabin all by itself on Jeter Mountain. Hell, you're like a damn fast-breathing teenager.

But there was something about her . . . she was made of ice, but maybe that ice wished it could melt. Maybe it just didn't know how. It would take time, but . . .

Grow up!

He tried to imagine taking Gerry back to the farm to meet Mama, like he'd been thinking of doing with Allie. Mama would . . . what? She'd probably take a good, narrow-eyed look at Gerry, be extra, extra polite, not say much about anything, and give Hack questioning glances. With Allie, on the other hand, it would be two happy sisters getting together after a long separation. They'd get so involved talking about church, children, gardens, quilts and farm problems that Hack would feel like a stranger at a family reunion. If he married Allie and moved back home he'd be a member of that family. Hell, he'd be *head* of it.

Yeah, well maybe he didn't want to go back and grow tobacco. Maybe he wanted a . . . a *different* life.

Maybe, hell. He just needed to grow up.

Ten minutes later the whole lawn looked like an unbaled hay field, but at least it was cut. He put the tractor in the garage, went to his pickup and sat behind the wheel wondering what to do next. Maybe something useful, like digging a hole then filling it back up, or trying to drain the river with a bucket.

One thing he couldn't face was going back to his office, where everybody would look at him and wait for him to say something. He cranked up the truck, jammed it in gear and left the parking lot in the direction of town. When he reached Buncombe Street, where a left turn would take him to the square and his office, he turned right, down toward the river. Three minutes later he pulled up in front of a tiny cabin stuck back in some pines a hundred feet from the river's edge.

He leaned out the pickup window and bellowed, "Aunt Ola, you there?"

At the station, Melba coped. To outside requests to speak to the chief, which always seemed to come in bunches when he wasn't there, she said, "He's not available at the moment. Can I take a message?"

To members of the department who asked for him, she said, "He stormed out of here two hours ago without his beeper. No telling *where* he is now."

At 5:46 a caller for Hack identified himself as Jack Lange, of Asheville Gem and Mineral. "Chief Hackett told my wife that I was supposed to call him as soon as I got home," he said. "He wants to talk to me about a ruby."

"Oh yes, Mr. Lange. I know he's been waiting to hear from you. I'll tell him you called. At what number can he reach you?"

Melba had a much-exercised system for locating her boss when he wasn't wearing his beeper. First she'd try the radio in his pickup, then his three favorite places: the Rocking Chair Café, Bertha's, and Jumpoff Rock. About two thirds of the time she'd find him at one of those places.

His radio was, as usual, switched off, so she started with the Rocking Chair. Hattie Mae told her that the chief hadn't been there since breakfast. Melba was about to try Bertha's when the other phone on the desk rang. She picked it up.

"Police department."

"Louanne McLeod."

It was dog-food-for-brains. Melba told him to wait, fetched Louanne from her office and arranged the tape recorder. After giving Louanne a go-ahead nod, she listened to the conversation. "Hello," Louanne said.

"Louanne?"

"Yes."

In the long silence that followed, Melba listened for heavy breathing but heard nothing. When the caller spoke again his voice was a featureless monotone.

"There's something I've got to tell you."

"Tell."

"I love you."

"Oh, that's nice." Louanne made a face at Melba and rolled her eyes.

"You don't believe me. I understand. You don't know me. Yet."

"Oh, am I going to meet you? What's your name?"

"Be at the corner of Wyndham and Oak in five minutes. Come by yourself."

"I can't get there that quick."

"Yes you can. Five minutes, not a second more, or I won't be there. I know the fire-setter at the college. And I know the cat-killer. I'll tell you his name."

He hung up. The women looked at each other.

"*His* name?" Melba said. "They're the same person?"

Louanne looked at the clock. "Six forty-one."

"You're not going, are you?"

"Wyndham and Oak, that's right in the middle of the Little League fields. There's nothing there. No, there's the drink stand."

"I'll get Sam," Melba said.

Louanne stood up. "There's not enough time. I'll call you when I get there . . . before I get out of the car."

Melba watched her hurry from the building.

CHAPTER 25

Hack calmed down. Talking to Aunt Ola always had that effect on him. It wasn't that she'd done all that much talking, but then a priest at confession probably didn't talk a lot either.

Aunt Ola finished her second cigarette, carefully mashed it out in the pickup's ashtray and, not looking at the chief, pronounced her favorite word.

"Humph."

For most people "humph" is just a modified grunt. For Blue Ridge's oldest citizen it was almost a language in itself, conveying through tone and nuance every negative emotion from disapproval through disdain to smells bad.

"Why don't you just stop whining?" she said. "Whining don't ever get anybody anywhere."

"I'm not *whining*, Aunt Ola. I never whine. I'm just telling you how it is."

"Humph."

Hack had, after avoiding his office and picking up Aunt Ola at her cabin, wandered in a tell-it-like-it-is crawl around Blue Ridge for the next twenty minutes. He'd wound up on Jumpoff Rock, parked almost touching the railing at the cliff-edge. From the pickup they could see the whole town spread out before them like an elaborate model train set, an amazing set in which even the little people-models, as well as the trains and cars, moved around. Hack had often thought that being up on Jumpoff was like being a god, a helpless sort of god who could plainly see his world but couldn't touch it.

Today, for instance, he watched an accident happen. A bright red pickup backed out of a parallel parking space on the east side of the square and had its rear end crunched by a slow-moving, dark blue car. After the soundless impact the scene froze for ten seconds, then the overalled pickup driver got out and ambled back to the blue car. Traffic in both directions stopped.

"Humph," Aunt Ola said, the word this time dripping scorn. "Tourists. Probably some biddy older than me, if that's possible, still trying to drive, can't hardly see over the dashboard. Melba going to call you to come see about it?"

"No. The radio's off, she can't get me. They don't need me. See, look at the station, there comes Sam already." They watched the town's senior peacekeeper walk across the square to the accident.

"He'll straighten things out, and everybody'll leave the scene happy," Hack said. "Sam loves fender benders."

The pay phone mounted on the side of Jumpoff's refreshment stand rang. A dozen or so tourists stared at it but no one moved to answer it.

"Ain't you going to get that?" Aunt Ola said after the fifth ring.

"No. It might be for me."

After three more rings the phone quit trying.

"Humph. Take me home, then. *I* got better things to do than sit up here listening to a bunch a' damn whinin'."

Melba looked up when Hack entered the station half an hour later, then pointedly returned to her work. He went to the desk and stood beside it. She finished the page, reread it, then relented.

"Chief, you shouldn't hide from me like that. We needed you. I could actually *see* your pickup up on Jumpoff. Why didn't you answer the phone?"

"Sorry."

"I almost sent Billy up to get you, and that would have been . . . oh, well. The gem and mineral guy called from Asheville. Jack Lange. I told him —"

"Call him back."

Melba wasn't about to be hurried. "If you were all that eager to talk to him, you could at least have had your radio on. Also, the firebug called Louanne. He said he loves her. She went to meet him. He didn't show up, naturally. She just got back. I didn't want her to go by herself, but she did."

"What —"

"And there was an accident on the square, but you probably saw that. Sam handled it. For you."

"How does Louanne know it was the firebug?"

"She thinks so, is how."

Punishment administered, Melba went back to typing, and waited for penitence. Hack knew the script.

"Look, Melba," he said. "I really *am* sorry. I just *had* to get away and think. It's . . . well, it's . . ."

"That's okay. I'll call Lange."

The gem dealer wasn't there, but his answering machine asked for an after-beep message. He was told to call back. Louanne came from her office and joined them.

"What happened?" Hack asked Louanne. Melba answered.

"This guy called and asked for Louanne," she said. "It's the one that . . ." She turned to Louanne. "Here, you tell him."

"I think it's him, Chief," Louanne said. "And from the way he talked about both the fires and the cats . . . it's possible he's *both*. Maybe."

"Well, what *happened?*"

"He called —"

"Wait," Melba said, "you can listen to him." She took a moment to rewind the tape in her recorder, then turned it on. Louanne's voice was first.

"Hello."

"Louanne?"

"Yes."

"There's something I've got to tell you."

"Tell."

"I love you."

"Oh, that's nice."

They listened to the rest of the conversation, then listened again. Hack felt like saying "Humph."

"Okay, what'd you do?" he asked.

"I went where he said, got there in four-and-a-half minutes. They were having a game, lots of kids and people around. I wasn't there but a minute when the pay phone rang. I answered it. It was whisper-voice. He told me to look under the brick on the ground to my right, then hung up. I found this."

She handed Hack a sheet of notepaper in a clear plastic evidence bag. The penciled message was written in small, wavery, backward-leaning printing.

You came alone. Thank you. I am looking at you right now. You are the most beautiful girl in the world. I love you so much. I know you will learn to love me. When you really get to know me.

I am very happy now.

I will call again soon my love.

Melba read the note over Hack's shoulder. "Ugh! 'I'm looking at you right now.' That's horrible!"

"Yeah," Louanne said. "All the houses up on the ridge, including about half the college, look down on the field. It really gave me the creeps."

"You really think he's our guy?" Hack turned the note over. The back side was blank.

"Well, I don't know, Chief. Anybody could have said what he did. He's not the first weirdo I've, uh, attracted. But there's something about that voice, something, you know, not right, really sick, don't you think?"

"Were there any other bricks on the ground?"

"Other bricks? I didn't notice."

"Come on, let's go look."

Hack went into his office and came out wearing his beeper. He looked at Melba and pointed to it.

Two Little League games were underway when Hack and Louanne reached the fields. Though it wasn't yet dark, the field lights were on. Four groups of apparently immobile tiny people in glowing blue, red, yellow and green uniforms labeled Utes, Cherokees, Choctaws and Pawnees stood around infields and outfields, or sat on long benches. Knots of fathers and mothers watched from the sidelines. On the field, a pitcher moved. The ball reached the plate and was sent looping into left field. Everyone began running and screaming, or just screaming.

At the wall-mounted telephone Hack found another note under a brick to the left of the phone. Touching only the edges, he unfolded the paper.

You did not come alone. I told you to come alone. Love can turn to hate, you know. You. I know everything you do. Next time don't try to play tricks on me. Be ready.

Hack slid the sheet into a plastic bag, then turned and searched the hillside that overlooked the fields. A hundred windows, at least, stared back at him. Was he looking into the unseen eyes of a maniac?

A crimson-clad Ute hit another long ball. Over the noise that erupted, Hack barely heard his beeper. He and Louanne went to the pickup and its radio.

"It's that guy Lange, Chief," Melba said. "I'll connect the call."

After a moment a high-pitched voice with a pronounced Southern twang came on. "Chief, this is Jack Lange."

"Mr. Lange," Hack said, "I've got some questions —"

"My wife told me about your visit. I've been up in the hills. I didn't know about the poor Winoskis until I got home. I've got their ruby right here."

Louanne grinned and gave a thumbs up sign.

Hack decided against questioning over the phone. He wanted to be looking at the rock hound when the ruby was produced, since people's eyes often gave him more information than their voices did.

"Are you in your office?"

"Yes sir."

"Wait right there. We'll see you in about forty-five minutes."

Hack made a last slow scan of watching windows. He reread the printed note, then started the pickup and looked down at Louanne, whose fists were clenched in her lap and her eyes eager.

"Let's go get the Winoski file," he said.

When they entered the station five minutes later, Melba pointed toward the open office door and mouthed, “Visitors.” Hack went to the door. The sheriff was perched behind the desk smoking a cigarette. Harold Pell, in a visitor’s chair, looked up and smiled.

CHAPTER 26

Harold had tried not to smile when the chief came into the room — into his own office — but couldn't keep a smirk from his face. It was all so funny. These two great big men — the chief was Burt Reynolds with maybe a little Robert Mitchum thrown in, the sheriff, a hundred percent John Wayne — were clearly agitated with each other, all because of him. Harold loved it.

Since the day *it* had happened Harold had had no clients, not one. The scheduled appointments were simply ignored. Except for a young woman who claimed through the locked door to be a reporter, the only people who had come to the studio were the sheriff and the chief.

Harold giggled. Both men scowled at him. He met their eyes, in turn, then looked down, but his quick glances had been enough for him to read their expressions, which were to him as obvious as headlines. Both men thought he was losing his mind.

Well, maybe he was. He didn't care, and it didn't bother him that he didn't care. What difference did it make? He stifled another unplanned laugh, then realized the sheriff was speaking to him.

". . . again why you waited so long to get help."

The giggles came again. When he saw the chief's transparent expression change to one of pure disgust, Harold almost laughed out loud. Then, with as straight a face as he could manage, he began for what seemed to him the thousandth time to retell his story.

"Like I said, I didn't know what to do. I was sure they were dead, but I hated to go away and leave the poor things. I —"

"Come out here, Tom," the chief said, his voice a growl. He turned and left the room. The sheriff followed.

Alone, Harold pictured the bodies again. He saw the blood on the rocks, the fog all around. But the picture was fading, and he didn't want it to fade. The other thing, the one he wanted to forget, was effectively gone, now little more than the memory of a memory. But Corliss and Doreen were so . . . so poignant. He didn't want to lose that.

The sheriff, wearing an undisguised sneer, returned. "Come on, come on, let's go."

"Anything you say, Sheriff." Harold caught the next giggle and turned it into a sweet smile. He knew what had happened. The chief had kicked them out of his office.

Hack and Louanne left for Asheville as soon as the sheriff had removed Pell from the station. In the passenger seat of the cruiser Hack leafed through the Winoski folder, whose meager contents he could have recited, eyes closed.

Melba had, through polite persistence and many phone calls, pieced together much of the past and present lives of the murdered couple, but nothing had turned up that could, even by straining, be taken as a reason for murder. There had been no personality clashes, no financial crises, nothing. Nothing, that is, except the ruby. The famous jewel whose very existence Hack had questioned. And now they were about to see it. Great. But why was there still so much doubt in his mind? Doubt of what?

He closed the folder and stared at the endless stream of oncoming traffic, which seemed literally to grow every day. He wondered what driving I-26 would be like in ten years.

Louanne glanced his way. "Uh, Chief," she said, "I guess I'm a little confused. I see how this Jack Lange could have been given the ruby by the Winoskis. When he saw it was valuable, he could have gone to their house and killed them. But if he'd done that, would he just show us the ruby now? It doesn't seem rational."

"Not to us. But we don't know him, maybe he's not rational. Maybe all rock collectors are round the bend, or over the ridge, or up the gully, or whatever. Hell, I don't know. With us looking for it, what else could he do with it?"

"Well, I guess."

Louanne drove the next two miles in silence, then, "I watched Harold Pell when the sheriff was leaving the station with him. He couldn't stop chuckling, like somebody who had just eaten the last cookie. Somebody else's cookie."

"Tom is trying to drive the pitiful little bastard over the edge, and it looks like he's succeeding. Nobody'll ever be able to prove he killed the women, and Tom just can't stand the thought of him walking away from it, rich and grinning. Good luck to Tom, but I'm not getting involved with it. We got our own problems."

Lights were on in Jack Lange's office when they pulled up in front ten minutes later. Hack was struck again by the place's similarity to Harold Pell's studio. The door opened before they reached it. A thin, sandy-haired, balding, deeply tanned man of medium height stepped aside and motioned for them to come in. "Hi, I'm Jack Lange," he said. "Come on in. Sit down. Pardon the mess."

The brightly lit room was as cluttered and rock-filled as it had been on their earlier visit, but two chairs had been cleared. Lange sat down at his desk and gave Hack a broad, teeth-showing smile. He picked up a ballpoint from the desk and, without looking away from Hack's face, began to click its little on-off button.

"Okay, Chief, uh, Hackett," he said. "How can I help you?"

Hack leaned forward and studied Lange's face in the unrelenting silent scrutiny that often induced twitching and sweat beads during an interrogation. It had no more apparent effect on Lange, however, than it had had on Harold Pell. Lange simply looked from him to Louanne and back, clicked the pen a dozen times, let his smile fade, and finally broke the silence himself.

"Terrible about the poor Winoskis. Really hard to believe. My wife told me what happened, I didn't even know about it until I came down from the mountain. I just can't imagine . . . it's the times we live in." He reached in his pocket and brought out a key ring. "You're interested in their ruby, aren't you?"

Hack realized he was holding his breath as Lange unlocked the desk drawer, reached in, took out a fist-sized reddish-brown rock, and held it out.

"Rubies," he said. "Beautiful specimen."

Hack was surprised by the rock's heaviness. He saw that the red appearance was caused by many small dark crystals embedded in a coarse, light brown matrix. The crystals sparkled in the light of the desk lamp. He passed it to Louanne, then turned back toward Lange.

"Valuable?"

"Oh, yes. A unique specimen. A lot of collectors would give . . . well, probably not their right arm, but . . ." Lange retrieved the stone, picked up a round magnifying glass from the desk and held it close to the red sparkles.

"Mr. Lange?"

Hack waited until the balding man put down the rock and looked directly at him. "Yes?"

"Where did you get the ruby?"

"Why, the Winoskis gave it to me, of course. I thought you knew. They came, both of them, the day before I went up to Craggy. They were so pleased with their find. They wanted me to assess it."

"How much is it worth?"

"Oh, I can't say exactly. It's pretty valuable."

"How much?"

"A hundred dollars, at least. Some collectors might go as high as two. As I say, it's a unique specimen."

"It's not useful for, uh, jewelry?"

"Oh no, not at all, nothing like that. The rubies are much too small." Lange peered at Hack. "You didn't think that . . . that somebody killed them for it, did you?"

CHAPTER 27

Sam was waiting outside the office next morning when Hack got there. Often left out of the flow of events, which usually suited him fine, Sam every now and then needed a pat on the head and a "good boy," which in his case meant being listened to. Hack sat him down in a visitor's chair and took a mental deep breath.

After selecting a toothpick from the assortment in his shirt pocket, Sam began the methodical, frowning mastication that always preceded serious speech.

"Go ahead, Sam," Hack said. "What you got? Tell me."

"Another dead cat. Out in Pisgah Shadows."

Pisgah Shadows, on the west edge of town, was Blue Ridge's most recent upscale development, a dozen four-hundred-thousand-dollar houses filled with newly born, golf-playing mountain lovers from the flatlands somewhere, all anxious, now that they were in, to shut the gate and not let anybody else up the hill.

"Oh? Cut up like the others?"

"Naw. Woman found it in her shrubbery when she went out to get the paper. She's got two Persian cats. I could see 'em in the living room window. She was havin' a real hissy fit when she called about the dead one."

"Was it a Persian too?"

"Naw, just some old tomcat."

"It was cut up?"

"Naw, bit up."

"Bit up?"

"Yeah, dogs. I could tell easy. Dogs chewed it up, then it crawled in the bushes and died."

"What did the woman want us to do?"

"She was havin' a hissy fit. You know how them women are. I brung the cat in and threw it in our dumpster."

"Good. That's that." Hack opened the Winoski folder and pointedly began to read.

Sam examined and reinserted the toothpick. "Found another pot patch up on Jeter. Probably Jake Boatwright's. Jake senior, that is. Can't read his own damn name, but ol' Jake's a smart 'un. He ain't booby-trapped the patch yet, though, or at least there ain't no trap there now."

"You going to pull the plants?"

"Naw."

"Why not?"

"There's a place across the creek where I can see the whole patch. I'm gonna watch. Sooner or later . . . I catch just one glimpse of ol' Jake-boy, or whoever it is, and I'll snatch his ass up so quick he'll wish he'd gone on and finished second grade like his mama always wanted him to."

"Okay, but don't take any chances. Those guys are animals. But you know that. Now I got work to do."

Sam was undeterred. "You want me to work on the Winoski case for you? I got a idea."

"What's that?"

"All that chemistry stuff in their garage, I bet Winoski was makin' some kind of drugs. Competition for Jake, you know, and Jake killed 'em. Maybe if I put on a disguise or something, and tried to buy . . . I don't know, something. From somebody."

"Hm, making drugs. That's an interesting idea, Sam. I'll think about it. But right now I've got other work to do."

Officer Bailey, who was seldom accused of having had *any* kind of idea, left the office with his shoulders a little higher than when he came in. Louanne and Melba, both waiting to take his place, entered the office together. Hack nodded for Melba to go ahead. She put a yellow folder on the desk.

"This is the background on Gerry Smith you asked for," she said. "The report from the Rochester police came in last night.

Three-and-a-half pages. Our little Geranium was certainly no shrinking violet when she was growing up. No blushing rose either."

"What'd she do?"

"Oh, mostly she protested things. You know how a lot of them are at that age, girls especially. There was a sit-in at the National Guard armory where she chained herself to a post and had to be hacksawed loose, for example. Then she got arrested once for assault when she and some other girls crashed a fraternity house they objected to. She hit a guy over the head with a baseball bat, sent him to the hospital."

"Life in the modern world. She —"

"Then drugs, of course. For the life of me, I just can't see why so many young people seem to think that *drugs* . . . I don't know. They seem to go through an absolutely stupid stage. Anyway, she was convicted of possession twice, intent-to-sell once. She claimed she was just trying to make money to help local AIDS victims, but she actually spent three days in jail on the intent-to-sell conviction. It's just the same old horrible story we hear so much today, but it looks like in her case she escaped in time." Melba gave Louanne a wry look and left the office.

Hack stared at the yellow folder, picturing the blood-soaked almost-corpse that Gerry Smith had been that gray morning in the Rocking Chair parking lot. He knew well that the drug world, particularly those who dealt in the business side, had long, long arms, never-fading memories, and claws that pinched real hard. He would call Rochester and talk to somebody about young Gerry. But of course all that had been years ago.

He looked up and saw that Louanne had perched herself on the edge of her chair. "Go ahead," he said.

"Chief, I've got an idea about the Winoski case. Of course you've probably already thought of it, it's so obvious. But anyway, I woke up at four o'clock this morning and couldn't get back to sleep. It just came to me out of the blue."

Hack, who had no ideas at all about *anything* at the moment, waited. Louanne opened the little blue notebook she always carried, touched a finger to her lips, and hesitated. Hack was contrasting his bright-eyed, fresh-faced youngest with his sag-jowled, toothpick-munching oldest when she continued.

"Jack Lange told us that the ruby is only worth a hundred dollars, but he also said that a collector would give his right arm for it. Does that make sense? I admit that the rock he showed us didn't look like much, but who's to say he hadn't switched rocks. The *real* ruby might be worth —"

Melba came in the room and held up her hand.

"Louanne, your creep's on the phone again. I told him I'd look for you. You can take the call in here, but don't pick up the phone until I tell you. Chief, come on out to my desk and listen. I'll try to get the phone people to trace the call, and I'll tape it."

A bare minute later, phone company alerted, tape recorder running, Hack holding a phone to his ear, Melba called to Louanne. "Okay, we're ready. Go ahead."

"Hello," Louanne said.

A low resonant hum lasted several seconds then stopped. A male voice whispered, "I feel much better now."

"Oh, that's good."

"You don't know me, but you do care about me. I know because you came when I asked you to."

"Yes, I care."

"You're so beautiful."

"What's your name? It's hard to talk to —"

"I can't talk long. I know they're trying to trace our call."

"I want to meet you. Where —"

"In the mall, outside Belk's, by the fountain. Be there in eight minutes. Come alone. But you know to come alone. You were alone last time. I'll be watching."

"I don't think I can get there in —"

"Oh yes you can. Louanne, no tricks, now. Please. When you get to know me . . . I really love you."

"Oh, don't hang up yet. I want —"

"You're trying to give them time to trace the call." The voice lost its softness. "Don't do that. You mustn't make me angry."

"But, I'm not —"

"Listen. I've got a question for you. You listening?"

"Yes."

"You know what hasn't happened since I realized that I love you?"

"No, what?"

"There haven't been any more fires at the college."

"Oh."

"And no more kittens. The last one, the one you buried, had a black spot behind its left ear. Don't make me angry. Eight minutes. Alone." He hung up.

Louanne came out from Hack's office, her face pale, her mouth a thin line.

"The kitten," Hack said, "did it —"

"Yes."

Hack glanced at the wall clock, which showed 9:12. He stood up.

"Go on," he said. "Meet him. Doubt if he'll show, but if he does, bring him in. Go, it'll take you eight minutes. He's timed it. We'll alert mall security."

Louanne stared at him a second then ran from the building.

Hack turned to Melba. "Get me the phone company, the call-tracer that you were talking to. Then call mall security. Tell 'em what's going on but have 'em hang on until I finish the other call."

As Melba dialed and waited, Hack closed his eyes and tried to put himself in the place of the caller, to guess what a maniac would do. Would he just come out to the fountain and say, "Hi, Louanne, it's me, I love you," or would he be watching from one of the shops? How could he be sure a dozen cops weren't right behind Louanne? Or would he not show and call later to set another rendezvous? Probably. But he might not be rational. Was he really the firebug? And the kitten killer? How else could he have known the cat's markings?

"Here's Chief Hackett," Melba said to the phone, then held it out to Hack. "Phone company. They tried to trace his call but didn't have enough time."

Hack skipped preliminaries. "You got six minutes this time. Get ready for a call that might come in to the pay phone by the Belk's fountain at the mall. I don't know the number. Can you do that?"

"We can try," a woman said.

"It's important." Hack handed the phone back to Melba and reached for her other one, which she was holding out.

"Mall Security," she said. "Robert Garner."

"Bob?" Hack knew all the mall cops personally. Garner was the day supervisor.

"Yessir, Chief."

"I want you to watch the fountain at Belk's but not be seen doing it. Right now. Louanne McLeod should be arriving there in the next two, three minutes. Be ready to respond if you're needed."

"Yessir. I'll go myself."

Hack handed the phone back to Melba. "Call the McFees. Ask for Brent. Talk to him. Trace him down on the campus if he's not home. Find him."

Louanne approached the splashing fountain in its little jungle of potted shrubs and blooming flowers. Half a dozen people, mostly old, sat on the marble ledge around the pool. Nobody there could possibly be the caller. A little boy standing on the fountain ledge showed his mother pennies on the pool bottom. The big clock over the Belk's entrance said 9:19.

Louanne didn't know how to act. She tried to look nonchalant, whatever that meant, but felt that she stood out like . . . like a cop at the mall.

If he was really here, he would be looking at her right now. She resisted the urge to stare at people and shop windows. The image of the mutilated, furry little blood-soaked bundle came to her mind. She saw the patch of black behind an ear. Several fountain edge-sitters stared at her. She tried to smooth out the horror that must be showing in her face. At 9:21 the pay phone outside Belk's rang. Louanne reached it first.

"Hello."

The humming on the line was louder than before. It went on for several seconds. With a shock, she recognized the sound. He was purring!

The hum stopped. "You came, and you came alone." The voice had taken on a faint singsong. "Thank you. You really do care about me."

"I told you I care."

If he knew she had come alone, he must be able to see her. He *was* watching! From a place where there was a phone. There couldn't be many such places.

"I had to be sure," the voice said, "but this is my last test. Next time we'll meet. Face to face."

"But what's your name? Do you live in Blue Ridge? Are you a student? Tell me about yourself. Really, I would like to —"

"Are you trying to give them time to trace this call? You aren't doing that, are you, Louanne? I love you, but I couldn't stand it if you tried to trick me."

"Oh, trust me. I want to meet you. I want to help. I want —"

"I know all about you. I've watched through your window. Did you know that your drapes don't quite close? You have a little red birthmark on your right hip."

Louanne felt her face begin to burn.

"I know where you go during the day. I've followed you everywhere, because I love you. So you see, you mustn't try to trick me, you just mustn't."

Louanne groped for something to say that would keep him on the line, but nothing came. After a moment the purring resumed, faint but clear, then stopped again.

"I'll call you again tomorrow. You *will* love me, I know."

He hung up.

At the station Hack waited, Melba's phone at his ear, for the phone company's tracing results. Sam had come up from downstairs and was watching. At 9:32 the word came through.

"Got it, Chief!" the call-tracer said. "The pay phone up on Jumpoff Rock."

"Thanks." He shoved the phone at Melba. "Sam, go block Jumpoff Road. Don't let anybody down the mountain. Or up. And be careful. Now, hurry! Go!"

Hack followed Sam out of the building, ran to his pickup and headed toward Whiteoak Mountain, to the gravel road that ran behind the college up to where the foot trail to Jumpoff Rock started. The trail and Jumpoff Road, which Sam would be blocking, were the only ways to get down from the rock without using climbing gear. If they were in time, they had him trapped. Jumpoff, he should have thought of that. The one place where you could see the whole town. From up there Mr. Whisper could have watched Louanne leave the station, could have seen if she left alone, and could watch her enter the mall. He'd have been a god up on a cloud, looking down. Well, if the god hadn't hurried down from his cloud this time . . .

Hack called Melba on the radio. "You find Brent?"

"Nobody answered at the McFees," she said. "I'll keep trying."

His hand jerked when he hung up the phone behind the refreshment stand, and he couldn't keep his left shoulder from twitching. He realized he was humming again and stopped. He pushed thick blond hair away from his eyes and stared unseeing at the phone on the wall.

Did he dare meet her next time? She said she cared.

She might be lying, they all lied, all the time. But she sounded like she really cared. No, she was a cop, she would do her job. He had to be realistic.

But she could still care for him even while she was trying to trick him. Women loved things they could pity. She didn't know him, couldn't know what he was really like. But once he had her all to himself, away from things, somewhere — he hadn't thought that part out yet — he could really talk to her. He could take all the time he wanted. Do anything he wanted. She would be his.

He realized, almost with surprise, that he actually didn't want to kill her now. Not at all.

At least not for a long time.

The fleeting glimpses he'd had of her through the crack in her drapes flashed before his eyes. He shook his head and looked at the observation point at the edge of the rock. He'd waited until no tourists were there before making his call and apparently none had come. At least the parking lot was empty. He strolled toward the woods, casually, in case there were any hikers or rock climbers that he'd missed who might have seen him.

When he was out of sight of the rock he ran to the start of the path and, backpack bouncing, wig displaced, began a scrambling descent. The cops might have been able to trace the call. She had kept him talking too long. Hurry!

The steep climb up the trail to the rock had taken more than half an hour, the slide down took only fifteen minutes. As he had anticipated, he met no one. Near the end of the narrow path, where it leveled out and approached the gravel road, his left shoe began to flop, its lace untied. He sat down to retie it and straighten his wig. Except for his ragged, panting breath the woods around him were dead-quiet.

A car crunched to a stop on the gravel below him, beyond the line of bushes at the edge of the woods. He moved to where he could see through the underbrush. It was a green pickup, the chief's.

The big cop got out, listened a moment then, moving slowly, entered the trail. He had a gun in his hand!

Hide! Hurry. Behind that rock.

No, no, not the rock! That's where he'll look first.

He moved off the trail, crouched low behind a thick clump of mountain laurel, opened his pack, and took out a revolver wrapped in a tee shirt. Teeth clenched, blond wig again askew, heart crashing against his ribs, he waited.

The chief, gun in hand, came a short distance up the trail then stepped off and began to climb through the woods. Toward him! But he was looking down at that rock, not up the hill.

When the chief was only ten feet away, the watcher raised his pistol and with trembling hand tried to aim.

CHAPTER 28

Hack pushed through the thick growth at the forest's edge. Tall oaks, hickories and poplars spread a flickering green canopy high above the open understory. He could see far ahead the path bent sharply to the left and began its steep ascent toward Jumpoff Rock. Dark clumps of mountain laurel and rhododendron marked the trail's diagonal way up the mountain. At the bend in the path a huge shagbark hickory grew beside an outcropping of gray rock. Hack studied the rock. It was big enough to hide a man.

His nerves tautened and his thoughts began to come in sharp little snatches. He was back in the jungle. In Vietnam. The rock . . . field of fire. He stepped off the path.

Something was wrong. It was too quiet. Where were the woods sounds?

With eyes on the ambush rock, he stood and listened. A silent minute passed, then a locust high in a tree took up his rasping autumn love song. A small brown bird flitted from one nearby bush to another, and a bee buzzed away from a stalk of yellow goldenrod near his feet. A squirrel high in the branches of the shagbark suddenly began a raucous chur.

Hack had spent much of his youth in the woods with a rifle, usually hunting squirrels, whose habits and language he knew. This one was screaming bloody death at something or somebody on the ground. A hickory nut, still in its green outer husk, dropped from the tree and bounced off the gray rock.

Raising his chief's special, Hack moved slowly up the hill toward a tangle of mountain laurel. From there he would be able to see behind the rock.

A gun cracked from the direction of the laurel and a bullet thudded into a tree trunk close by. Hack sprinted towards a fallen log to his right. Before he reached it a second bullet ripped through leaves above his head. Then a third slammed into his leg.

He fell behind the log and hugged the ground. Silence, deafening after the gunfire, returned. A moment later someone began a noisy run downhill through the dead leaves. Hack rose to his knees and caught a glimpse of a man disappearing in the bushes at the bottom of the slope. The squirrel in the hickory tree, hushed only briefly by the gunfire, resumed his swearing.

Hack looked down at his right thigh. The cloth just above the knee was ripped and bright blood had already soaked his pants around the rip. He felt the first sharp thrusts of pain. Then his own swearing shocked the outclassed squirrel into silence.

CHAPTER 29

At the station Melba snatched up the phone when it rang. It was her chatty cousin at the college again.

"I can't talk now, Lurleen," Melba said. "I'm expecting a call from the chief. Things are happening and —"

"What's happening?"

"Gotta go, I'll call back." Melba hung up and waited, tense.

When the chief's radio call came a few minutes later, he spoke in a low, slow, gritty voice that she had heard only a few times before. She knew from those earlier times that the correct response to whatever he said was, "Yes, sir."

He told her to send Billy, and anybody else she could grab, to the start of Jumpoff trail. They were to begin at the laurel bush just above the big boulder at the bottom of the hill and track whoever had been there, but to take care. The person they were tracking was armed and would shoot. She should tell Billy to pull guys off traffic to help, anybody he could find, but they were to locate the shooter, then wait there for help.

"Okay, Chief. Where will you be?"

"At the damn hospital."

"The *hospital?* Are you hurt?"

The radio went dead.

Melba yelled for Billy, told him what the chief had said, then called the emergency room at Pisgah Memorial. The duty nurse, another cousin, said that the chief had just limped in. One of his pants legs was bloody, but at least he was walking.

* * *

Twenty minutes later the nurse called back. It was a flesh wound above the right knee, she said. Nasty-looking and painful, but not very serious. The bullet had cut a big gash but had gone on through and hadn't stuck in his leg. Against advice — the way he was glaring at them, nobody felt like insisting — he'd just driven off in his pickup. They'd got him bandaged, but he hadn't even let them take off his pants. And the things he'd *said* . . .

Six minutes later the wounded warrior stumped through the station door, his bloody pants bulging above the right knee, his face pale, his mouth a hard straight line. Melba braced for earthquakes and explosions.

"They wanted to cut off my pants but I wouldn't let 'em," he said. "Anything from Billy?"

His voice, which carried neither tremor nor snarl, could have been ordering barbecue for lunch. Melba took a deep breath and relaxed.

"Not yet," she said.

"Where's Louanne?"

"She went with Billy and Ferguson."

"Beep her. Tell her to stop whatever she's doing and come here. Get me Art Taylor on the phone — no, I'll call him. You call the sheriff, say emergency. Call Sam. I suppose he's still out blocking Jumpoff Road. Tell him to go up to Jumpoff. If there's anybody there, take their names and find out how to contact them, then come see me. Then you go and get me some pants. In my bedroom closet."

He dropped a set of keys on the desk, went into his office and got Art Taylor on the phone.

"You think its our fire lover?" the college president asked after hearing the morning's events.

"Yes."

"You know who he is?"

"No, but it's very likely one of your students."

"What makes you so sure?"

"Art, I don't *know* he's a student," Hack said, "but I'd bet my pension and pickup on it."

"Huh. Lurleen just heard you'd been shot," Art said. "Three times, once in the neck, twice in the chest next to the heart. Sounds sort of serious. You going to live?"

"Clipped my leg. Nothing."

"What do you actually know about . . . him? It *is* a him?"

"The voice that called Louanne was male, low pitched, clearly disguised. From the way he ran down the hill, he must be fairly agile — he'd already climbed all the way up and back down the mountain. His calling Louanne from up on Jumpoff where he could watch both the station and the mall was smart. He knew details of the last kitten that was cut up, so he must be —"

"A clever, athletic, homicidal pyromaniac who may be enrolled in freshman English, or organic chemistry, or —"

"Take it serious, Art, damn it. Get everybody you have —"

"Oh, don't worry, I'm taking it very seriously. But he does sound like the kind of boy who would liven up my Philosophy 101, which tends to get a little samey."

"One of my guys will be on the campus. Use him any way you can." Hack hung up. A few minutes later, Billy came into the office.

"Easy to see where he ran down from where he was hiding to the edge of the woods, Chief," he said, "but we lost the trail there. I got two guys from traffic knocking on doors for witnesses and sent another one up on Jumpoff to talk to anybody they find there."

"I'll get the sheriff to send his dogs," Hack said.

Melba tapped on the doorframe and came in with a pair of gray work pants over her arm. Sam followed her. She handed Hack the pants, then, carefully not looking down at his bloody leg, left the room and shut the door.

"Nobody up on Jumpoff, Chief," Sam said. "Parking lot empty. I checked the rest rooms."

"Okay, sit down." Hack stood up but when he tried to slip his pants over the bandage he realized why the doctor had wanted to cut them off. He winced and almost asked Billy for help, but after much maneuvering managed to get the bloody ones off and the clean ones on. He limped to the door and called Melba.

Louanne came in with her. The women's eyes went directly to the bloody wad stuffed in the wastebasket. Louanne grimaced and quickly looked away. Melba picked up the wastebasket and carried it outside. Hack's phone rang. It was the sheriff.

"Tom, we got a problem," Hack said. "I need your —"

"You want my dogs. Okay, but you know they won't do much good in town. From what I hear, you didn't even shoot at the bastard. Why not?"

"Didn't have time. When —"

"They're getting 'em ready now, I figured you'd call. Have somebody meet my guys out where the trail starts, in about twenty minutes. By the way, I'm going to need you in the morning."

"Why?"

"Harold Pell. We're going to reenact the crime, as they say. The weather is supposed to be the same as it was the day he pushed 'em."

"I can't get away, Tom, not as long as I've got a maniac running around shooting people."

"No, I need your help. I think Pell's about to crack, I really do. It's got so he bubbles all up with giggles whenever he sees me. I think the two of us together can push him over the edge. The mental edge, that is. We'll go back up to the parkway, in the fog and all. I'll pick you up early — say seven o'clock — at the Rocking Chair."

"I can't do it, Tom. I —"

"Hey, Hawgy boy, you say you want my bloodhounds? Right now? This very minute? Well, gee, buddy, I don't know, we're just real busy. Maybe next month, though."

"All right, all right, if it's that important to you, but you're just kidding yourself. Pell'll still be giggling at you when he collects the insurance, and he'll probably fall all the way off his damn chair laughing when he gets title to those eighty acres. Hell, Tom, *you* may be the one to crack first, not Pell."

"You just be ready in the morning, Hawg." The sheriff hung up.

Hack put down the phone and glowered at the crew arrayed before his desk, their mental mouths open, waiting to be told what to do. Hell, it was about time for him to tell *somebody* something useful to do, instead of him stumbling around like a blind bird dog getting himself shot, risking Louanne's life, playing stupid damn telephone games with a would-be killer.

And he knew what to tell them. He actually felt like a police chief today, for the first time since he couldn't remember when.

"Louanne, I want you out of the way. No more using you as bait."

"Out of the way? What do you mean? I —"

"Go to Hope Springs. Stay there. Inside."

"Chief! That's not fair. I'm the one that —"

"Hope Springs. With a crazy loose in town, we *ought* to have somebody out there, and you're the obvious one. You can keep talking to Geranium. We've still got her shooting to worry about, remember. Keep your eyes and ears open."

Louanne half rose from her chair and turned toward the department's number-two man. "Wipe that grin off your face, Billy!"

"Who, me?"

"Yeah, you! You —"

Hack slapped the desk hard. "Stop that. Now."

For a moment the only sound in the room was heavy breathing. Hack made his voice low and calm when he spoke next.

"Melba, I want you to start calling people, start a — what do you call it? — phone chain. Start with your relatives. No, start with the fire department. Start with your relatives in the fire department. I want *everybody* in Blue Ridge to know about Mr. X. Have the whole town watch for him and report anything suspicious. You be here to take the calls. There'll be a lot of them. Get somebody in to help you."

Hack looked deliberately at each face, in turn, pausing at Billy and Louanne. "Any questions?" he asked, spacing the words.

There were none.

"Okay, the firebug is now number one, but we can't forget the Winoski killings. Sam, I want you to go to Asheville and bring in Jack Lange. I'll let the Asheville cops know what you're doing. Louanne will tell you where he lives. Just ask Lange to come with you. If he refuses, call me, but stay there and watch him."

"You think he —"

"Don't know, but the ruby — maybe he didn't show us the right one — is really all we've got to go on. Anyway, get him in here."

"Okay, Chief."

"Ferguson, find the McFee's son, Brent. Bring him in. He's the only . . . no, change that, don't bring him in. You'd probably have to bring his mama too, and that . . . just find him and watch him. Try to keep him in sight or at least know where he is. If X calls again — and I'll bet he will — I want to know where Brent is when the call comes.

"And Sam, when you get back from bringing in Lange, go up to the college and stay out where people can see you. Stay there until I tell you.

"Billy, you go meet Tom's guy with the bloodhounds. And don't forget X is desperate. Okay, now go on, all of you, get started. Go."

Looks passed among the troops, but no one said anything. Billy avoided Louanne's death ray as they filed out of the office. Sam, for once toothpickless, was the last in line. Hack called him back.

"Before you go, tell me again about the pot patch you found up on Jeter, the one you think is Boatwright's." He held out a box of red-topped pins. "Here, mark it on the map."

Sam went to the map, studied it a moment, then stuck in a pin. "Right here on this path, Chief. It ain't big. There wasn't no booby trap there last time I checked."

"Okay, thanks. Now go get Lange."

Hack waited until Sam left the office, then went to the window and stood, right foot in its accustomed place on the windowsill. Raising his leg to the sill had made his wound hurt, but he kept it there anyway.

He watched different sets of tourists do touristy things — eat ice cream cones, read brochures, stare at Johnny Reb, slump exhausted on benches, peer at the overalled farmers sitting in tilted-back chairs on the sidewalk outside Huskey Hardware. Hack knew both farmers and tourists well enough to imagine the choice comments each group made as they perused the other.

With a grunt he took his leg down and hobbled across to the map, where with a finger he traced known paths, both marked and unmarked, on Jeter Mountain. He went back to his desk and reread the contents of Gerry Smith's now fairly thick folder, then closed it and went out to where Melba was activating the town's early-warning alarm system.

"That's right, Wanda, he shot the chief. No, no, he's okay. Anyway, we think the one that shot him is the firebug at the college *and* the one who's killing the poor kittens all over town. The chief wants you to watch out your window and call us if you see anything suspicious. The chief said to . . . well, I guess he's still going. Yes, he's taking Allie. No, no, Honey understands. I gotta go now, Wanda. You just call if you see anything, you know, funny."

Hack left the building and went to his pickup. The pain in his leg was increasing, and it felt like the wound had begun to bleed again. After driving around the square, he turned onto Buncombe, followed it to where it became Jeter Road, passed the Rocking Chair Café with its now-bloodless parking lot, and continued up Jeter Mountain.

He drove slowly, his eyes searching the brush on the uphill side of the road.

CHAPTER 30

As Hack looked for obscure paths in the brush on the side of Jeter Mountain, Marie McFee stood in the middle of her living room, her hands clenched in a hard knot against her chest, her face pale. She was alternating between anger and fear. A car driven by a policeman had just pulled away from the curb in front of the house and followed her son's Mazda in the direction of town.

They knew.

To set fire to his *own house* . . . the fires in the college buildings had been cries for help, and she hadn't listened. She'd been too busy. She, of all people, who should recognize . . . in her own son . . .

And for it to happen right now, just before her book came out. She could imagine the sniggers from some of her "colleagues" when they heard.

It wasn't her fault. She hadn't known there was insanity in Hammond's family when she married him.

Earlier in the day she'd heard of the shooting on Whiteoak Mountain and had immediately looked for Brent. She hadn't found him. Then later he'd come into the house and gone straight upstairs and shut his door.

She'd thought of following him and . . . what? Telling him it wasn't his fault? That together they could work it out? Work what out? How? Where'd he gotten a gun? Did he still have it? She'd gone as far as the bottom of the stairs but then turned around and come back to the living room.

Brent came downstairs a few minutes later and left the house. She'd called to him, but her voice was weak and he hadn't heard, or he'd ignored her. Then the police had followed him.

Marie went into the kitchen and sat down at the table. Her face scrunched. Tears, the first in many years, spilled from her eyes and rolled down her cheeks. She knew well the futility of self-pity, but couldn't stop herself from crying. She put her head down on her arms on the table. Minutes passed, then a noise caused her to look up.

Hammond was standing in the doorway, his face drained of color, his eyes blank. She realized she was actually glad to see him.

"The police are following Brent," she said. "They know." She looked closely at her husband. "What's wrong, Hammond?"

He held out a long, thin-bladed knife. "I found this in Brent's room. In the back of a drawer."

"Oh, no!" Marie stood up and backed away, but couldn't take her eyes from the shining blade's point.

Hammond stepped around the table. "Look, you can still see blood."

She took another step backward and felt the wall with her hands.

Hammond began to hum low in his throat. He moved forward. "Look," he whispered.

She raised her hands to her mouth, unable to speak.

Hammond jammed the knife into the center of her chest.

At the station Melba's phone rang again. She was keeping count of the I-saw-something-suspicious calls. If this was another one, it would be number thirty-seven.

"Police Department," she said.

"This is Hammond McFee at the college." His tone was brisk. "I'd like to speak to Louanne McLeod, please."

"She's not here right now, Mr. McFee. Can I take a message?"

"She gave me her number and said I should call if I had any thoughts on our firebug."

"You can give me a message. I'll pass it on."

"I guess I'd rather speak to her, if you don't mind. Where can I reach her?"

"Well . . . it might be hard to get in touch right now. Do you want to talk to someone else in the department?"

"No. She told me to be sure to call her."

Melba considered for a moment. It should be okay to give out just the phone number if she didn't say where Louanne was. Maybe Mr. McFee knew something important.

"Okay, I guess," she said. "Just a second."

She consulted a telephone list and found Hope Springs Shelter. "You can reach Louanne at this number, Mr. McFee."

The phone in the kitchen rang. Violet Turner picked it up. "Hope Springs Shelter."

Click.

CHAPTER 31

Hack pulled off the road and parked in the shade of an ancient hemlock that grew beside a picnic table on the banks of Brightwater Creek. The stream, really only a small brook this high up on Jeter Mountain, formed a shallow gravel-bottomed pool almost big enough to hold trout. Hack half-sat on the edge of the table for a few minutes listening to the rush of water over mossy stones, his thoughts gray.

He shouldn't be where he was, of course, he should be directing the maniac-search he'd started in the valley below. But with his bad leg, there was nothing he could really do to help, just be there. His team knew its job, and if they needed him they could call on the damn radio . . . if he were to turn it back on, that is. The creepy-crawler pistol shooter and house burner wasn't the only bad guy they had to worry about. The whole nightmare crime wave had started with a shooting up here on Jeter, and Hack was pretty sure he knew how and why the shooting happened. Now he wanted to see where.

He picked up a little brown hemlock cone that had fallen on the table and frowned at it, unseeing. A crow swooped in, landed on a low branch over his head, then with a loud caw and much flapping, flew away. Hack shook his head, tossed the cone aside and limped across the road.

Walking along the low bank that bordered the pavement, he peered closely at the underbrush on the uphill side of the road, for once not seeing the butterflies — burnt orange monarchs and both yellow and black swallowtails — that flitted among the golden daisies, deep purple asters and the rusty rose billows of Joe Pye weed that turned mountain roadsides into flower beds in early fall. He stopped at a narrow, barely discernible trail through the brush, examined the hard dry ground a moment, then stepped through the gap into the forest. There the trail, worn smooth by countless generations of deer, was plainly visible.

He followed the narrow track a quarter mile to where it intersected a larger, man-made, trail. He turned right. Occasional broken green weeds showed the path to have been used recently. In a damp place by a tiny spring he stopped and examined several clear footprints, then continued, deliberately, along the path. Every few steps he paused and looked around, his eyes moving from the ground on either side of the trail up into the trees, then back down to the ground. After ten minutes of stop-look-and-go he reached an open grove of ancient oaks, where he halted and didn't advance.

Ahead and to the right, in an area of dappled shade largely hidden from above by the trees, some two dozen feathery-leaved plants, five or six feet tall, grew in a weedless, cultivated garden. Hack wondered what the so-called "street value," so loved by newspaper reporters, would be when the public read about it. Probably a lifetime's legitimate earnings for the troglodyte who planted the stuff.

Well, the troglodyte — if that was the word for caveman — was going to be disappointed this time. They would make a big deal of digging up the plants and burning them, and Hack would insist on having Sam's picture in the newspaper, maybe in color. The story would surely make the front page.

Fine, but that wasn't why he was here. He turned around and made his way back along the trail, even slower and more watchful than on his approach. After a dozen yards he stepped off the trail and up to a sprawling rhododendron. He pulled the branches apart. A short piece of heavy black thread dangled from a thick, head-high limb. He turned and sighted from the thread toward a tall, straight poplar tree on the other side of the path. He went to the poplar, examined its smooth gray bark just below eye level, then reached out and touched six little round holes there. His scowl turned blacker.

He searched the area around the punctured poplar and found, in a leaf-filled depression, a large black plastic bag almost completely hidden by newly fallen leaves. In the bag was a set of heavy lopping shears, the kind gardeners use to prune shrubbery and fruit trees. They had light-colored wooden handles with black molded rubber handgrips, and the curved steel cutting blades were stained from use.

He closed the bag without touching the shears, nodded, and limped back the way he had come.

CHAPTER 32

In the Hope Springs kitchen it had taken some coaxing to convince Johnny Peebles to sit in Louanne's lap, but once there he wouldn't leave, and he was heavy. She hadn't realized a four-year-old could weigh so much, or be so demanding.

"Read it again," he said.

"Oh, Johnny, let's read something else. We've read —"

"No, read Tuffy again."

"Okay, but just one more time." The pistol on Louanne's belt was a small log against her right hip. "Here, let's move you over to my other knee."

She shifted the stocky little body, then turned back to the start of *Tuffy The Tugboat.* The kitchen was a warm, pleasant place this afternoon. Violet Turner puttered at the stove, two of the four current residents sat at the table nursing babies, another sliced carrots at the sink, and another unloaded the dishwasher. One of the recent mothers was Mary Louise Peebles who, in addition to Johnny and two-month-old Allison, had back in her trailer somewhere up Dutch Cove a husband who drank.

Louanne knew that the women all wondered why she was there. She'd told them without elaboration that the chief wanted her to stay with them a while. They hadn't asked any questions, but she knew they still wondered.

Well, *she* knew why she was there. It was because the chief had ordered — not asked — her to come. She understood the reasons, but still she fumed inside.

"No, no!" Johnny cried. "Tuffy said, 'chug-chug-chug.' You didn't read it right."

"Oh, I'm sorry, Johnny."

She reread the offending passage and had just turned the page and begun the heroic rescue of the big, blue-eyed, storm-tossed, sinking ocean liner when a loud banging on the back door stopped her in mid-word. A long, drawn-out, gobbling screech followed the banging, then the door burst open.

Louanne jumped up and grabbed for her gun. Johnny slid to the floor and let out his own screech. Violet Turner dropped a pot in the sink.

A grizzly, bearded man in dirty overalls lurched into the room, fighting with a huge flapping bird. "Help me with this darn turkey!"

Louanne slid her gun back into its holster.

Violet stepped up, grabbed the gobbler's neck, managed to find its legs, and held it away from her face. It struggled wildly at first, then after a few dispirited wing-flaps and clucks became still.

"I had him tied up good, or I thought so anyway." The man, ancient, gray and stringy, backed away, stood up straight and looked at Violet. "You all want him? He's a young one, nice and tender. He ain't very big, but —"

"Why sure we want him, Mr. Welch," Violet said. "You bet we do."

"I should 'a killed him for you, but I thought maybe . . . here, keep holding, I'll tie him back up." He took some cord from a pocket and tied the turkey's legs together. "But I *should* 'a killed him for you."

"No problem about that, Mr. Welch," Violet said. "We'll fix him. And we thank you, sir, we really do." She turned to the women at the table. "We're gonna eat good tonight! Right, girls?"

After profuse and repeated thanks, Mr. Woodrow Welch, eighty-seven years old and charitable, departed, still mumbling apologies for not having killed the bird for them. Violet explained that he lived on the farm that adjoined the Hope Springs property to the south. The farm was now run by his oldest grandson, but Woodrow still raised a big garden and a small flock of free-range turkeys. He had brought vegetables to the shelter before but never a turkey.

"That was real sweet of him," Violet said. "I know he loves those birds like pets. No wonder he didn't want to kill this one. I wasn't planning to fix anything but macaroni and cheese for supper. We'll pretend it's Thanksgiving."

"I'll dress him for you, Violet," Mary Louise Peebles said. "Where's a hatchet?"

"You don't mind, Mary Louise? I could be getting ready to cook him. There's a hatchet in the shed, on the bench by the tractor, and there's a chopping block out back."

Louanne, who had been watching the trussed turkey's unblinking eyes, spoke. The words came out almost before she realized what she was saying.

"No. I'll do it."

Billy and the chief thought she was too tenderhearted to be a cop, too nice to run over squirrels. They thought the sight of a little blood would make her faint. What did they think she ought to do, go to work in a library? Okay, maybe she wasn't bloodthirsty — like Billy — but when the time came, she would do what she had to do. She was positive.

From far in the back of her mind a little uninvited voice piped up. "Unless you faint, of course."

She frowned at the turkey and shook her head sharply. The women in the room exchanged looks.

"Here, Violet, give him to me," she said.

She knew how to "fix" a turkey. She'd seen her grandmother do it. There was nothing to it. When she accepted the bird from Violet, Mary Louise, who was square, thick, muscular and red-cheeked, handed Allison to her neighbor and stood up.

Louanne, her own cheeks pale, her jaws clamped and her lips squeezed together, carried the turkey by the feet, upside down, unprotesting, out the back door. Mary Louise followed.

Five minutes later Louanne held the turkey's legs up so that its neck lay across the face of a much-used oak stump. She lifted the hatchet she had found in the garage, squeezed her eyes shut and . . . did nothing.

She opened her eyes. Another eye, a gleaming, brownish-yellow circle surrounded by red lumpy skin, regarded her calmly, coolly. Sadly. It knew what was going to happen. It knew!

She just couldn't do it!

But she *had* to!

She couldn't.

DO IT!

Several hatchet-poised seconds later Mary Louise stepped up, said, "I'll do it," and took the hatchet.

Louanne turned her back and reclosed her eyes but couldn't help hearing the heavy "thuck" and the wild flapping that followed.

She returned to the kitchen, picked up Johnny and hugged him so hard he said "Oof." Then, holding back tears, she started reading Tuffy again. The women in the room carefully avoided looking in her direction. No one said a word.

Half an hour later the bird was in the oven and the table set for supper. Without asking, Violet had put an extra place for Louanne. Johnny, astride the rocking horse, was mumbling, pretending to be Tuffy, while Louanne slumped in a chair by the window thinking about libraries and turkeys, wondering if she would be able to eat any of the latter. The phone rang. Violet picked it up. "It's for you," she said and held out the phone to Louanne.

"Louanne? Is the chief there?" It was Melba.

"No."

"You know where he is?"

"No."

"He's gone off without his beeper again and his radio doesn't answer. Sometimes that man . . . maybe you can help me."

"How?"

"It's about that Jack Lange, in Asheville. Sam just called from his house. Lange's not there. His wife thinks he's in New York. Lange never tells her his plans, she says. She imagines he'll be back tonight."

"Oh?"

"Sam asked her if Lange had taken the Winoskis' ruby with him. She said she didn't know, but then they went in the office and found it, all labeled and everything. She wants Sam to take it."

"She does?"

"She hopes giving it to him will make the cops go away, Sam thinks, like throwing meat to wolves that are chasing you. He asked if her husband owns a gun. She doesn't know of one, she says. Sam wants to know what he should do. Should he take the ruby? And I can't find the chief. What do you think?"

It was the first time anybody in the department had ever come right out and asked her advice about anything that mattered. She felt a little better. Maybe she could be a *police* librarian. "I guess I don't see why not," she said. "He can give her some kind of receipt. If Lange actually switched rubies, which is what we believe . . . yeah, I think Sam ought to take it."

"I'll tell him. You staying at Hope Springs?"

"Well, Melba, you heard what the chief said. It sounded like a direct order to me, and I can see the reason for it."

"I got everybody in half the county peering around curtains looking for a monster. And that monster may well be somewhere looking for *you*, Louanne. So you stay right where the chief told you to, you hear. And keep your eyes open too."

"Well, I guess."

"Oh, yeah, another thing. Hammond McFee wants to talk to you. He wouldn't tell me what about. I'll bet he knows it was Brent that set the fire at his house and wants to talk to you about it. I gave him the Hope Springs number and said he could call you there."

"Well, he hasn't called."

Louanne put down the phone and went back to her place by the window. A few minutes later loud meowing came from behind the basement door, followed by the sound of rapid scratching.

"Those cats," Violet said. "They're hungry all the time. No telling how many of them are down there, but they keep the mice and rats away. Must smell the turkey. I'll give them the gizzard, that ought to keep 'em busy a while."

She reached in the sink and held up a brick-red, fist-sized lump. "We really ought to put 'em out of the basement and close up that hole, but the little kittens are so cute. I'd let the kittens in here, but Gerry'd have a sneezing fit if I did. In all my born days I never saw anybody as allergic —"

"Where *is* Gerry?" Louanne asked.

"Asleep. She took a pain pill. Her shoulder still bothers her a lot, especially late in the afternoon. Sleep's what she really needs most right now, poor thing."

Violet went to the basement door, opened it a crack and, blocking the entrance with her foot, tossed in the gizzard. The meows stopped.

Hammond McFee heard the women talking upstairs and heard the door open and close and the cats stop yowling. He was sitting on the cold basement floor, head down, eyes squeezed shut, hands pressing against his temples. He gave a barely audible moan. A long shiver shook his whole body. His brain was about to burst. He was dying.

No. Not here. Not yet.

Half an hour earlier he had approached the building from the west side, where shades on the two windows were drawn. The basement door had opened at a push. He didn't think any of the women had seen him or heard him, and after listening a while to their idiot kitchen-jabber he was sure.

He'd put the gasoline can on the floor beside a stack of empty cardboard boxes and checked the ceiling to make sure there was no smoke alarm this time.

Then pains — stabbing fire behind his eyes — had suddenly hit him, and he'd had to sit down. He knew the hurt would go away, it always had, but it had never lasted this long before. It seemed to him he'd been sitting there for hours. Maybe this time the pain wasn't going to stop . . . ever.

No. It would. He just had to wait.

A little later it had begun to ease, then drained quickly away. It left him weak and quivery, but then exhilaration, as always, rushed in to take the pain's place. He opened his eyes. A big orange cat, thin and emaciated, crouched over something at the base of the stairs in the middle of the room. Two kittens, one gray and one orange, watched the big cat.

Hammond carefully stood up. All three cats turned their heads in his direction. Pains now forgotten, his heart racing, he knelt back down, held out his left hand, and began to purr softly in the way he had learned.

In the kitchen, turkey aroma had begun to overpower the other cooking smells. Louanne realized with surprise that she was starving. Violet had just basted the nicely browning bird when, after a tap on the back door, the chief came into the room.

Talk stopped abruptly and all eyes turned to him. Without a word he nodded to Louanne and limped painfully to the table. He pulled out a chair, dropped into it and, with a grimace, raised his right leg onto another chair. His face was drawn and gray, the scar on his cheek red and prominent.

"Gerry Smith here?" he said to no one in particular.

"She's asleep," Violet said. "Took a pain pill. I really don't think I ought to wake her up."

The chief scowled but didn't say anything. He slumped a little lower and sat staring at his elevated foot until Louanne broke the silence.

"Chief, Melba called a little while ago looking for you. She wants to talk with you. Jack Lange's left town. He —" She shouldn't be talking police business in front of strangers. Not that it mattered. The chief's mind was clearly elsewhere.

"Okay," he said. Then, using both hands, he lifted his wounded leg down from the chair and stood up. "Violet, where's the key to the room in back of the garage?"

"The store room? On Gerry's key ring."

"Get it for me."

"You want it now?"

"Yes."

"I'd really hate to wake her up. She needs —"

"Then I'll get it myself." He took a limping step toward the door at the back of the room.

"No, no, no, that's okay, Chief," Violet said. "I'll get it."

She left the kitchen and returned a moment later with a key ring. "It was on the dresser. Gerry's dead asleep. I think this is the one." Holding out a little silver key she handed the ring to the chief.

"Is she staying here now at night?" he said.

"No, she still goes up to her cabin, but at least now she uses the van, not the bike. I've tried to convince her to stay here and let us take care of her, but she won't. Maybe you could convince her, Chief."

Louanne thought for a second that he was going to respond to that, but instead he shook his head and limped to the back door. With his hand on the knob he turned back to Violet.

"Tell her I need to talk to her. I'll leave these keys on the tractor seat." He left the room.

"I don't like him," Johnny Peebles said. "He's mean."

"No he's not, Johnny," Louanne said. "He's not mean at all. He's got a hurt leg. He's *nice*."

"Oh."

"Well, what in the world was that all about, Louanne?" Violet said. "I never saw him like that. What's he want in the garage?"

"I don't know."

"Why is he interested in Gerry's cabin? You think he's going there?"

"I don't know."

Johnny, book in hand, patted Louanne's knee. "Will you read to me again?"

"Sure, Johnny."

She scooped him up, kissed him on the forehead and arranged him on her left knee. She had just reached the scary part about the fog when a cat in the basement let out a long wail. It ended abruptly. Louanne stopped reading and looked at the basement door, but the sound wasn't repeated.

"Cat fight," Violet said. "I ought to chase 'em all away."

"Read," Johnny said.

"Okay. 'When Tuffy saw the giant ship looming above him in the fog, his heart sank. He knew he was too little . . .'"

CHAPTER 33

Hack left Hope Springs intending to go back to the station. But as seemed to happen more and more often these days, he turned toward the mountains instead, an action which he realized was very close to dereliction of duty. With a mad arsonist and shooter on the loose in his town, he should be back at the command and control center, his office, barking out orders. Or if he didn't bark, he could at least be visible, jut-jawed and grim, to inspire the troops.

But hell, he could give orders just as well by radio, and he felt anything but jut-jawed right now. And his team could cope better without him breathing on their necks. What he needed was help with *his* problem. But there wasn't anybody who could help.

What he had found in the Hope Springs storeroom — what he'd expected to find, and what was now on the seat beside him — had brought him face to face with a decision, a moral decision. And moral decisions were best addressed from mountains, not valleys.

Many times in his life he had faced situations where temptations pulled him one way, his sense of right and wrong — his conscience — the other. Usually, after a struggle, his conscience won. And even when it lost, it wouldn't let him really enjoy his forays off the path. The decision before him now was different. He didn't know which way was right; his conscience muttered at him out of both sides of its mouth.

Would it be right to shut down Hope Springs and put those women on the street? No.

No? That's what he had sworn to do when he became a cop, wasn't it?

Aunt Ola often accused him of whining. Well, how could he help it if his own conscience whined in his ear about everything he did these days. Take unhappy Louanne back there at Hope Springs. Was what he'd done with her right?

No. It wasn't professional to hide her away like that. She was a member of his team; he shouldn't make exceptions just because she was too little, too nice, too pretty to be a cop, not somebody to go out and look for a knife-carrying weirdo who said he loved her.

But how could he face Allie if something unspeakable happened to her daughter? What if, instead of picking Allie up to take her to the church supper, he'd have to go to her door and say, "Allie, I've got bad news. It's about Louanne."

He didn't want to hurt Allie. Or Louanne. Or the poor women back in the shelter. Or Gerry Smith. He wanted to protect them.

Okay, all very well in principle, but had it reached the point where the principle got in the way of his doing his job? Could he still make hard decisions? Or was he too old?

Louanne might be too softhearted to be a cop, but what about himself? Was "softhearted" just another word for "chicken"? He really didn't have to keep the damn job. Didn't he maybe owe it to the town to let somebody else have it, somebody still young enough to be tough?

What if he went ahead and courted Allie and down the road asked her to marry him. Assuming she said yes — and in the light of day he supposed she probably would — he could take her back to the old Hackett farm, to Mama. Mama who would *love* Allie. Then he could spend the rest of his life deciding tough questions like how many acres of tobacco to plant next year or whether to go back to growing a little cotton. And if something happened to Louanne, at least somebody *else* would have to tell her mother. And Hope Springs Shelter could go its way without him even knowing if that way was up or down.

Hack suddenly realized where he was. He had driven all the way up Pisgah Mountain and was on the Parkway. He had no memory of getting there. Twenty miles. Another damn you're-too-old sign.

He parked at Looking Glass Mountain overlook, walked to the low gray stone wall and looked down at his valley spread out before him as clean and neat as a Norman Rockwell painting. You wouldn't think there could be arson, murder and animal torture down there. He could just make out Hope Springs Shelter. From a mile up it looked like a country school that should be full of barefoot boys and girls with pigtails, not beaten women and their babies.

And there in the distance Jumpoff Rock hung out of the side of Whiteoak Mountain like judgment day about to happen to the valley below it. From the square in Blue Ridge Jumpoff was a towering cliff, but looking down from where he was it was just a pebble. It all depended on your perspective.

Did *everything* depend on your perspective? Did the question of right and wrong?

Stop whining. Think what Aunt Ola would say if she could hear your thoughts. Maybe you ought to just ask her what to do, let *her* be your conscience.

Oh, come on, act your age. No, *stop* acting your age is more like it. Why didn't he just forget about "courting" and go on and ask Allie to marry him? Even if they'd never had a real "date," they spoke the same language. Allie would understand. He could propose Sunday night, between the mashed potatoes and the peach pie, like Hattie Mae had suggested. Deep down, he knew he wanted to, so why didn't he do it?

But what about Gerry Smith?

He should just keep remembering that her name was Geranium, and that she was a Yankee do-gooder. That'd keep her in perspective. He should forget how she looked, just do his duty, and stop wondering what she would look like if she really smiled. At him. He should marry Allie and get on with his life. He should forget the damn gray-eyed save-the-worlder. What if she were ugly instead of beautiful? What would he think of her then? Hack shook his head and went back to his truck. He switched on the dead radio and called Melba, who didn't give him time to say hello.

"Chief, where in the world have you been? I've been trying to —"

"What you got?"

"Jack Lange. He walked in here awhile ago, says he wants to talk to you."

When Hack entered the station half an hour later he found Lange sitting beside Melba's desk. The two of them were laughing.

"Chief, I just found we're related," Melba said. "Third cousins-in-law or something like that. Small world. Jack's wife's mother was my mother's . . . oh, it gets too complicated. It's —" She stopped when she saw her boss's expression.

"My wife tracked me down in New York," Lange said. "It sounded like maybe I ought to come on home."

"Yes. Come in the office." Hack turned to Melba. "Sam here?"

"Just came in. I'll get him."

"Tell him to bring the rock."

In his office Hack motioned for Lange to take the visitor chair, sat down behind the desk, put his stiffening leg up on an open drawer, fastened his eyes on his suspect, and waited. When Sam came in with the rock, Hack took it, put it on the desk in plain view, and nodded for Sam to sit behind the suspect.

"Now, Mr. Lange," he said, "tell us why you left town."

An hour later Lange's face was red, his collar damp and his voice dead. He was reciting once again the whys, whens and whats of his New York trip. He had described the gem auction and his hotel, and was trying to remember the names of restaurants he'd been to when Melba tapped and came into the office. Without looking at her relative-in-law she handed Hack a sheet of paper, then left. The paper gave the results of her telephone checks of Lange's New York story, the main features of which had been confirmed. But not everything.

"Now, Mr. Lange, tell us again what you did between three and five-thirty in the afternoon."

"Really, there's nothing more I can say. I walked in Central Park. No particular reason, didn't have anything better to do. Just walked. But I can't prove it."

"You sure you didn't go somewhere and sell a big ruby? Under a false name maybe? You didn't —"

"No. And I didn't kill poor Frances and Paul, and that rock right there is the great 'ruby' they found. But I can't prove that either."

Hack stared hard at him for a moment, then forgetting to favor his wounded leg, stood up too quickly. He grimaced.

"You can go now, but don't leave town," he said.

The suspect left the room. Hack sat back down and looked sourly at Sam. "What do you think?"

"Well, I don't know, Chief. Maybe —"

"Hell, this isn't getting us anywhere." Hack stood up again. "Check in with Billy," he said, "then go on back out to the college. I'll keep the damn jewel."

"Okay, Chief." Sam left the office.

Hack picked up the red-crusted rock, frowned at it, weighed it in his hand, then slipped it into his jacket pocket and went out to Melba's desk. She was on the phone. Hack could tell from her tone she was talking to her mother.

". . . no particular reason, he just turned up in one of our investigations. No, not George Lange, it's his younger brother, Jack. Yeah, Jack. Right. Sort of blond, but almost bald. Hold on a second, Mother." She put her hand over the phone and looked up at her boss.

"Chief, I talked to Louanne awhile back," she said. "She wants to know how long she has to stay out at Hope Springs. Really, it hardly seems —"

"Until I tell her otherwise. I'm leaving for a while. I'll take the beeper this time."

"Well, okay. I'll tell Louanne just what you said. That'll make her happy, I'm sure."

Hack left the building, considered driving back out to Hope Springs, decided he'd just upset things there, and went to the college instead. He'd reached the what-in-hell-should-I-do point where he *had* to talk to somebody, even if that somebody couldn't really help, and there were only three names on his okay-to-talk-to list. The first was Art Taylor.

The philosopher wasn't at his house on Faculty Row. At this time of day he was probably lecturing to a room full of half-hypnotized freshmen. Hack considered finding the class and sitting in the back of the room. He'd done it before, but listening to one of Art's lectures wouldn't help him right now. He left the college and drove to the little riverside cabin of his chain-smoking, humph-saying conscience. Aunt Ola was number two on his list.

He usually just leaned out the truck window and called to her when he needed to talk, but today he got out of the truck, went to the cabin's front door and knocked. There was no response. He went inside — Aunt Ola never locked doors — but she wasn't home either.

The need to talk having by now grown to a vibrating compulsion, he drove back to the square, parked and went into Dewhurst Realty. Honey was the last on his talk-to list, nobody else in town came even close to being suitable. There was no one at the reception desk but the door to Honey's office as usual was open. Hack looked in. The county's champion home-seller raised her eyes from the perpetual paper stack on her desk but didn't put down the pen in her hand.

"I don't want to bother you," Hack said.

"No bother. Come on in, sit down. Close the door." Honey knew her role. She put the pen down, sat back in her chair and waited.

Hack, even though he had no fear that Honey would repeat what he said, still couldn't bring himself to talk about his *moral* dilemma. But that didn't matter since plenty of non-moral ones — murder, arson and ambush to start with — floundered around in his probably calcifying, too-old brain like frantic fish in a draining boat box. Right now he just needed a listener to talk at. Talking always calmed the flounderers. Subject matter didn't matter much. Just talk.

Fine, but now that he had a superb listener poised before him, he didn't know what to say. Where should he start? His eyes ranged around the home-buyer-friendly room. He looked at the array of for-sale houses on the wall, then passed on to the mountain activity collection. He stopped at the remembered picture of a younger

Honey holding a greenish rock. Her rock was the same size as the reddish one in his pocket.

"You said your husband was a rock collector?" he asked without looking away from the picture.

"Is, as they say, the Pope Catholic?" Honey replied. "Harvey would have gladly eaten rocks for breakfast if I'd found some way to soften them up a little."

"You went on collection trips with him?"

"A few times. Like I told you, I tried, but Harvey . . . you don't want to rehash *that* story, do you?"

"No, no." Hack returned to his chair. "It's just that I've got this situation . . . two bodies . . . that looks like it involves rock collecting." He took the "ruby" from his pocket and showed it to Honey. "If you've got a few minutes I'd like to tell you where this rock came from and . . . uh . . . get your thoughts."

"Sure, go ahead," Honey said. "I've heard the rumors, of course. I know John Redding and Janet Benjamin and all the rest of the Scrabblers, and I've heard about the great ruby ten times at least by now, each version grander than the one before, but I'd really like to hear the official one."

"Okay, good," Hack said. "Here are the facts. I'm assuming they're facts anyway. This rock was found by the Winoskis, serious rock collectors. These little red specks they tell me are rubies. Sometime after the Winoskis found it they were shot to death in their kitchen. A gem dealer —"

"Jack Lange," Honey said. "I've known him for years."

"Oh. Anyway, he assessed its value at $200, then took off for New York . . ." Honey listened without interruption as Hack told of finding the bodies and searching the house and talking to Janet Benjamin and Jack Lange. He ended his recital with, "We're wondering if maybe this rock is a substitute. Maybe the real ruby the Winoskis found *is* worth a fortune. Or something. It sounds so unlikely when I tell it."

Honey took the ruby and examined it closely, then reached behind a pile of file folders and brought out the ruby's emerald twin. She held the two rocks up, one in each hand. They were both the size of large lemons, one with a red crystalline streak, the other with a green vein about the width of a pencil running through it.

"My emerald was only worth $85 back then," she said. "Maybe with inflation it would go $200 today too. Anyway, it makes a good paperweight."

"Where'd you find it?" Hack asked.

"Harvey stumbled over a 'source' up near Grandfather Mountain. A source is a place that's never been picked over, where the next rock you find might be the Hope Diamond's emerald sister or something. It's that the-next-rock-might-be-*it* feeling that captures people."

"What kind of source?"

"Usually a rock slide. It doesn't have to be big, just new rocks exposed. Happens every winter on the slopes. Harvey found one. In the end there turned out to be nothing there but a few pieces like this one." She held up the green rock. "But at first Harvey acted like he'd found El Dorado or something. If a collector finds a good source, he — or she — keeps it secret. At all costs. Harvey would have killed to . . . no, that's overstating it, but he might have maimed. Say, Jim . . . are you with me?"

Hack realized he'd been scowling purple doom at Honey. He smoothed his expression. An idea had stepped right up and thumped him on the nose. The possibility that there were gem sources that the finder might *kill* to protect . . .

The idea was farfetched, but then the whole mess was farfetched, and his idea joined together facts he had thought unconnected, facts that, if the connection were true, would stamp a great big X right between the eyes of a multiple killer.

"Sorry, Honey," he said. "Something just occurred to me." His scowl returned. "Tell me, are there special parts of the mountains where gems occur? Is it just around Grandfather, or over by Sylva?"

"Oh no, anywhere," Honey said. "It's just that some places are more likely than others."

Hack rubbed his scar. "I've got to go," he said. "I'll see you. Thanks."

He stood up and returned the red rock to his pocket. Without looking back he strode from the building. His farfetched idea had over the course of the last three minutes strengthened from impossibile to maybe conceivable, but he was damned if he could see how to prove it even if it were true.

In his truck the radio crackled to life.

"Chief! Shooting at Hope Springs! Hurry!"

CHAPTER 34

Hammond woke up. The waking process was incremental, little waves of consciousness advancing and receding like an incoming tide climbing a beach. He spread his hand and felt the surface he was lying on.

Cold and damp. Concrete.

He opened his eyes. The room was almost dark. Racing panic suddenly filled his mind. Where was he? Why was he here? How long had he been here? Then he remembered.

The pains had hit him again with no warning, right after the cat. So soon. They had never come so close together. And he had never passed out before. It had been afternoon. Now it must be almost night.

He was dying, the next pains would surely take him.

He sat up and rubbed his forehead. But there was no trace of pain there. Maybe he wasn't dying. Right now he felt *good.* He saw Sammy lying on the floor beside him, next to the orange cat. He studied the cat-object a moment, then picked up the knife and carefully got to his feet. He wasn't even dizzy.

He remembered the kittens and went to the box where he had put them. They started to make their nasty little squeak-noises. He thought of silencing them, but the women upstairs would hear. The women . . . oh! Now he remembered why he was here.

Was she still up there? She might have left!

He went to the base of the stairs and listened. Women were talking and moving about. He couldn't hear Louanne's voice. She was gone!

He climbed the stairs to the dark landing at the top and pressed his ear to the door. No, she was still there. It sounded like she was reading to a child, her voice low. He strained to pick out words but couldn't, but that didn't matter. She was there. He could open the door right now and run in and just grab her if he wanted to. He began to purr deep in his chest. One of the women made a stupid comment about the cats in the basement. He almost laughed out loud.

Their cat. They should see it now.

He held Sammy in the thin beam of light that showed at the door edge. Blood, mostly dried but still wet in places, made him catch his breath.

He pushed back the wig that had slipped down almost over one eye and tried to will his trembling hands still, but he couldn't. Squeezing Sammy's handle, he pressed the flat of the blade against his cheek. He wanted to throw the door open and rush into the room and scream.

Stop thinking that! That's not the plan. That's insane.

The pain behind his eyes suddenly welled up again and erased all thought. Squeezing his eyes shut, he leaned on the wall to keep from falling, held his breath, and waited. The pain receded and his breath returned in little pants.

That's a hemorrhage starting in your head. You're about to die.

I don't care. I've got to kill her.

Why?

Shut up.

The most important thing in the world for him, the *only* thing that mattered, was for Louanne to come to the basement. That was clear in his mind, but the whiny voice kept trying to whisper things to him.

The pain is blood packing your skull. You're about to die.

Someone just on the other side of the door spoke. Hammond froze.

"You know, Violet," a woman said, "if we don't get some rain soon I ain't gonna get enough pole beans off my late patch to be worth pickin'."

"Well, at least the weeds've stopped growing," someone responded. "They Kentucky Wonders you planted? Ain't it too late?"

"No, not Kentucky Wonders, some fancy new kind. No, it ain't too late. Leastways, that's what they claim on the seed pack."

Idiots! Chattering like a flock of cowbirds, Louanne reading drivel to a child. If only they knew . . . Hammond clenched his teeth and pressed a fist to his mouth to keep from crying out.

Of course he wasn't going to just *burn* Louanne. She had to see him and *understand* before he killed her.

Understand what? Why do you want to —

Why? Because what he was doing to Louanne was the whole point of everything.

What are you talking about? You were going to capture her, put her in a cage, love her. What happened to all that?

He grabbed the lower part of his face and squeezed until it hurt.

Just shut up.

You're purring again. You're crazy.

A wave of dizziness came and passed. He crept down the steps. It was time.

Gerry Smith came into the kitchen from the bedroom. She looked surprised to see Louanne there, but didn't say anything.

"Chief Hackett came by to see you, Gerry," Violet said. "I told him you were resting. He asked if you were sleeping nights at your cabin now."

Everybody looked to see Gerry's reaction. There was none. She went to the stove, looked in each of the pots and opened the oven door.

"Where'd we get a turkey? Looks good."

"Mr. Welch brought it."

"Good for him. I'll send him a note. How long was I asleep? I must have been dead."

"You needed it," Violet said.

Gerry yawned, went to the window and stared out at the fading twilight.

Johnny Peebles tapped Louanne's knee. "Tell me a story."

"*Tell* you a story? Okay, Johnny, what kind of story do you want?"

"A tugboat story."

"A *tugboat* story? Oh, my goodness, I don't think I know a tugboat story."

"Better check those potatoes, Violet," one of the women at the table said. "I think they're scorching."

"Oh, lord, yes." Violet lifted a pot off the stove. A thin cry came from the basement.

"There's them cats again," Mary Louise said. "I never heard such yowling as they do. It's a pity we can't bring the kittens in here and —"

"Well, I'm afraid we can't," Gerry said from the window. "Not if I want to keep breathing."

"You girls want to go on and pour the tea?" Violet said. "Let's eat. I'm starved."

The whine from below suddenly rose to a screech. Mary Louise stopped what she was doing and stared at the basement door. "What in the world?"

"Probably a strange cat wandered in," Violet said. "Ours doesn't like visitors. Let 'em settle it."

The screech came again, then a loud bang and clatter.

"Sounds like it might be a coon that come in this time," Violet said. "Could even be a wildcat, we've got 'em. I'll go —"

"No, I'll go," Louanne said. She put Johnny on the floor, stepped to the basement door and opened it. No sound came from the darkness at the bottom of the stairs.

"Pull that light cord," Violet said, "and watch them steps. The third one from the bottom is loose."

Louanne pulled the string that dangled above her head. A single bulb, forty watts at most, came on at the base of the stairs. Without conscious thought she loosened the strap that held her pistol in its holster, then went slowly down to the pool of dim light at the base of the stairs. The room around her, mostly filled with stacked crates and boxes, was in deep shadow.

"You got a flashlight, Violet?" she called.

"Yeah, somewhere. I'll look."

Something red at the edge of the light caught Louanne's eye. It was a round can with a handle and a spout, partly hidden by a stack of old boxes.

Loud purring came from close behind her, almost in her ear. She whirled around.

Something furry jammed into her face, covering her eyes. It tore at her cheek. She felt skin rip as she jerked the furry thing away.

A man with long blond hair that half obscured a twisted face stood close enough to touch her. He held a knife, low, pointing upward. A remembered voice, now cracked and jerky, whispered, "You came."

Louanne slapped at the knife with her left hand and dropped to her right, drawing her pistol as she fell. She fired one shot at the man's face. The sound was deafening in the closed room. She saw a hole appear over his left eye before he fell backwards. The knife clattered to the floor.

The women in the kitchen screeched. The orange kitten that had been thrust in her face wailed. Louanne scrambled to her feet, realized her left hand was spouting blood, then fainted.

CHAPTER 35

Hack slid to a stop in the shelter's parking lot just ahead of the ambulance. He ran limping into the kitchen expecting to find a clutch of hysterical women and wailing babies. He found a tableau of calm. Louanne sat with her back to the table, her head down. Her left hand, loosely wrapped with a bloody white cloth, lay in her lap. Gerry Smith, her face chalky, stood beside the open door to the basement.

Louanne raised her head. "It's okay, Chief."

"Where are the women and —"

"Violet took them back to the bedrooms," Gerry said. She pointed to the basement. "He's . . . uh . . . down there."

"Alive?"

"No."

The ambulance crew pushed into the room, Billy and Sam right behind them. Their arrival shattered the eery calm. The next two hours passed in a blur of people rushing around and vehicles coming and going. It wasn't until almost midnight that Hack was able to disengage and drive to the McFee house to inform the widow, a job he'd done too many times in his career, a job that didn't get easier with practice.

He found a man and woman on the McFee's front porch. The front windows of the house were dark.

"We heard what happened," the man said. "We're the Willards from next door."

"Did you ring the bell?"

"Yes, and knocked. Nobody. We don't know if we should —"

The door opened. Brent McFee faced them from the doorway, his eyes wide and unfocused. Before anyone spoke he turned around and, leaving the door open, went back into the house.

With the neighbors trailing, Hack followed him through the living room to the kitchen, where a light was on. At the kitchen door Brent stopped. Hack pushed around him.

Marie McFee was slumped against the far wall, the front of her light blue dress soaked with dark blood. Her eyes were open.

Brent reached out and touched Hack's forearm. "You've got to catch my father," he said in a scarcely audible voice. "He's sick. I should have told somebody."

CHAPTER 36

Two men waited on the porch when Hattie Mae unlocked the Rocking Chair's front door at 5:31 next morning. A cold, thick, drippy September fog filled the still-dark parking lot behind them.

"Lord, Hattie Mae, what you been waiting for?" one of the men said. "I gotta have my coffee."

"Ah, Jimmy, you know Hattie Mae don't care 'bout us," his companion added. "She's been in there all warm, drinkin' coffee while we —"

"Well, don't just stand there like a couple of wet turkey buzzards, come on in."

Hattie Mae stepped aside and let the day's first customers enter as another pickup pulled into the lot, its headlights illuminating the gravel where a week ago . . . no, it hadn't even been a week.

Hattie Mae counted back. Just last Tuesday. It seemed longer. In her mind she saw again the black-clad body in the glare of the bus's lights, the bicycle on its side, the chief kneeling by the body, the blood. She shivered and turned back to the bright warmth of the dining room.

An hour later, at about his usual time, the chief came into the café. By then of course everybody in the county had heard of the shooting out at Hope Springs and the discovery of Marie McFee's body in her living room. The room became dead quiet and all eyes followed the chief down the serving line. Forks paused on the way to mouths and cups hovered in midair, but for once no one yelled out questions. It just wouldn't have seemed right.

"Morning, Chief," Hattie Mae said, but after one look at his gray face and unsmiling eyes, she didn't go on to the usual girlfriend teasing.

He took his regular breakfast and sat down at a table close to the door, where he lowered his head and began to eat. The activities of the room resumed, but at a noise level much reduced from normal.

Five minutes later Aunt Ola came in, peered at the lone policeman, then slid her tray down the rack. When she was opposite his table she leaned toward him. Hattie Mae strained to hear what she was going to say, but needn't have bothered. Aunt Ola's voice, loud and grating, filled the room.

"Hey, what's wrong with everybody in here, you all dead or something? Mornin', Chief. I hear you done shot you a nut case last night. Or was it that little girl that works for you done it? Don't matter. Good goin'!"

She straightened up. "Gimme an extra biscuit this morning, Hattie Mae, to celebrate all these great doin's."

The chief gave the white-haired granny a cold, sour glance but didn't comment. She took her breakfast to his table, said "Thanks for the invitation, don't mind if I do," sat down, looked straight at the NO SMOKING sign, lit a cigarette and took a couple of puffs, then leaned back in her chair. Her eyes narrowed.

"They say his wife, the great professor, would have drove Jesus Christ crazy," she said to the chief. "Like she done her husband. Not that she deserved what she got. Why didn't you figure that out earlier? Seems kind of obvious to me."

The chief made a low noise but didn't stop eating. Hattie Mae went to the table and refilled his cup, even though it was only half empty. Aunt Ola was just warming up.

"From what I hear, if you'd'a just talked to that son of theirs, he'd'a told you what was going on. He knew his daddy was sick, just like his great-granddaddy had been. He knew about his daddy being in the mental hospital and all. The Willards heard him tell you last night. He thought his daddy was probably the firebug but he was afraid —"

"Aunt Ola, just hush."

"Why, what's the matter with you, Chief? You ain't feelin' sorry for yourself, are you? You ain't mad cause it wasn't you that solved the case, are you? Hell, don't let it worry you, you got plenty left to work on." She tapped ashes onto a saucer and leaned across the table.

"That poor white-hairy girl out there in this very parking lot, for example? Any idea who shot her? And them nice Winoskis, why they was in here not a week ago buyin' grits and eggs, just like us, and now they're dead. Ain't you got no idea about who shot them? Hell, even *I* know 'bout their ruby that was stole. Big as my fist, at least. Why don't you look for that? Then you —"

"Hattie Mae! Bring her another biscuit, will you? Maybe she'll stuff it in her mouth to celebrate."

"Just trying to help," the old woman said. "Seems to me you need it."

For the next five minutes each new customer stopped after entering and looked around to see why the room was a funeral home on Monday morning. When they came down the line to Hattie Mae, they whispered their breakfast orders.

At 7:05 Louanne came in. She had four wide bandaids on her face, and her left hand was a big ball of bandage. The quiet of the room got quieter. She took only grapefruit juice and two pieces of whole wheat toast. Up close Hattie Mae saw puffy, red eyes. Louanne managed to pay one-handed at the register, then looked at the chief and started to carry her tray to the other side of the room.

"Hey, come sit here," Aunt Ola called out. "Come on."

When the chief nodded assent, Louanne joined them. Aunt Ola leaned toward her and stared.

"You should'a stood in bed this morning, honey," she said. "You don't look good. Your boss wouldn't of minded."

"I'm okay."

"Humph. Violet Turner said you couldn't even kill their turkey for supper last night, but you got the maniac right between the eyes. Good for you."

"Aunt Ola," the chief said, "why don't you just hush up?" He gave the white-haired little smoker his deepest scar-faced scowl.

She returned a grandmotherly smile.

"That's okay, Chief," Louanne said. "It's all right."

"Just kidding about the Winoski ruby, Chief," Aunt Ola said. "Don't be so sensitive. I know you found the ruby in Asheville, but the guy that stole it's done skipped town. Gone to New York or somewhere."

"Who told you all that?"

"Oh, I got my ways."

"Well, 'your ways' better try a little harder next time. He's come back. He's Melba's cousin."

"Well, humph."

The old lady stopped talking long enough to grind out what remained of her cigarette in her saucer. She lit another, inhaled deeply, deliberately blew smoke in the chief's face, then turned to Louanne.

"That's okay, honey, don't let shooting that guy bother you. I remember when I killed my first hog. I thought I'd —"

"Aunt Ola." Louanne leaned over the table and with squinting eyes peered at the wrinkled old face.

"Yeah?"

"What's wrong with your nose?"

"My nose?" Aunt Ola reached up and felt the questioned appendage.

"It's . . ." Louanne's widened eyes showed real horror. "It's turning green!"

"Green?" Aunt Ola stood up and frowned at the mirror over the cigarette machine.

Somebody at a back table laughed, then the whole room exploded. Hattie Mae laughed so hard she had to lean on the counter. Aunt Ola turned away from the mirror, looked around the room, felt her nose again, then started cackling as loud as anybody. When she sat back down Hattie Mae clearly saw her wink at the chief.

People were still chuckling when a few minutes later the sheriff came into the café, nodded to Hattie Mae and went straight to the chief's table.

"You ready?" he said. "Let's go."

"Okay." The chief stood up and tapped Louanne on the shoulder. "You come with us," he said.

Then he looked down at Aunt Ola. "And you, you just be careful where you stick that green nose of yours."

CHAPTER 37

They went out to the sheriff's gray county car with the big gold star on its side. Louanne climbed in the back and huddled in a corner, and Hack took the passenger seat. The sheriff drove. On the way down toward Blue Ridge he described, with obvious relish, Harold Pell's increasingly wobbly mental condition.

As the sheriff talked, Hack tried to spark up his own mental condition. After a sleepless night of blood, death, and rushing around, his mind had settled into a deep, gray, go-away-and-don't-bother me state. Breakfast caffeine had given it a jab, and sunlight just piercing Jeter's morning fog helped, but still it took deliberate effort for him to formulate useful thoughts.

He made the effort.

The idea he'd had in Honey's office last night — the literally off-the-wall idea — lay in a heap in his mind just where he'd dropped it when the frantic Hope Springs call came. He picked it up and examined it in daylight. Improbable, wishful thinking, as solid as butterfly breath, but . . .

Fate, he realized, had actually arranged a free test of the idea. All he had to do was keep his wits about him this morning and his eyes open. He glanced at the all-set-to-go sheriff and decided the best way to proceed right now was to keep his thoughts to himself. Then, if his great idea turned out to be nothing but mountain mist, nobody would know he'd even had it. He spoke to the sheriff.

"Pell know you're coming?"

"No. Let him think he's got a day without me, get all relaxed and —"

"Tom, what do you really think he'll do up on the mountain? He's not going to confess to killing those women just to get you off his back. And your pestering him isn't going to drive him out of his mind."

"Oh, I don't know. You keep picking at a wound long enough and it'll get infected. That's what I'm doing, picking. And I really think I am driving him out of his mind, or at least he's acting that way, giggling like an imbecile half the time. Actually, the main reason why I want you along this morning is to be a witness."

"Witness?"

"In case he decides to jump off the cliff himself. And he *might.* If he thought we had found something that would actually . . . pin him. Anyway, Louanne being there is all the better."

"You planning to push him over the edge and expect us to lie for you?"

"Sure, why not?"

Hack turned to his detective in the back seat and contemplated her ash-pale bandaged face and dead eyes. "How you doing?"

"Okay."

"Aunt Ola needed that little come-down you gave her back there. Sometimes she —"

"She was just trying to get you and me to stop moping."

"Yeah, I guess. You sleep any last night?"

"No."

They drove on in silence. Before they reached the Pell driveway Hack said, "Tom, if we're actually going through with this, we should know what we're doing. To start with, where do you want Pell to sit, front or back?"

"Front. Then you can ask the back of his head questions. Make him keep turning around."

"All right. How about when we get up to the cliff?"

"Oh, just be around looking like a wolf about to bite or something, but be close enough to hear what's said. I'm not kidding about witnesses."

"You realize I've got a case just as hopeless as this one?"

"Yeah, the Winoski killings. I heard about your boy Lange switching rocks on you and running off to New York."

"Lange came back from New York last night, came to see me. We checked his story. There's a three-hour time gap when he says he was just out walking in Central Park, but the rest is confirmed."

"Hell, even if he sold a big ruby up there, he'll just say he found it himself. It's just like with Pell. Unless you find the gun, or a witness . . . what'd you do with Lange?"

"Let him go. It turns out he's Melba's long-lost cousin or something."

"What's that got to do with anything?"

"I don't know, last night it just seemed so incredible. Mysterious missing ruby . . . like a bad detective story from back in the thirties. Anyway, I turned him loose, but I'm probably kidding myself there too. Like I did when I sent Louanne out to Hope Springs yesterday to keep her away from the firebug. Hell, Lange's probably as guilty as . . ." Hack realized his voice had become a whine. That wouldn't do. He brightened his tone. "Tom, I'll tell you what, if you can make old Harold-boy jump off the rock today, maybe we can try the same thing with Jack Lange. Hell, with him and Jakey Boatwright *both*. Get 'em up there on the edge of the cliff and look real stern at 'em, then their bad consciences'll make 'em turn around and —"

"Nah, there'd be too much mess to clean up down at the bottom." The sheriff glanced over his shoulder at Louanne.

"Your way's better," he said. "That was some shot. Cat clawing your eyes out, guy coming at you with a knife, cut hand, room practically dark. Right in the old bull's-eye. Cat really did a job on your face, though, looks like. Hope it doesn't leave scars. Did you —"

"I don't want to talk about it."

A light was on in the Pell studio when they pulled up at the edge of the gravel. The sheriff insisted that all three of them go to the door together, to make it look like an arrest. "Little bastard'll be sitting at the desk staring at the door when we go in," the sheriff said. "I think he sits there all night."

He knocked — banged — on the door, then rattled the handle. This time the door was locked.

Harold Pell opened it, then went behind his desk and sat down, his face showing no expression other than a brief look of surprise when Louanne followed the two men in.

"Get the camera you used when the women 'fell' off the cliff, and come on," the sheriff said. "Fell" was a four-letter word.

Hack expected a protest, but Pell got up, calmly took a camera from a shelf by the door and flashed a twinkly-eyed smile for everyone's benefit.

"All right, Sheriff," he said. "Say, maybe we can have a picnic in the mountains. That would be fun, don't you think? I'd take your pictures for you. No charge, of course. Let's go. I'm ready."

He left the room. The others, caught off guard, followed. At the car the little photographer turned around.

"Oh, Sheriff, there's something I've been meaning to ask you. A favor. I'm planning to develop this land when all the, uh, paperwork is finished, you know. Put in a subdivision. I do hope you'll help me get planning board permission. You will, won't you?"

They passed from drippy gloom to brilliant morning sun halfway up Pisgah ridge. There was considerable fall color in the woods now. The leaf-peepers would soon be out in force, but when the sheriff turned right onto the Parkway, no other cars were in sight.

Despite the sheriff's intention to bombard Pell with insanity-inducing questions, they drove in complete silence to the turn-off toward the fatal cliff. After passing the remains of the rock slide that had blocked the road, they came to the parking area at Bear Wallow overlook. The sheriff turned to Pell in the seat beside him.

"Where'd you park?"

Pell pointed to a spot away from the stone wall at the cliff edge.

The sheriff drove there and stopped. "Okay, out," he said. "Bring your camera."

Hack and Louanne got out too, but stayed by the car and watched the county's keeper-of-the-peace try to convince one of its citizens to kill himself.

"Okay," the sheriff said, "now, what did you do first?"

"We've been through this a hundred times, Sheriff. Do we really —"

"Yes. Where did the women go? Were they beginning to suspect by then? Did the look on your face show murder?"

"Sheriff, you know this isn't going to work, whatever you're trying to do. I didn't *touch* Corliss and Doreen that morning. That's the absolute truth. What do you expect me to do, say I did?"

The sheriff ignored him. "Hack, Louanne, you two be the women. You've seen the pictures. Go over there and stand by that boulder like they did. Look at 'em, Pell. Think about it. Now where exactly were you standing?"

Hack waited beside the almost vertical rock as the sheriff switched between bullying and insinuating, all of which his suspect mocked with pretty smiles and mild protests, clearly enjoying himself.

Hack began to relax. The sun, which in the clear air at their elevation turned the sky an improbable dark blue and sharpened all images, sparkled back at him from the red, crystalline streaks in the beige boulder. He leaned back on the rock.

Louanne sagged beside him. Her bandages reminded him of his own black state after his first line-of-duty killing two decades earlier. And he had already served in Vietnam at the time. And *he* had never minded chopping the heads off turkeys.

Ah well, time heals. He'd just keep her busy, she'd get over it. At least they had solved two of the crime wave's cases, the firebug and cat killer, solved them with one bullet. Real neat. They were making progress. Wonderful!

Then why was he feeling as happy as a truck-squashed possum? He supposed it was because all that progress had been made despite him, not because of his efforts. And the dead Winoskis, what had he done about them? Other than wait around until his only suspect presented himself, then turn him loose because he was Melba's cousin. Last night in Honey's office he'd had his wonderful solve-everything idea, but out here, in bright daylight, straw-grasping was the best you could say about it. Pathetic. Forget it.

Damn! He really *ought* to quit and go back to driving a tractor. Or maybe he should ask Louanne to cheer *him* up. Maybe she could tell him his nose was green and make him laugh. Aunt Ola had just been trying to make him stop whining, bless her.

Hack couldn't get his mind off Jack Lange. A good cop would never have let him go, even if the whole scene *was* bizarre. He pictured the gem dealer at the station last night and suddenly realized for the first time that Lange actually resembled Harold Pell. Maybe he was as crazy as Pell too. He was probably somewhere right now, laughing his head off, just like Pell was, silently.

Lange would have to have known he was a suspect after their first official visit to his place. The audacity of his going away, more or less right under Hack's nose, and selling the real ruby — it was a way of sneering. Just like Pell. Hack began for the first time to understand how the sheriff felt.

Unless there never was a real ruby.

He'd have to find Lange, drag him back to the station, keep him as long as the law allowed, maybe a little longer, and have everybody in the department take turns asking him the same questions. Then maybe take him to the murder scene, show him pictures of the Winoskis' bodies. Let him go then, but a few hours later bring him back to the station and do it all over again. He could make his life miserable for a while, sure, but . . .

The sheriff finally got around to the actual photo-taking with *his* murderer.

"All right, Pell, there are the women," he said. "The chief is Corliss, Louanne is Doreen. What'd you do?" He pointed to the camera in Pell's hand. "Do it again."

Pell shrugged. "There's no film in it."

"Take the picture anyway."

"Whatever you say, Sheriff."

The photographer grinned apologetically at his subjects and pointed the camera at them. Hack, rebelling against posing, frowned and looked at the ground. He picked up a rock at his feet and considered throwing it off the cliff, just to see how long it would take to hit bottom. The rock, heavy and rough, showed the same red streaks as the boulder. Hack pulled last night's idea out of his mental trash can and let the sun shine right down on it again. This time it showed a few tiny glints.

"Okay Pell, what did you do next?" the sheriff said.

"The wall shots, them sitting."

The sheriff motioned to Hack. "Okay, you two come sit over here."

Hack and Louanne went to the wall, which was still wet from the fog. Hack felt it. Cold. He started to protest, but after a glance at the sheriff's blood-and-thunder face, mentally shrugged. He tossed the rock he had picked up over the cliff into the fog. Three long counts later, he heard a muted clack, followed by the receding sound of the rock bouncing its way down the steep slope. He sat down beside Louanne and felt the chill through his pants.

"Get closer," the sheriff said.

Hack half-slid six inches to his right. He put his cold hand in his jacket pocket, the one that contained Lange's ruby. He took it out and looked at it again as Pell pretended to take pictures.

Hack realized that for somebody watching, the whole charade would have been hilarious. The idea of him pretending to be the pretty woman in the pictures he'd seen — or Louanne pretending to be the thickening, unnaturally red-headed mother-in-law — was as insane as Tom's whole drive-him-crazy plan.

"What'd you do next?" the sheriff said.

"They stood up on the wall." Pell's voice showed some emotion for the first time. Remorse? Fear? Desire to jump? Desire to push? Just excitement?

"Okay, you two," the sheriff said. "Up."

Hack turned and looked over the cliff at the white ocean stretching to the east as far as he could see. He thought of how long it had taken the rock to hit, then of the two apparently unsuspecting women.

"Come on, *up*." A note of exasperation had crept into the sheriff's voice. "I won't let him get close to you."

Hack stepped onto the wall, the ruby-rock still in his right hand. He transferred it to his left and reached down to help Louanne.

The sheriff turned to Pell. "Now what?"

"I made one shot then went back to the car to change film."

"Do it. What expressions did they have when they finally realized you were going to push them off?"

"I didn't *touch* them, sheriff."

Hack looked over Pell's head. In the far distance the high peaks of the Smokies stuck up out of the fog. In the foreground the unweathered face of the broken boulder seemed out of place against the timeless gray stone of the mountain. He looked up the slope to where the boulder had originated in the rock slide of last winter.

Rock slide.

Gem source. Something a rock hound would kill to protect. Or maybe just maim.

He looked at the ruby-rock in his hand, then held it up in the sunlight. It sparkled red fire. Fuzzy, unconnected jigsaw pieces in Hack's mind, unbidden, rearranged themselves and snuggled together to form a picture. It was the picture his straw-clutch idea had been trying to sketch last night. Was the picture true?

He could find out right now or at least he could try. And if he wound up looking like a dope, so what. And if he didn't try it now, he'd never get another chance. Passing up the opportunity would be spitting in the face of fate. So do it. Now.

He stepped down from the wall.

"Come on." He held out a hand to Louanne.

"Wait," the sheriff yelled, "stay up there. I want him to —"

Hack ignored him and walked over to the boulder. With Lange's stone in hand, he explored the big rock's surface until he found a vein of tiny reddish crystals. They looked like little bits of dark sand, the color of dried blood.

He turned and faced Pell. A broad grin — the lopsided one that terrified tourists — spread across his face. He walked slowly toward the photographer.

When Pell looked into Hack's eyes, his love-me smile melted and his face seemed to sag. He flicked a glance over his shoulder toward the wall.

Without taking his eyes from Pell's, Hack gestured to Louanne, who nodded understanding and stepped between the photographer and the cliff. The sheriff didn't understand, but knew Hack too well to interfere. Hack held Lange's rock up before Pell's face.

"The Winoskis went up in the mountains that morning to their secret ruby source, a place where new rocks had been exposed. This rock slide is the source." He pointed to the boulder behind him.

"They found this." He held up the Winoski's rock and moved it to within inches of Pell's eyes. "It's their ruby."

Pell's mouth opened but he didn't speak.

"They found something else," Hack said. "You. They probably heard you, down there with the bodies, maybe talking to yourself. They called. You panicked. You climbed back up here and made up some story for them — taking fog pictures or something — that satisfied them. They left. But the bodies would eventually be found, and then the Winoskis would talk. You couldn't let that happen. You followed them home and killed them. The times fit. Where's the gun?"

Pell said nothing, but his lower jaw began to quiver and his eyes to dart this way and that.

Hack's clutched-straw idea had suddenly become rock-solid ground.

He remembered the photos on Pell's desk the first time he'd been to the studio, shots Pell had made and developed on the day his wife died. Why would he be in the darkroom when he should be in mourning? Hack leaned close to the photographer.

"Did you take one last picture of the women that day? Is that what scared them off the wall? Is the picture in your studio?"

For several seconds no one spoke or moved. Hack didn't blink. Jerky motions began to snatch at the edges of Pell's mouth. He threw the camera at Hack's face and with surprising agility darted toward the wall.

Louanne dived and tackled him just as he reached it, in the process falling against the rough stone. The sheriff grabbed Pell and wrestled him away from the edge.

Louanne got to her feet. Blood poured down her left cheek, and Hack could see that his department's brightest member's nose was not quite lined up with the rest of her face.

CHAPTER 38

Aunt Ola, having had to give up regular coffee a decade earlier, finished her fourth cup of decaf. She usually spent all Sunday morning at her regular table at the Rocking Chair, finding that preferable to spending it alone in her little house by the river. She lit her third cigarette of the day and watched Hattie Mae's do-it-like-you're-killing-snakes approach to cleaning up from breakfast and getting the café ready for the Rocking Chair's Sunday dinner.

The few Sunday-working people and early churchgoers had all left the café; now there were only leaf-peeping tourists and people who didn't go to Sunday School relaxing over coffee. Outside, a bright sun climbed into a cloudless sky above the crest of Jeter Mountain. Its rays had melted the fog and turned to flame a clump of red and yellow sassafras across the road.

The aroma of frying chicken filled the room. Hattie Mae had taken away the last of the pans of grits, scrambled eggs, sausage and other breakfast items and was attacking the steam table top with a polishing cloth. She looked up, right into Aunt Ola's smoke-narrowed eyes.

"Aunt Ola, do you *have* to smoke in the no-smoking section?" she said. "The boss says we're going to have to rearrange the whole café if you insist on sitting there. Anyway, you know as well as I do, you smoke too much."

"Hattie Mae, honey, I'm ninety-two years old, maybe ninety-three, I don't know. Been smokin' for 'bout 91½ of 'em, far as I remember, and I ain't gonna quit now. Besides —"

"People complain."

"Bunch of whiners. Let 'em complain to me, if they got the nerve."

"The boss says —"

"Besides, if I moved to another table I couldn't gossip with you, and you know *that* wouldn't do. The chief didn't come in this morning, did he?"

Hattie Mae laughed. Actually, Maureen was happy to have Aunt Ola do whatever she wanted. The tourists and retirees got a kick out of watching and listening to her.

"No, he didn't show up," she said. "And no wonder. That Pell guy. You never did trust him, I remember. I thought he was cute, like a little doll baby. Just think of him killing *four* people in one morning. For the life of me —"

"I hear it was Louanne kept him from jumping off the cliff. Broke her nose and loosened some teeth in the process, and all that on top of the cat scratches from the night before, and her cut hand. She should have pushed him instead of grabbing him."

"Or just shot him. For somebody that looks like a doll herself — or used to, anyway — she must be something with that gun of hers. Billy Holloway was always telling everybody she was too chicken-hearted to be a cop, too worried about her looks. Wonder what he's saying now?"

"Ol' Billy'll think of something," Aunt Ola said. "He won't change, you can bet on that. Look, here they come now."

A Blue Ridge police cruiser pulled into a spot in front of the window, Billy driving. The chief, Billy, Melba, Sam, Ferguson, and a just-dug-up mummy got out. They came into the café. At the serving line they all stood back to let the mummy go first. The dozen or so people scattered around the room watched, in several cases open-mouthed.

"Morning, Hattie Mae," the chief said from the back of the line. "You still got any of that good coffeecake back in the kitchen?"

The words he used were cheerful, but his voice was dead. Aunt Ola, who after two decades of being his private conscience and better judgment, knew the chief at least as well as his own mother did. She frowned at him.

He was trying to have a little celebration for the troops. That was nice, but why did he look like he just came from a mass baby funeral in the rain?

Hattie Mae spoke to the mummy. "Hi, Louanne, can you chew? How you doing?"

Aunt Ola could see two brown eyes and one side of a bandaged mouth. The mouth grinned.

"Okay," the mummy said. "It doesn't hurt too bad, only when I talk. Or breathe. I'll just take little bites."

"Looks real good to me, honey," Aunt Ola called. "Come sit with me. Billy'll bring your tray. Come on, Chief." The six newcomers pulled chairs around her table.

Aunt Ola opened the conversation. "Pell confess?"

"That's police business, Aunt Ola," the chief said. "You know we can't talk about things like that. You're gonna have to wait and read it in the newspaper like everybody else."

"Well, humph on your police business. Now tell me."

The chief grunted a little half-laugh. "Okay, I guess. It'll be in the paper tomorrow anyway. Yeah, after we found the gun in his car he couldn't wait to talk. He's proud of the picture and wants to —"

"What picture?"

"Oh, it's quite a shot. From just two, three feet away. The women clearly knew they were falling when he took it. Their expressions are, well, 'shocking' doesn't do it justice. Come to the office sometime, I'll show you. Pell keeps trying to explain to us how he didn't even *touch* them. He feels that makes all the difference. And of course he didn't touch the Winoskis either, his bullets did."

"And that little rock you had was the famous ruby?"

"Right. The kind of thing only a real rock person could love."

"And that Jack Lange guy . . . ?"

"Didn't really know what we were talking about until we told him. He's another total rock hound, not completely tuned in to the rest of the world. He'd been to a gem auction in New York just like he said. He's okay."

Aunt Ola sat back in her chair and looked around the table. "Well, you guys must think you're something. Solved the whole damn crime wave, didn't you? Just wonderful, ain't you? Everybody patting each other on the back and grinning."

"Oh, I don't know, Aunt Ola," Melba said. "Routine police work, keep plugging away, you know. We —"

"Well, don't go feeling so damn smart. What about all them pot patches in the woods? And the booby traps out there. I ain't heard of no arrests."

"We're working on it," Sam said.

"Workin' on it, eh? Wonderful. Then what about poor little Geranium? Who shot *her*? Right out there in this very parking lot. That's what started the whole shebang."

This time it was Billy who responded. "We're still looking for a red pickup on that."

"I see. Red pickup. Well that must make Geranium feel real good. You know, real safe. I got just one thing to say."

"Well, go on, say it."

"Humph."

CHAPTER 39

After the grand coffeecake hurrah at the Rocking Chair, Hack returned with his crew to the station. He went into his office, shut the door, sat down at his desk and propped his foot on the open bottom drawer. His leg had begun to throb again. Outside his door Billy said something and Louanne actually laughed, a first.

With four — no, with Marie McFee it was five — murders solved, not to mention the firebug and cat killer eliminated, departmental morale soared. Everybody on the force looked forward to walking around town with heads up for a change. Actually, "walking" wasn't the right word. "Sauntering" was better. "Moseying" might be better still. Anyway, they'd try hard to look bored for the citizens, as if multiple-murder-solvings happened every day.

Great for the department, but with all that good feeling floating around like happy butterflies, why was it that the boss of it all felt like looking for the lowest cave in the mountains, crawling in and pulling the rocks shut behind him?

Who was he kidding? Hack knew exactly why he felt the way he did. It was because he had something to do that he didn't want to do, something that required a decision he didn't even want to look straight at. It was a decision that only he could make, one that he couldn't discuss with anybody, not Art, not Honey, not even Aunt Ola.

What should he do about Gerry Smith?

There was no longer any doubt in his mind. He knew how she'd been shot, and why, and where. He had proof, courtroom-solid proof. Now he had to decide what to do about it.

And that decision was all tangled up with another one. Although he had never faced the question head on, had never spelled it out word for word to himself, he knew he was approaching a crossroads in his life. What he did today was going to bring him right up to that intersection. He'd have to turn one way or the other, or else try to keep going on the road he'd been stumbling along since Mary died.

Oh, don't be so melodramatic. It's just a damn church supper, not the end of the world.

Yes it was. Or maybe it was the beginning of a new one.

Hell.

He struggled to his feet and went over to the window. Across the square, beyond the bank, he could see the Methodist church steeple, thin and white, with a dark slate roof and tall gold cross at its peak. He pictured the church social hall, a pleasant, low-ceilinged room, where generations of people — people like Allie McLeod, *his* kind of people — had laughed and sung and had fellowship and church suppers. He'd been there many times.

He looked back at his desk, to the flip calendar in its place beside the picture of his wife and daughter. Under today's date Melba had written, underlined and circled in red: *SINGLES' SUPPER AT 6:30. PICK UP ALLIE AT 6:15*

From the window, by leaning forward and looking left, he could see most of this side of Jeter Mountain, now September green-red-gold in the hot midday sun. He could plainly make out the Rocking Chair Café and, much higher, just below the crest of the mountain, the hollow where he knew Gerry Smith's cabin was hidden in the trees.

He pictured Gerry. Not the cold, unbending protector of beaten women, nor the dark, bleeding bundle in the Rocking Chair parking lot. He saw instead a lost, hurt, frightened little girl, her pale hair spread around her head on the white hospital pillow, slowly regaining consciousness.

He could arrest that little girl and send the Hope Springs women back up to the coves where they came from. He could do all that. In fact that's what he'd sworn to do when he became a cop. Or, he could close his eyes.

Quit feeling sorry for yourself, damn it. Get up and do it! No, no, wait. Think about it some more.

Several people on the sidewalk were peering up at his window. A woman smiled broadly and waved. A man grinned and shook his fist in a way-to-go-Chief gesture.

Wonderful. He was their hero.

With an audible groan he went back to his desk and sat down. A phone outside his office rang every few seconds — with congratulations, he was sure.

Melba tapped and opened the door. "Professor Taylor just phoned, Chief," she said. "He wants you to call him."

"Later."

"Oh." After a close look at her boss she backed out of the room and closed the door quietly.

Hack stayed at his desk, mostly frowning at nothing, until the church clock struck four. Then he struggled up from the chair and, without even nodding to Melba, left the building, got in his pickup, drove down to the river and stopped in front of Aunt Ola's house. He didn't get out of the truck or yell for her, just sat slumped in his seat, half-hoping she'd come out and climb in beside him, half-hoping she wouldn't. She didn't.

He wanted to explain his problem to her. To whine, in other words. No, that wasn't right. He wanted her advice. Without saying the actual words, she'd tell him what to do. At least, after talking to her, he'd know what to do. It had happened often enough in the past.

Oh, don't try to kid yourself again. You can't talk to Aunt Ola about it. You know that. You can't talk to anybody.

He didn't see why he couldn't just *talk* to her.

Yes you do see. Don't kid yourself.

After waiting ten minutes for his ninety-something-year-old better judgment to come out and rescue him, he cranked up, rambled around Blue Ridge for half an hour, then headed up Jeter Mountain.

Ten minutes later he pulled off the pavement onto gravel near the mountain's crest and stopped behind the old Dodge van from

Hope Springs. A trail that had clearly earlier been a road of sorts led from the pull-off into thick woods. He could probably have managed the rutted, grown-over drive with his pickup, but preferred to arrive without fanfare.

Carrying the black plastic bag he had found in the Jeter woods and ignoring his aching leg, he made his way up the trail, emerging after five minutes into what had once been a clearing but was now a thick grove of young maples. Gerry Smith's rented log cabin stood in the middle of the clearing. For all Hack had heard about the place, he'd never seen it.

A Virginia creeper vine, its leaves already showing red, spread from the rough stone chimney on the north end of the small rectangular building and half-covered the window there. Saplings as thick as Hack's wrist grew around the cabin, some only inches from the cabin walls. From somewhere to his right a bird gave three piercing single-note calls; then a red, black and white pileated woodpecker left a big oak and, in its wavy, looping way of flight, disappeared down the mountain. Hack sighed and followed a leaf-cluttered gravel path to the cabin door and rapped three times with his knuckle.

As he waited for a response he put a finger on one of the huge squared logs that made up the cabin wall, and pressed. The wood was mushy with rot. His finger sank in an inch.

Gerry Smith opened the door. She wore a loose gray blouse and almost-ragged jeans. The left side of her face was red and marked with a pattern of dimples. She didn't speak.

"I need to talk to you," Hack said. "Can I come in?"

"I guess. I was asleep. Come in."

Hack followed her into a small, dark room. The bare, wide-plank floor needed sweeping. A couch covered with a thick, coarse brown-and-black blanket faced two wooden chairs. Between the chairs a low table, from its rough looks, handmade, held a lamp with an age-stained shade. Gerry reached down and clicked on the lamp.

"Sit down," she said, gesturing to the couch. She remained standing.

Hack put the black plastic bag on the couch but didn't sit. After an awkward moment Gerry said, "Uh . . . you want something to drink?"

"No. Sit down."

She perched on the edge of one of the chairs. Hack, without bending his aching leg, lowered himself to the couch and looked around the room. There were no pictures on the walls, no decorations. The only extraneous thing he could see was the couch blanket, which looked as if it had in younger, brighter days probably graced a horse or mule.

The air in the room was heavy with the scent of rotting wood, mildew and damp ashes. At the north end of the room a wide stone fireplace, constructed long ago for utility, not looks, needed cleaning. An open door opposite the couch showed the cabin's bedroom, where a faded red chenille bedspread — the kind with little cloth balls all over it — had been pulled loosely up over an unmade double bed. The spacing of the balls on the bedspread matched the dimples on Gerry's face. A patchwork quilt, of a pattern he recognized from Aunt Ola's cabin as "Mountain Sunrise," was draped over a chair.

Hack turned to Gerry. "How's your shoulder?"

"Oh, okay. Hurts sometimes. What about your leg? I heard —"

"How are the finances? Is Hope Springs going to make it?"

She raised her hand and slowly massaged her right temple a moment before responding.

"Yes, we'll make it," she said. "The bank is putting us on their charity list. The woman who called mentioned your name. And the Elks Club is sending a committee to see what they can do for us. I'm sure you talked to them. And the *Charlotte Observer* is planning a feature on us. Did you call them too? Anyway . . ."

When she raised her eyes the usual hardness was gone, replaced by an expression Hack knew well. All cops — at least all old ones — knew it. It was the look of someone in trouble, someone who thought that, just maybe, they had caught a glimpse of hope, but who were afraid to believe it.

The look said, Are you going to hurt me? Can I trust you? I want to trust you. I need to trust you.

The mute appeal was there for only a second, but was unmistakable. Gerry shook her head as if to clear it.

"What do I call you, by the way?" she said. "'Chief,' or what? I know your name. You . . . you must know how much I thank you. All the women down there thank you. They all know what you've done. I . . . I . . ."

Her voice caught, but then she smiled, really smiled, for the first time in Hack's presence. She reached out and put her hand on his. Her hand was icy. She pulled it back and squeezed her eyes shut. A gulping sob escaped.

She hit the chair arm with a tight fist. "Damn it! I don't want to cry!" Her face crumpled, her shoulders shook and tears appeared on her cheeks.

Hack didn't reach out, pull her up from the chair, take her into his arms, and say, "It's all right." But holding back left him drained.

She stopped crying, sniffed a few times, let out her breath in a whuff and stood up. She whispered, "Can I call you Jim?" and held out both hands.

Hack looked into her upturned face, his thoughts a swirl of memories, hopes, promises, desires.

And duties.

"Do you remember anything else about the red pickup from that morning?" he said. "The one with the dented fender?"

"Oh!" Hope died in Gerry's face. Something like death replaced it.

"I found something of yours," Hack continued. "In the woods, halfway down the mountain."

He took the pruning shears from the black bag and held them out, handles toward Gerry. She drew back and raised her arms.

"You must have dropped them on one of your Jeter hikes," Hack said. "They've started to rust, but a little oil and some rubbing will fix it. Here, they're yours."

She didn't respond.

Hack dropped the pruner on the couch. "Another thing," he said. "I poked around your garage down at the shelter and found this in the storeroom." He took a plastic bag from his shirt pocket and held it out. The bag held three dried leaves. "Marijuana."

"Oh. Oh. Are you —"

"Some vagrant must have been using your storeroom to stash the stuff before he sold it in Atlanta or somewhere. The word going around the hills these days is that somebody's been stealing from people's patches. Dangerous thing to do, steal from somebody's pot patch. They've started setting booby traps in the woods, and it's only a matter of time before somebody'll rig a shotgun to a tripwire or something. A person could get his head blown off, wandering around out there in the dark."

"Oh."

"And you'd better change your storeroom lock, or whoever's been using the room might come back."

"Oh."

"And, you know, it's really not a good idea to carry sharp tools like that on your hikes." He gestured to the pruners. "You understand?"

Gerry looked directly into Hack's eyes and said, slowly and distinctly, "I understand. I really do. I was just doing it for the women. They're . . . they need . . . I know what you're doing. For me. You're doing it for me." She opened her arms and took a small step toward him. "I . . . I wish . . ."

Somewhere in the valley far below, a church bell chimed, its notes faint but audible. Six o'clock. Church suppertime. Allie time. Hack pictured Allie's smiling blue eyes and rosy cheeks. He looked at Gerry's ivory cheeks and somber, tear-damp, gray eyes, then he raised his own eyes to the rumpled bed with its red tasseled spread in the room behind her. A moment later he made his decision.

CHAPTER 40

Hattie Mae opened the kitchen door a crack and looked out over the social hall, which was as bright and welcoming as the Rocking Chair on a sunny morning. Big bunches of yellow dahlias stood on each windowsill, and an arrangement of patterned gourds and miniature pumpkins formed a mound on a blue cloth in the middle of the table. Blue lettering on white place cards matched the cloth's color. If the dahlias had an aroma it was overpowered by the peach pies baking in the kitchen.

All twenty-two places around the table were occupied except two, where the place-cards read "Jim" and "Allie." Conversation among the waiting "singles" — thirteen women and seven men, whose ages looked to range between the late thirties and early sixties — had subsided after beginning as self-conscious chatter of embarrassed people trying too hard to sound cheerful. Hattie Mae knew all of the waiting diners, at least by sight. Two of the women, a librarian and a schoolteacher, had never married; the rest were about evenly divided between widows and divorcees, one of whom Hattie Mae knew had five children at home. Two of the men were widowers, the others divorced. It was 6:42.

"Reckon I should start passing out salads?" Hattie Mae asked.

"Not yet," Melba replied. "Give it a few more minutes. "Aunt Ola, *please* don't smoke. The whole church is non-smoking."

Aunt Ola said, "Humph," but pushed an unlit cigarette back into its pack. "You still think the chief's coming?"

"He promised," Melba said. "Allie's expecting him. You think he's not?"

"I don't know and you don't know. Nobody knows what the chief might do. Doubt if he knows himself."

"Well, that's *ridiculous.*"

"I think we ought to start serving," Hattie Mae said. "They're looking at their watches. Nobody's talking. Go on out and make your speech, Melba."

"Wait one more minute. No, two." Melba raised her wrist and checked the time.

"Just think of Allie," she said, "all dressed up, waiting. Sometimes I'd like to . . . I don't know . . . just quit trying, I guess. I actually thought he was building up to ask Allie to marry him. Fat chance. You know, it really is mean of him just to ignore —"

"Ah, Hack might not show up," Aunt Ola said, "but he don't do mean things."

"I say it's *mean*. You always take up for him. He —"

"What you going to talk about tonight, Aunt Ola?" Hattie Mae deflected the about-to-go-to-war conversation.

"Ah, I don't never know." Blue Ridge's last living pioneer was also its best storyteller and a frequent after-dinner speaker. "I just start babblin' about old times. People seem to like —"

"Where do you suppose he is?" Melba said. "Up some god-forsaken creek out in the back of the sticks, I guess. Without his beeper, of course."

Hattie Mae glanced at Melba but could think of nothing to say. She mentally shrugged and turned back to the storyteller. "Why don't you talk about the night the bear came in the bedroom?"

"Oh, I couldn't tell that in church," Aunt Ola answered. "We should *never've* stored honey under the bed. Damn old bear . . ." Her voice trailed off.

"It's five of seven, Melba," Hattie Mae said. "We've just got to start. Come on, perk up. You look like this was 'suicides anonymous' or something."

Melba squared her shoulders, bared her teeth and snarled. "That cheerful enough for you?" she said; then she gave a little laugh and added, "You're right, Hattie Mae. Start the salads. Here goes."

She left the kitchen, stepped onto the low raised stage that held the piano, and faced the audience.

"Good evening, everybody. Welcome to the first meeting of Howdy Neighbor Club. I'm Melba Johnson. Now, if you haven't already done it, I want you to turn and meet your neighbors. Just say 'howdy' and —"

The door at the back pushed open and the chief leaned in. "This the right place?" he said.

"Ah, Chief, welcome, welcome." Melba's fake cheer became real. "Come on in."

He held the door open and stepped back. Gerry Smith came into the room. She had on gray slacks and a pale blue, short-sleeved blouse. She wore no jewelry or make-up, but her cheeks showed pink, and her hair, pulled back, gleamed like platinum. On the podium Melba forgot to close her mouth. All color drained from her cheeks.

Hack took Gerry's arm, led her to the table and pulled out one of the vacant chairs. In silence so thick you could have heard butter melt he nodded brightly to Melba then spoke to the group.

"Folks," he said, "let me introduce Gerry Smith, a newcomer to Blue Ridge. I'm sure you've all heard about her recent . . . uh . . . adventure up on Jeter. Now you can get to know her for real. She's a special friend of mine. When you shake hands with her, don't shake too hard, though, and if you want to pat her shoulder, pat this one."

Grinning, he put his hand on Gerry's left shoulder and squeezed. Then he sat down, reached across her plate and turned the "Allie" place-card on its face.

Hard red spots formed high on Melba's cheeks. Hattie Mae, who was close enough to hear breath hissing through clinched teeth, put down her salad tray and braced.

At that moment the door at the back of the room opened again, and Allie McLeod came in. The chief saw her, stood up and looked a question at Hattie Mae.

"Uh . . . we got another chair maybe?" he said.

Hattie Mae brought one from the kitchen, and the people at the table squeezed together to make room. The chief sat down between Gerry and Allie. Melba finished her welcoming speech, but with words that held all the warmth of last night's grits.

The meal proceeded, with the chief the center of attraction. Melba retreated to the kitchen with Aunt Ola. Hattie Mae served the table, reporting each time she came in from the dining room.

"The chief's being a real life-of-the-party," she said after a round of coffee replenishing. "His girlfriends aren't saying much. Gerry didn't eat her dinner, just the rolls. She looks real pretty tonight, doesn't she?"

"What's Allie doing?" Melba asked.

"Nothing much, but she ate like *she* was hungry."

Melba went to the door and peered out. "He just leaned over and whispered in Allie's ear. Allie nodded. Now he's doing the same to Gerry. She smiled. I hate men."

"Don't take on so, Melba," Aunt Ola said. "What's he doin' wrong?"

"I know that man. He's going to string them both along and string them along, then . . . lose interest. Then he'll yack about it with Art Taylor at Bertha's."

"Chief's not like that," Hattie Mae said. "Maybe he just wants to be friends."

"*Friends.* He's got plenty of friends. He needs a wife. He's got to *pick* one and —"

"Melba," Hattie Mae said. She waited until Melba stopped talking and looked straight at her.

"Yes?"

"You want the chief to choose between those two out there?"

"What do you mean?"

"I bet *I* can make him choose."

"What are you talking about?"

"You just watch this." Hattie Mae picked up a tray, set two saucers on it, put a serving of food on each saucer, then pushed the kitchen door wide open. She went directly to the chief and punched him hard on the shoulder. He turned around and looked up.

"All right, Chief," she called out, holding the tray in front of his face. "Who gets these?"

On the tray were servings of mashed potatoes and peach pie.

* * *

Hattie Mae finished washing the last of the big pots and handed it to Allie to dry. Melba sorted silverware and replaced it in a cabinet while Aunt Ola sat in a corner sipping decaf.

After watching Allie a moment, Aunt Ola said, loudly: "So tell me, Allie, how'd you like that second piece of pie?"

"It was good," Allie said. "But . . . was that some kind of joke or something, Hattie Mae? You trying to fatten me up?"

"No joke, Allie, just a little game between me and the chief." Hattie Mae, keeping her eyes down, began to wipe the sink. A short, awkward silence followed; then Aunt Ola, who on principle never pussyfooted around things, posed the question that was hovering over the room like a homing bat.

"Allie, tell us, why did Hack bring Gerry tonight and not you? When he came in with her we thought . . ."

Allie deliberately folded the dishtowel and hung it up before answering. "Jim didn't tell you? He . . . uh . . . questioned Gerry in her cabin this afternoon. About the shooting, you know. She was in really bad shape, he said. Down, you know, depressed. He didn't want to leave her alone up there. He had to practically force her to come down here to the dinner."

"Well, that was nice," Aunt Ola said.

"Jim says she never had a home or a family or even a hometown, and she's lonely, needs friends. He called me from her cabin and asked if I'd mind meeting him here; his pickup's not big enough for three."

"Humph." Aunt Ola looked at her watch. "Is he coming back here to pick you up after he takes her home?"

"No, I've got my car, I'll drive myself home."

Aunt Ola drained her cup and glanced at Hattie Mae. "How long you suppose it takes to get to the top of Jeter and back?" she said.

Allie turned and faced the old woman. "I don't know," she said, "and I don't *care*. He's coming by my place later to talk about . . . things."

"Oh?"

"Yes. Louanne has night duty this week."